INSENSATE

Rob Pomeroy

To Rich & Mary,
With very best wishes to two lovely people!
Rob

To Miss Rigg, Mrs Hand,
Mr Capell and Mrs Cherrill
for inspirational teaching
and for infusing a love of language.

MORGAN JAMES PUBLISHING

Published by Morgan James Publishing,
PO Box 3500, Chester, CH1 9DX, United Kingdom
First published 2006

ISBN 1 84728 530 9
ISBN 978 1 84728 530 0

Characters

Jonathan Fenton	Son of Ron and Penelope
Isobel Fenton	His wife (parents Gordon and Faith)
Graye Lovel	A Hearer
Plykar Lovel	Husband of Graye
The Elders of the Etherean Guard	
	Yorgish bayle Prout, senior elder
	Garmon Weir
	Mekly Sur, administrator for the elders
	Ruith ru Contin, sister of Hesdar
	Gylan Gorph
	Jish Storbont
Members of the High Congregation	
	Hesdar ru Contin (Chair)
	Bars Medok (Director)
	Ti'par ru Masal (successor to Bars Medok)
	Resar Playne, associate of Gylan Gorph
	Jowl Ruban
	Dayle Rother
The Central Elect – Disciples of Belee'al	
	Klushere (Senior Preceptor)
	Sivian (Klushere's closest disciple)
	Jerud (organiser of the Chosen)
	Delturn
Al'aran Kytone	The Grand Preceptor; most senior servant of Belee'al
Martin Plowright	An Etherean
Ulsa Grabe	A bracarpium master
Elena Plowright	Martin's wife
Floom Medok	Wife of Bars
Neevairy Ewtoe	A persuader
Bravish Ha'ware	A gambling magnate

Prologue

The three figures paused, gasping for breath in the thin mountain air. The evil one they sought to elude was not far behind. A silver knife-edge glint of moonlight from behind a cloud revealed the silhouettes of two adults and a small child, all wrapped generously against the freezing air. From their deportment it could be seen that they were in a great hurry; more observant eyes would also detect a high state of agitation.

The taller of the two men turned and said something to the other, pointing far into the distance. With that, and with an embrace as befits two good friends who will never again meet, they parted company, the shorter man hurrying the child, who could have been no more than five, towards the place his companion had marked out. The other, seeming to sigh inwardly, set off at a tangent to the first. His was the weary trudge of a man who did not expect to see another sunrise.

Some five minutes later, a lone wanderer appeared at the point where the two friends had separated. Although only in his mid teens, he was dressed for battle and his stature bespoke a confidence of victory. He paused briefly, looking about and then followed the path that had been taken by the shorter man.

Over the brow of the hill, unseen by the pursuer, were the taller man and the boy standing beside a small shrine, hidden in a rocky outcrop. "Take a deep breath, little Chankwar," the man said. He closed his eyes for a moment and when he opened them again, his eyes were fixed on a point beyond the building and beyond reality. He took hold of the boy's hand and they stepped towards the building together. And vanished.

On the other side of the hill the pursuer had cornered his quarry within a blind ravine. The hunted bravely turned to face the hunter. He nodded slightly, as if he knew that he would surely be vanquished. He was not wrong. The teenager drew forth a sinister twin-bladed sword and with an elegant, complex but single stroke simultaneously disembowelled and beheaded the man he had chased. Turning from the loathsome spectacle, he then sniffed about in the air, as if searching for something. Realising he would not find it, he threw his head back and screamed in rage. In his bitter disappointment—or was it purely malice?—he wreaked his sacrilegious vengeance on the body of the man but twenty seconds dead.

1

It was the kind of thing that only happened in films.

Jonathan Fenton was driving to a meeting. He was not looking forward to the meeting. He was under orders from his immediate superior to convince the powers that be that the structured cabling at their server farm was obsolescent and should be replaced urgently with a fibre optic network at a projected cost of £2million.

The trouble was he was a little too good at his job. He had ensured the relatively smooth running of the company's network for a little over 12 months. Of course this good work went largely unappreciated. But he was running out of useful hacks to enable the hardware to keep up with the increasing demands made of it and he knew that disaster was imminent.

He wasn't looking forward to the meeting, because frankly it was going to be very boring. There was nothing exciting about fibre optic cabling. For sure, some people would disagree with him about this. *Some very weird people*, he thought.

As he joined the southbound motorway, he reminded himself that this job was a means to an end. He was hopping on stepping stones through the fast-flowing river of technology. Instinct and good fortune had thus far kept him out of the water. He was acquiring valuable experience. Pointless meetings with predestined outcomes were, no matter how irritating, an essential part of the journey.

He had scary diagrams coming out of his ears. His superiors would froth and foam and complain and contradict, but in the end they would reach the same inescapable conclusion. The fulcrum of their IT infrastructure was founded on ten year old technology and the company's younger competitors were far ahead in terms of capacity, simply because they started later with newer and more efficient resources.

The budget would be released; the meeting would conclude with a positive decision. But prior to that, a three hour charade was necessary in order for the purse bearers to justify their existence.

If Jon had known that the meeting would never take place, even if he had known the fraught and ultimately tragic circumstances that would prevent it, he would have smiled, ruefully.

It had been a mistake not to switch on the traffic announcement facility on his radio. His reverie was interrupted shortly after joining the motorway as he saw the flow of traffic becoming dense and sluggish like a post-courting swarm of drone bees. For the next six miles, the speedometer barely registered more than thirty miles per hour.

Eventually, he came upon the cause of the bottleneck. An extremely wide load was taking up the best part of two lanes, travelling slowly. The rest of the motorway occupants fought and jostled for the third lane, passing the hold up and then buzzing off at speed.

Jon experienced a pleasant feeling of relief as he anticipated passing the wide load. His hand dropped to the gear stick, ready to change down for some long-awaited acceleration. He looked over his shoulder, checking for a gap in the traffic in the outer lane. And then he almost drove his car into the central reservation in shock, as something shot over his right shoulder.

He snapped his head forward, trying to follow whatever it was, but it was gone. Perhaps a large bird had been sucked into the traffic stream and was now embedded in the radiator of one of the other vehicles. But it had seemed large for a bird.

Jon found his gap and pulled out. He was within six car lengths of the wide load and picking up speed, when something very ominous happened. The wide load consisted of three gigantic sections of pipe. The bore of these sections was so large that a lorry could comfortably drive through them. They dwarfed the vehicle towing them.

One of the sections was moving sideways off the trailer.

His actions of course defied all reason. As the gargantuan pipe rolled onto the motorway, the obvious, instinctive course of action would have been to brake and swerve away from the obstacle. Not to drive through it. But drive through it he did.

As his car flipped upside-down Jon's only thought was to protect his head. When the car hurtled out the other side, its passenger was unconscious and for the moment completely unaware of the carnage surrounding him.

Unconscious mind. Active mind. Why do horrors overwhelm at such times?

Ashley's fist pumped into Jonathan's nose twice and withdrew, pursued by a volcano of blood.

"*Déja vû*," thought Jonathan, falling to the ground as was expected of him. He rolled to his side and received a swift kick for his troubles.

Ashley towered over him, his bleached white face snarling and shouted, "Yer weird pansy!" He then covered Jonathan's bloodied face with phlegm.

Briefly Jon wondered if he should use his advantage against the bully. As always, he concluded this would only make life worse. Relief swept over him as he detected the crowd parting like waves in the wake of Mr Pratt. As Ashley's porcine fist raised itself to rain down once more, it was plucked from the air by the red-faced Pratt.

"He called me mum a fat slag!" bleated Ashley. And of course Pratt believed him.

"Yes, well that will do, thank you Ashley." Letting go of Ashley's arm, he turned to survey the damage and let out a quiet low whistle. "You really went for it this time, didn't you, you little psycho," he murmured. With unusual care, Mr Pratt assisted Jonathan to his feet and took him back into the building.

Jon took some pains to drip blood on Mr Pratt, but only on the back of his jacket, where he wouldn't notice until later. "I think I need to go to casualty, sir," was all he said. Pratt ignored him. So Jonathan fell to the ground unconscious. Thus ended one nightmare; now began another.

His alarm clock sounded odd. A single drawn out wail rather than short repeated chirps. Then a sound of rushing water joined in. *Why have I taken my alarm into the shower?* Jonathan thought sleepily.

The alarm became more insistent and the rushing sound louder and a Rottweiller was alternately biting his face and then licking it. The rushing became a roar and then the dog started hurling itself at Jonathan's right side. Thud. Patter patter patter. Thud. Patter patter patter. Thud. Patter patter patter. Thud. Patter patter patter. *Smash.*

And the dog landed on his lap. Only it wasn't a dog—it was a steering wheel. And it wasn't an alarm clock—it was his car horn. And the dog was licking blood off his face. No—there was no dog. But there was a buzzing in his ear. The biggest hornet in history was buzzing round him, buzzing angrily, buzzing, buzzing, saying, "ARE YOU ALL RIGHT MATE?"

Jon's eyes snapped fully open as his brain strove to shake off the visions that had briefly beset his bruised mind. An upside-down disembodied yellow head was six inches from his face—mercifully out of the path of Jon's arterial fountain, which was real enough and which was moistening the steering wheel. The steering wheel was inexplicably resting in his lap, detached from the steering column. Jonathan noticed that he was still clutching the steering wheel with both hands. He told his hands to let go but they resolutely maintained their grasp.

"He's opened his eyes!" shouted the head—a fireman's, it seemed—and disappeared.

Without his permission, Jonathan's eyes scanned about, surveying the wreckage. His car, a beloved but ancient Ford Granada Scorpio was now somewhat narrower than he remembered it to be. It was also shorter. Isobel's furry gremlin was missing from its usual position, dangling from the rear-view mirror. Ah—the mirror was missing too. *Not a bad day all in all!* he thought ironically, chuckling to himself and then he passed out from the effort.

His nose was broken in seven places—'mashed' would be a better description—and there was a steering-wheel dent in his forehead. He had broken several ribs and his right shoulder was dislocated. Broken ribs were a misery. The dislocated shoulder would mend quickly, but—the ribs! How could he hug Izzy in this state?

The hospital was apparently anticipating neurological damage. That was advantageous since he was accordingly receiving extra pampering courtesy of the NHS. The disadvantage was that there was no chance of being left to pee in peace.

Jon had no intention of disclosing the impossibility of brain damage. Something had happened during the accident that he could not entirely explain, but he knew that his head was safe. The medics would examine the x-rays and conclude that their patient had an exceptionally hard head. The truth about how he had protected his head was much stranger.

He could not presently remember much about the accident. His post-trauma hallucinations—including that horrible school memory—were his strongest impressions. The staff nurse, angel, whatever she was, had told him that a gigantic section of concrete pipe had rolled off a lorry in front of him, flattening several cars. It was loaded lengthways on the lorry and thus parallel to the motorway. He had allegedly driven his car through the centre of the pipe.

Of the four drivers who had a direct physical encounter with the pipe, Jon was the only survivor. He felt that his extraordinarily fortunate escape had caused him to be regarded with some suspicion by the staff and patients. It was almost as if they thought some witchcraft was at work. In Jon's mind, the good fortune of his escape was easily outweighed by the misery of being in the thick of the mêlée.

His wife was a long time coming. He hoped she would arrive soon. Wriggling to adjust himself in the bed, he felt himself losing consciousness again. *Blast, what a nuis...* was his last thought.

With the sweet, pure touch of consciousness came the pleasant awareness that he was looking into the most fabulous green eyes. Such eyes! Perfect white with grey-ringed irises and dark mottled green muscles linked to a further grey ring encompassing an ethereal blackness. Above and around these eyes swept extravagant lashes and high-arched light brown brows. A luxurious smile filled Jon's face at the proximity of his first love.

"Oh, my dear," she said and leant close to kiss him. Jonathan flinched involuntarily.

"They said you were in a bad way," she looked round almost guiltily, "but I thought maybe you had..."

"I didn't," Jon interrupted. Isobel relaxed visibly. "Only my brain, I think. Not sure how I did *that*," he continued. "But I seem to have lost some blood..."

"That was careless!" Izzy smiled sympathetically. Jonathan

smiled too, but only slightly. He was not eager to risk fainting again. "Are you all right though?" she continued.

"I think so. Don't think I'm going to manage my squash match with Mick tonight though." He raised an eyebrow. "Sorry to drag you out here like this, love."

Isobel smiled. But not her full-toothed heart-melting smile; just her lips-only smile. Jon knew that she must have serious concerns about him being in hospital. He shared those concerns. The underlying tension in their lives which they both tried to ignore, was always heightened in the presence of the medically qualified. "No trouble," she lied, "but I think a remarkable recovery is in order."

"How can I?" he questioned, looking down at the probes and devices attached. Isobel caught his meaning. What Izzy was suggesting was far too risky, especially here and now.

"How did you get here?" he asked, to divert attention away from himself.

"Doug dropped me off." Jon was slightly surprised by that. Her boss's personal assistant would rarely accept any disruption to his regimented schedule. "His mother is here in D wing." The terminal wing. That explained it.

"Oh, is she all right?" Jonathan wondered, slightly stupidly.

"Er—no. They're giving her only days. Doug has been coming in here every lunch time. He's looking awful..." She paused, reflectively. "Like you, actually!"

There was the sparkle he loved so much. Isobel was relaxing after her breathless arrival. Jonathan would recover, she had decided. Sensing this and not wishing the sympathy to end so soon, Jon let out a little whimper. Instantly Izzy's face fell. Jon grinned wickedly.

"Oh—you...!" and she started trying to tickle him through the bedclothes.

"Help! No! Aagh!" Jon let out a yelp of genuine pain, causing the six other occupants of the room to stare round.

"He deserved it!" Izzy announced to the ward—and the patients' eyes grew wider. They all looked away in very English embarrassment.

It would have been plain to see for anyone with eyes, that here were the best of friends. Both deeply concerned for each other's welfare, both trying to put the other at ease. Their banter continued for some time, until Isobel noticed that Jonathan was flagging.

"Are you okay?" she inquired. She sat gently on the bed, where she could best see his face and studied him intently.

"Um, I think I had better get some more sleep." He was feeling annoyingly worn out already. "What will you do now?"

She passed her hand over her face. "I'll have to get back to the office really. I've already cancelled two appointments—the work will be piling up..." There she was, her gorgeous but unmanageable auburn hair pulled tightly back, a few rebellious curls bursting out of the clip, dressed in a navy pinstripe trouser suit and appliquéd cream blouse, but girlishly sitting cross-legged on the bed and pouting most pleasingly. This was one of many moments when Jonathan wished he had his camera.

"I really meant tonight, though."

Misery descended over her face, only part mock. "I'll probably stay up festering until 3 o'clock, watching some useless Japanese B movie and then fall asleep snuggled on the settee with Mr Spencer." Mr Spencer was a four foot tall polar bear soft toy with frayed ears. He had become a substitute bed companion for Jon's wife whenever Jon was away from home overnight. Jonathan wasn't quite sure why only Mr Spencer's ears showed signs of wear. In truth, neither Isobel nor Jonathan liked to be separated from the other. But sometimes it was necessary, like now.

As an afterthought, Isobel smiled, as if she were making a joke. Jon didn't approve. "You've got work tomorrow," he said and frowned.

"You know I won't get any sleep though, so what's the point in trying?" Izzy retorted. Jon was aware that it was true. He counted himself exceptionally lucky to have such a devoted wife and was secretly pleased that she missed him and worried about him so much when he was away that she couldn't sleep.

They parted, wistfully; she to her office, he to his sleep. He prayed it would be dreamless.

2

There was an ominous silence in the temple of Belee'al. Klushere sat, crossed-legged in worship, resolved not to leave until he had his answer. He was concerned that they had been required to wait so long and he found that he was perspiring moderately in the intensity of the moment, although it was two hours before dawn and cool as yet. Inside he remained at peace. His disciples were becoming more nervous however and the cold stone floor drained their confidence along with their bodily warmth. They were fully aware that the longer the silence lasted, the more their own lives were at risk. And yet, to flee would incur greater risk still. And so they, the twenty Central Elect, remained kneeling a respectful distance from their Preceptor, anxiously awaiting his next word.

When Klushere spoke, it was in an ancient tongue, known only to the highest elect amongst them. He spoke in praise of the Ultimate Preceptor and begged him for a hearing. And then Belee'al replied. His voice was heard deep inside the blackest recesses of the hearts of all those present. Few besides Klushere understood the message.

I did not expect a meeting so soon my friend. There can be but one petition that brings you here. Often have we communed concerning this subject. You have pleased me greatly by your cleansing of the High Congregation. And so now your time of satisfaction draws near.

Klushere could not suppress a sigh. He had worked and striven hard to hear these words from his master.

Indeed you fast approach the point in your training that will take you Beyond. When you enter Beyond, there you will find the object of your hate. You must bring him to me. Then, in his destruction, will you reach the final initiation.

Klushere smiled.

Ah yes. You know it well. You have learnt much these two decades and yes, I am pleased with you. Prepare yourself, therefore. Sixty sunrises hence I will allow you to pursue him. Then will you bring him to me. Then will you take your birthright. Then will we commune deeply.

The smile that had been on Klushere's mouth disappeared into an indescribable beatified look. Today he was hearing the promise he had longed for. His whole body and mind reeled with the shock of at last approaching his life's goal. With a supreme effort of will, he stayed sufficiently focused to hear the remainder of his master's message.

I must have you pure before you can begin. Devote yourself to sanctification for two months. Bring to me the arch blasphemer and purify yourself in his torment before me. Now go. Leave with me the one called Delturn.

The last sentence was spoken in their native language clearly for all to hear. Klushere's eyes opened with a look of triumph and determination. All of his disciples except for Delturn arose with him and followed behind as he exited the temple. As they left, Delturn could not help lowering his head in despair. He crouched there, trembling on the unforgiving rough hewn flagstones, tears flowing in spite of himself as he awaited his fate and his departure from this life.

The remaining nineteen of the Central Elect were overwhelmingly relieved to find their Preceptor in high spirits having left the temple. They now journeyed through a dense forest, on their way to a less formal meeting place. They drew comfort from his evident satisfaction and this helped them to keep their minds away from the fate of their former peer.

Sivian, the closest of the group to Klushere and the one amongst the disciples who had heard Belee'al most clearly, spoke respectfully to his mentor. "Preceptor, the Great Lord seeks the removal from office of Bars Medok, does he not?"

"You discern correctly, son Sivian. For many years has Medok blasphemed Belee'al and now he will suffer and learn penitence! I have looked forward to the day my master would sanction the removal of this vermin. It brings me pleasure indeed to know that he will at last feel the touch of my sword." Involuntarily he touched the straps of his back harness that held his ever-present weapon of ritual cleansing.

Bars considered himself to be a straightforward man. He championed justice (at least his own personal idea of justice, since all view the concept through tinted glasses) and despised oppression. Although he did not chair the High Congregation, taking the lower role of Director, his voice was greatly respected by the majority and the Chair, Hesdar ru Contin considered herself almost permanently indebted to this wise, powerful and mostly humble man who supported her and her retinue.

Bars Medok was an outspoken member of the ruling Congregation. It was known that some others of the High Congregation had started to immerse themselves in the more arcane practices of this planet. Bars had been quick to denounce any such activity amongst the elected rulers, asserting that the roots of these dark traditions lay in anti-democratic ideals; the elevation of the individual at the expense of the community; the domination of one's will over another. Publicly all of the Congregation supported his views. Privately though, there were increasing numbers of people who sought the favour of Belee'al.

The Congregation was formed democratically, but the elected rulers were subsequently treated like royalty. The intention of the founders of this system was that those elected would aspire to just leadership. The incentives for those in office were supposed to encourage them to rule wisely enough to be re-elected. The success of the system was largely dependent on having a fair and benevolent Chair. Such was true at present. Amongst some of the lower ranks, there were those who were less scrupulous. Bars Medok was more aware of their murmurings than was Hesdar, the Chair—that was one of the things that made Bars so valuable to her. It was also the thing that made Medok more of a target.

The politics on Deb were largely peaceful at this time, thanks mainly to the brilliant and balanced team in office. Below the surface, however one could find the usual ambition, deceit and treachery and jostling for positions of honour, that may be found wherever one person has power over another and where humans are humans. Of late, the tension had increased since, while not publicly admitting it, some members of the Congregation had certainly been less private concerning their devotion to an ancient religion of Belee'al-worship—a religion understandably regarded with some suspicion and distrust by those not a party to it. Little was known about this religion by the uninitiated, but it was generally believed that the faith involved worship of a spirit presence who was said to sanction and encourage selfish ambition, psychological manipulation and even assassination.

"How will we take him Preceptor?" intoned Jerud, a lithe and muscular woman, much used by Klushere in covert kidnappings and assassinations.

"It must be by overwhelming force, in order to bring him into true humiliation before our Lord, my daughter." Klushere replied. Jerud smiled. Not an evil smile particularly. More a smile of devotion and eagerness to accomplish a task to bring her further into favour with her two Lords—the one physical and the other spiritual. "A conference is necessary with the Chosen. Arrange it."

"Yes, my Lord," Jerud replied subserviently and melted away from the group.

Turning back to Sivian, Klushere asked, "What of the hospital assignment, son Sivian?"

"My Lord, it is well advanced. We have Belee'ans in key positions within the main administration centres for hospitals Rebke-side and Norvesh-side." Sivian picked at his short, well-groomed beard. "I am inclined to believe that we will have no difficulty in achieving your desired objective at short notice."

Klushere paused for a moment, plucking a berry from an overhanging tree, simply because it was there. Then, symbolically crushing it between thumb and forefinger and looking at Sivian across the flow of juice he said, "There must be no evidence of our influence, my son."

"None at all," Sivian replied.

The meetings of the Chosen were shrouded in even more secrecy than those of the Central Elect, if that were possible. The call to meet was traditionally signified by a particular symbol being affixed to a central monument, such as a local public timepiece. The symbol was written using a chalk-like substance and resembled a smear. Therefore any uninitiated onlooker would presume it was simply dirt or debris.

Once the symbol first appeared, the Chosen were to make it their business to propagate the sign in other similar places. They were then to attend the meeting place, always by thirty degrees of the sun after nightfall. The next day, the Chosen must covertly remove all traces of the sign, thus avoiding any false alarms. The system worked surprisingly well.

Apart from Jerud the leader, the identities of the Chosen were a closely guarded secret. Members attended meetings hooded and cloaked and respected mutual vows of privacy. This was understandable, since their joint ventures were rarely lawful. Should one member be caught, it was crucial that he or she be unable to reveal the identity of other members, even under duress. Members of the Belee'al cult, those gifted with Etherean skills, were obliged to consider carefully whether they truly wished to join the Chosen. Once a part of that group, desertion was not an option. Belee'al himself would reveal the identity of the deserter and the price for desertion was high.

Jerud took herself to Sang's tower clock at Plaedon Central, rendered herself invisible while out of sight and then scaled the outer face. Sang's clock was as popular with the Chosen as it was with regular citizens. It stood over thirty metres high, as Earth reckons them and the exterior decorations rendered by the architect Javorn Sang made the clock easily surmountable. Jerud took the climb slowly. Like many of her colleagues, although endowed with the power of the Ethereans she still found the task of remaining invisible arduous. She conserved her energy by taking regular breaks during her ascent.

She never failed to marvel at the view from this point. To her left as she leant against the clock, all of Hulladon was spread beneath her, with its unfussy architecture and spacious gardens. She could almost imagine herself settling in that quarter, in time. Immediately ahead was Plaedon Central—an intense area fighting to march in time with the capital, Rebke. And as she looked beyond Central, she could see in the distance the six towers of Rebke. In amongst those towers she knew, was the Seat of the High Congregation. Perhaps even now they were deep in discussion, analysing the trends of opinion of the electorate; puzzling over the current waves of crime in a usually peaceful metropolis. Her Lord Klushere had initiated many ventures to keep the Etherean Guard occupied while he extended his influence there unnoticed.

She reached the clock's plinth and there daubed her sign. A thrill overcame her as she thought of tonight's conference.

⟹⟫⟫⟫

If a walker were to tarry awhile on the road between Plaedon and Rebke, at a certain point near a towering evergreen tree, she may be surprised to note a disturbance in the shady ground beneath that aged denizen. She might draw closer. Perhaps a small rodent is foraging amongst the fallen leaves; perhaps a large invertebrate has set up home there. And then a gust blows away the leaves and she can see neither beast nor plant there. Nothing grows or lingers where the tree alone has rights to the earth's nutrients. It is perhaps a figment of the imagination.

And yet—a strange sensation is experienced—as though one is watched by unseen eyes. An Etherean noting this feeling would, as a learnt reflex, flick spiritual eyes over the Ether.

Of course none of the Etherean Guard is here. The Chosen would never consciously enter their meeting place whilst the ever wary Guards looked on.

It is a wonder that the place had so long escaped the notice of those enemies of the Chosen. The site was, many aeons previously, a burial ground and an ancient temple. Perhaps such history provides some measure of protection. All Jerud knew was that the Chosen had never been disturbed here—not in living memory.

She took her place in the long underground chamber, near the vent through the hollow part of the tree above. It was natural that the leader of this group should select the most comfortable seat, but in truth Jerud had never noticed that she was in a prime position, as it were.

The Chosen tended to descend through the chamber ceiling at the opposite end, before materialising and illuminating their underground lights. Jerud had a good view from where she sat. The anticipation made her smile.

She glanced momentarily at her notes, although she had no real need of them. In the past, their operations had required careful planning and precise timing. This time, however, things would be much more straightforward.

Cloaked figures had begun to appear. They seated themselves round the chamber and took a moment to meditate before the meeting began. It was not long before all were assembled. The Chosen were pathologically punctual. Often their lives depended upon it.

One of the Chosen, as if on cue, opened the meeting with a word of dedication to Belee'al. And then Jerud began.

"My friends; warriors and spies; thank you for coming tonight. I will not labour in lengthy introductions; my purpose is simple. Belee'al has requested that Bars Medok be captured, humbled and brought to him and Preceptor Klushere enjoins us to this task."

Murmurs of assorted varieties were heard in all quarters. Some of disdain, some of relief; but all expressing approbation.

"We will take numbers for this assignment and all of you will be needed." Jerud called out "one" and in turn, the others called out ascending numbers in a clockwork sequence round the chamber. These would be their assigned identities for the duration of the mission. Anonymity was retained so far as possible.

Jerud continued, "The Ethereans have been kept busy. I am delighted to note some of our own handiwork and would give credit where it is due!" This was something of an in-joke. Being one of the Chosen meant by definition receiving neither praise nor criticism for one's actions. Jerud could feel the twinkles in the eyes of her comrades without needing to see them.

Although without exception all of the Chosen could technically call themselves "Etherean," they preferred not to. That designation was reserved in their minds for their natural enemies, the Etherean

Guard.

"I also see that many others have rallied to our cause," Jerud proceeded, "although how much they are in support of us and how much in support of plain *insurrection*, I cannot say. Certainly though, having walked the paths around the Seat of the Congregation, I can tell that the Ethereans' presence is much diminished. I therefore favour a direct concentrated strike at the Seat. Do the Chosen concur?" This was an indication that the plan was open for discussion.

A few places to Jerud's right, a man's deep voice questioned, "It seems to me that a strike will require all of our efforts. How then are we to ensure that the Ethereans do not call the reserves to assist?" It was a good question. Only with the bulk of these protectors of order occupied at other places away from the Seat, could the Chosen hope to stand against the Congregational guard. "Member twenty-three," he appended, so that Jerud could address him direct if she wished.

A somewhat shriller male voice interjected from across the room, before Jerud could respond, "Member five. Twenty-three need not be concerned. I have reason to believe that the gambling community may be relied upon to begin a recruiting campaign at a moment's notice." That would certainly assist.

"The Ethereans won't like that!" a woman concurred, with a chuckle, without identifying herself.

Jerud sounded hopeful when she asked, "Are you sure, five? I had considered approaching a magnate for whom I occasionally freelance myself with a direct request."

Five replied, "We need not stoop to begging, my lady. I have certain influence there and I know that the leaders shall be glad of an excuse to begin an incursion within Rebke. There are many who feel that the time is right." In a relatively short time, the Ethereans had become deeply unsettled by the outbreaks of violence seen in and around Rebke. The truth is that after decades of peace, few had thought it likely that the Guard would be required to engage in combat of any sort. They were never to be underestimated of course. But at present, it was true that they appeared to be sufficiently stretched to allow the Etherean Guard contingent at the Seat to thin perceptibly. This was an obvious cue of sorts, evidently seen by Belee'al. Little if anything escaped the Ultimate Preceptor's notice, particularly where it concerned the Ethereans.

"Very well then five. I would request the campaign begin at nightfall two days hence. Could the gamblers be ready in this time?" Jerud asked.

"My lady, I am certain of it," five replied simply.

And thus was the only known obstacle overcome. The rest of Jerud's briefing contained little for discussion. The Chosen were each assigned their places for the attack. It would take place late at night. Bars Medok would no doubt still be hard at work, but there would not be many others around. There were a few places where diversions and smokescreens would be required—more than one might imagine, since there were more than just the three dimensions to contend with. But the Chosen were not strangers to such things.

Most of those not engaged in diversions would be required to fight Ethereans hand to hand. A couple of members were assigned projectile weapons, but these would be reserved for use against the regular security corps since Ethereans are for all intents and purposes immune to bullets and suchlike. Even the fighting would be diversionary. Not many of the Chosen would hope to succeed in sustained combat against superior numbers of Ethereans—not even complacent Ethereans.

By their shape and size, Jerud could loosely recognise some of the people around her. This helped her in selecting two particular members whose skills she knew she could rely on to assist her in the delicate task of the kidnapping itself.

The plans concluded, Jerud gave the redundant order for all to rest and meditate. She closed with a brief commitment to Belee'al and they then left as silently and secretly as they had come.

3

When Jon met Isobel, he was a naïve undergraduate of Stone University, in his final year of a software engineering degree. She was a postgraduate at the same university, on a one-year business administration course. Jonathan was rather too wrapped up in computing to have any time to consider romance; Izzy was emerging from the tatters of a failed marriage and was at that time firmly convinced that all men were scum.

All men? No. During her life there was one man who had been ever constant. He had supported her through her various romantic dramas—culminating in a grand disastrous finale: her marriage part way through her first degree to a charismatic but thoroughly irresponsible art student. Her father had never criticised, except in a constructive sense. Although he expressed concerns and reservations, when eventually he was proved right he never took the opportunity to claim psychic prowess or perceptive superiority. Isobel knew that her lovely dad would never let her down or abandon her. Indeed he doted on his effervescent daughter. Yes her father was okay. *But to hell with the rest of them!*

Neither Jon nor Isobel were looking for a relationship. This meant that they were both ideally placed to begin a friendship without romance or sex getting in the way.

As is often the case, an ultimately great and tender romance had an inauspicious and commonplace beginning. They could both trace the start of their relationship to an incident concerning the communal printer in the chemistry department's computer room. The chemistry department was unique amongst the university's departments in this respect: The department heads appreciated that if they opened up a facility to the wider university community, this would give them a material advantage when petitioning for finance. This was the only area in which any department of the university saw beyond its own self-interests.

It was a homely autumnal day, with no meteorological menace about the air—just the sleepiness of nature post-breeding and undergraduates pre-essay deadlines. Contributing to the lethargy of the moment, more importantly, was the fact that it was nine o'clock on a Saturday morning. Most of the university community was not due to rise for at least another two hours.

Izzy was having trouble printing. No—it is unfair to say that of such an intelligent young lady. The printer was militantly and belligerently refusing to cooperate with a simple request. If that were not enough to irritate her beyond expression, the geek on the other side of the room doubtless knew the appropriate incantation to utter in order to cajole the machinery into submission. He was at that moment smirking over her impotence, letting her stew for a minute before he strode over and asserted his masculine dominance over all things mechanical. She was persuaded that this must be his attitude at least—she would not humiliate herself by actually looking at him to check.

Isobel refused to give any impression that she was a damsel in distress, requiring rescuing. Indeed, she endeavoured by strategic use of body language and looks of concentration, to convey the message that she was entirely in control of the situation.

Two observations had led her to deduce that he was of the IT inclination. Firstly, he had arrived shortly after her, at eight a.m. Only a serious computer freak could be that desperate for computer contact. And secondly, he had been tapping away furiously, in distinct mockery of her hunt-and-peck two-fingered style.

As the frustration deepened, she walked over to the Hewlett-Packard (for that was the fiendish company responsible for spawning this obnoxious creation), muttering dark imprecations under her breath. The printer sat there oozing supreme indifference. No lights were flashing, but the power light was on. She knew enough to appreciate that this indicated it had either not received her request, or had chosen to ignore it. She strongly suspected the latter.

"The queue's jammed," the other occupant of the room offered helpfully. Drat the man. She gave a grunt in reply that could have meant anything from, "Of course I knew that," to, "Drop dead you technofreak." He tapped away loudly and then suddenly the printer sprung into life.

He's made a pact with Satan, she concluded. Right on cue, the voice in her head told her not to be so ungrateful. As a penance, she flashed a slight hint of a smile and said, "Thanks." It wasn't worth it—he was long since past the moment and deep into programming.

Jonathan had been aware of the problem for some time. Although not conscious of this, Isobel had started tutting and groaning the moment it became apparent her printout would be delayed. Jon found tutting very distracting, so he looked for a way to end it. Covertly he noticed that the woman kept looking across at the printer. He decided to investigate.

To start with, he found out who was currently logged on, from the central server. He filtered this list so that it only showed the computers in the chemistry department. There were few people logged on at that time. One of them was him. Several others showed hung processes, suggesting failures to log out. The only other active login process must be hers. He made a mental note of the user id associated to the process.

Next, following his hunch, he listed the spooled printer jobs and saw in the list a job bearing the same user id. There was one job ahead of it in the queue that seemed to have been sat there for many hours. *Bingo.*

Jon had picked up several administrator passwords during the course of his studies. They were less powerful than the superuser's, but they gave access to many useful facilities nevertheless and they were less frequently changed than the superuser's. He logged on as pg12rg, a CompSci postgraduate called Russell Grew. Russ's account—unbeknown to its owner who was at that moment blissfully dreaming of a beautiful young undergraduate called Helen—was then responsible for removing the stalled print job.

Shortly after this he was vaguely aware of someone thanking him, but he had by that time switched back to his text editor and was compiling a large chunk of program code in the background. He wasn't generally obsessive about computers, but when he was programming, all other reality faded around him.

Around ten o'clock he was recalled to consciousness by the lady rising and saying, "Well, it's been a blast." Although only four words had passed between them in the previous two hours, he felt confident that this comment was directed at him. He was unsure whether she intended to be sarcastic or ironic, but being a generous-hearted fellow, he assumed the latter and therefore looked up and smiled broadly at the joke.

Isobel, who hadn't decided whether she was being sarcastic or ironic, or even whether she was talking to the computers or to the man, smiled back. Her smile was less reluctant than the last one, because she was pleased to have amused someone. She berated herself all the way back to her room for smiling at him, but the damage was done.

The woman had looked away quickly after the smile and Jonathan gazed after her for some minutes when she left the room. Without being wishy-washy or unduly sentimental, he was telling himself that he had never before seen such a pretty face lit up so brilliantly by so slight a turning of the lips. His memory had taken a snapshot of the face at that instant and he was playing it over and over. He couldn't believe that he had been so engrossed as to overlook how stunningly attractive this curly red-haired, green-eyed lady was.

His thoughts lingered on the woman and the little that had passed between them. Then, with resolve, he turned back to his screen. He had memorised the user id with little effort—these facts stuck in his mind whether he told them to or not. A quick directory query elicited her name from the university's LDAP server. Mrs Isobel Leary. *Mrs. Oh well.* Telling himself to forget it, he continued with his programming. Very quickly, Mrs Leary was a million miles away from his thoughts.

Izzy had not been so lucky dismissing him from her mind. She had not taken him in at all really, but she knew that there had been a connecting moment. It was this that irritated her. *Don't start that foolishness again,* she told herself.

Their paths crossed again, not long after this and under similar circumstances. The following Thursday, Isobel made her way to the open computer lab in the campus library to continue working on her project. Although there was no formal reasoning behind the decision, she had decided to avoid the chemistry department, since she now associated it with a man who for the past five days had tormented her remorselessly. Jon was oblivious to the trauma he was inflicting.

Unfortunately, shortly after Isobel had told herself not to start 'that nonsense' again, the face of the man impressed itself on her consciousness, without her bidding. Before she could replace it with a less male-centred image, she noticed how full it was of life, tenderness and fun. In truth, none of these characteristics could readily be discerned by any other observer. The fact was, Izzy was irrepressibly romantic, in spite of her past bitter experiences and these briefly suppressed feelings were surfacing again without her permission. Her romantic sensibilities imputed noble virtues on a man who was reasonably attractive and who indeed did possess those virtues. But how such diverse and nebulous emotions could be identified on a face that was concentrating deeply on programming a new optimised network protocol library in C++, the average dispassionate onlooker would not be able to say.

The experience was leaving her feeling displeased with the poor young man and unwilling to renew his acquaintance. On this Thursday, she was less keen than ever to see him.

Evidently a higher power had induced her to enter the library at that time. She stood for a moment on the threshold of the computer room, unable to accept what her eyes were telling her. That *man* was sitting directly opposite the door and worse still, her entrance had coincided with him looking up from his work. The end result was that Isobel stared directly into his intense blue eyes for several long seconds, blinking in consternation.

The first thing that leapt into Jonathan's head was her user id. The second thing that appeared were two terrible words. Mrs Leary. *Alas for that 'Mrs!'* He blanched and looked back at his screen.

Isobel was now in a dichotomy. To leave the room would be to admit everything—to admit, even, things that were not true. Leaving would tell him that she was desperately in love with him and was in fear that she would faint in his presence. She could not allow his ego to reach such conclusions. But on the other hand, to stay was equally intolerable. Their eyes would be sure to meet. He would be sure to persuade himself that he could conquer her with one, deft phrase: "Do you come here often?" And he would doubtless flash her a brilliant smile, made all the brighter by the contrast of ivory teeth against his ebony skin.

At times like these, it is fortunate indeed that the human mind moves swiftly. Isobel made her decision in less than two seconds—although to her, it felt like two minutes. She resolved to pretend that the man meant nothing to her—less than nothing—and she would take her place in the room like any ordinary person. She noticed that he seemed a little flustered, having met her gaze. This comforted her; it meant that she had the upper hand. He was embarrassed, so she would pretend to be oblivious.

As she moved into the room, she noticed initially to her dismay (which she tried not to show) that the only free computer was adjacent to her nemesis. *Even better,* she thought ultimately, *I can feign disinterestedness at close quarters.* She did not quite believe herself, though.

When Isobel sat down next to him, putting her bag on the desk in between them rather firmly, he noted, Jon offered a quick, "Hi," in recognition. She may be married, so he thought, but she had smiled at him, after all. The greeting was returned, but the conversation proceeded no further.

After having said, "Hi," Isobel cursed herself a thousand times. How much better it would have been to look at him in puzzlement and revulsion, with an expression that could only have meant, "Do I know you? If not, I don't want to." But no, she had said, "Hi," and in so doing, she had admitted that she recognised him, that the chemistry department incident had taken place and that she had made the oft-regretted error of smiling at him.

Jonathan had a terminal window open. Although he was physically at a Windows machine, he was electronically running programs on the Unix server, in another room. To do this required a terminal window. The advantage of this is that most of the screen becomes black and a black screen reflects objects much better than a screen full of multicoloured images. He was therefore able to sneak glances at Isobel in the reflective surface of his monitor, even though he knew he shouldn't.

She was dressed in an exceptionally fetching cream linen trouser suit. Beneath the jacket was a jade top. She wore no socks or stockings, just fine-strapped cream sandals. The overall effect was devastatingly charming. *Mr Leary is an extremely lucky man, he thought.*

It is hard to say why it never occurred to him that she may be widowed or divorced. Perhaps it was because she was so young. Equally unfathomable is why he never checked the ring finger of her left hand—for he would surely have found it empty. Perhaps he was so far involved in computing, that he had only a passing understanding of women and relationships. Certainly any other man would have looked to the left hand before anywhere else.

Jon had no serious thoughts of romance, or even friendship. But that did not prevent him from looking and from being civilised. His coffee break was nearing. University policy was that drinks were not allowed in the computer room. All the employed computer technicians broke this rule however and the students followed their example. The room was rarely visited by anyone who would particularly care. So Jon rose to fetch himself a drink and it occurred to him that it would only be chivalrous to offer to obtain one for his neighbour.

He gently imposed himself on her consciousness. "I'm going to get a drink—can I get you one?"

Isobel was instantly wary, defensive and closed. "No thank you," she politely but firmly returned.

"Would it make a difference if I told you I was gay?" Jon asked, shocking himself and the lady equally. He covered up his controversial question with a huge smile.

Eventually, Isobel chuckled to herself and then relented. "I'm sorry. It's a very kind offer. I would love a cup of tea—no sugar, if that's all right—but you must let me pay for mine." She had that look about her of a woman asserting her independence and taking on all male chauvinists who would dare to challenge her. Jon thought it prudent to accept the compromise.

"Sure. Back in a sec."

And so did the friendship begin. Very simply; no pomp or ceremony; no excess of hormones to announce the arrival of something new and exciting. There was an element of attraction on both sides, admittedly, but there so often is between a man and a woman and it so rarely comes to anything.

No—this relationship developed from Jon showing common courtesy to Isobel as she gradually defrosted, reluctantly accepting that she could not shut off all men forever. They grew closer as friends and discovered how to trust one other. Jon soon learnt that Isobel was divorced. He discovered with surprise that there was life beyond computers, while Isobel was reminded that there can be life after marriage.

Their friendship matured, teetering on the brink of deep romance, where it hovered for some time. And then Jon broke the news that would surely make or break the relationship.

4

"Ah, Delturn."

It was definitely not Belee'al's voice. The Ultimate Preceptor's voice was always heard with the spiritual rather than physical ear; its tone was generally smooth, silky, oppressive, dark and sometimes menacing. This voice however was thin, croaky, rasping and laryngitic and definitely human. The first syllable of his name had been spoken with considerable contempt, Delturn felt, as if it meant the same as 'rodent faeces' or 'latrine scum'.

Why wasn't he dead yet? Or at least in unspeakable torment? Delturn could not initially locate the speaker. It was dark in the temple and the tears still stinging his eyes encumbered his view. Automatically though, he looked round.

A sneering little grey-faced elf-like human was leaning on a short staff, glaring at him. He was dressed in the most ridiculously pretentious manner with a flouncy blouson, three-quarter length flared pantaloons and yards of bouffant trimming at every incongruous opportunity. Kneeling down, Delturn was about the same height as the diminutive croaking man. Delturn was considerably better dressed. The man spoke.

"Were the decision mine, I would surely not let you live. You disgrace the Elect with your conniving ways." He raised a withered hand to halt Delturn's protest and continued, "You know that Belee'al sees all and yet you flagrantly denounce him to your family and friends, as if he would not know! Yes, long slow torture and agonising death is too good for you."

Drops of spittle left the creature's mouth as he spoke, some of them landing in Delturn's face, making him blink involuntarily. Delturn had been about to defend himself, but he knew the accusation to be true. Who wouldn't denounce Belee'al publicly? On the other hand, this evil gnome was apparently suggesting that Delturn would be allowed to live—under what restrictions he could not imagine—but at least there was a glimmer of hope.

Two beady grey eyes looked out at Delturn from folds of flesh barely attached to the thin frame of the dwarf's head, with its oversized brow. How old was this creature? One hundred would have been Delturn's conservative estimate.

"Well, Vomit-stain—what have you to say for yourself?" it squawked. It was managing to cough, splutter and sneer at the same time. Under different circumstances, the effect would have been highly comical.

Delturn's brain had seized and his thoughts were coming slowly. This must be Al'aran Kytone. He had heard Klushere speak of a noble and long-standing servant of Belee'al who went by this name—indeed Klushere had mentioned that he had personally been trained by the venerable and respected Preceptor. To Delturn's certain knowledge, Al'aran had never revealed himself at any of the meetings of the Central Elect, not whilst Delturn had been a member. But this must be him. He felt a profound sense of disappointment—he had hoped for a stately warrior figure, not this shrivelled barely living carcass now standing before him.

"Grand Preceptor Kytone?" Delturn inquired, obeisantly.

The little man snorted, which appeared to be affirmative.

The kneeling disciple chose his words carefully, correctly guessing that his life depended on it. "It causes agony to hear that I have grieved Belee'al. Please tell me how I may atone?"

Al'aran smiled briefly to himself. A cunning, selfish smile. "The Ultimate Preceptor has a task for you. If you complete this task successfully, you may turn away his anger and he may yet spare you." Delturn was more than ready for whatever was to be required of him. If it meant going beyond the end of the world for his Lord, he surely would do it. He expressed his willingness, by a nod.

"Do you know what your master Klushere desires more than anything?" A trail of sputum was collecting on Al'aran's chin. Delturn tried not to look at it.

"Grand Preceptor, Klushere wishes to possess all the powers of an Etherean, I believe—does he not?" Delturn asked the question as though he were unsure of the answer. He was determined not to seem in any wise threatening to the learned man before him. In truth, he knew full well that this was what Klushere had striven for, for the last twenty years. It was no secret.

Al'aran moved in close to Delturn until his eyes were six inches from Delturn's. Delturn, still kneeling struggled not to flinch from Al'aran's rancid breath. And then he bellowed into Delturn's face, "BE NOT SNIVELLING WITH ME! ANSWER FULLY!"

Delturn's heart started pounding again. For a moment he had forgotten the precariousness of his position. He thought hard—his memory was not serving him well at that point. "Erm," he stammered slightly, "Klushere wishes to capture a person that he believes—no that will," he corrected, "confer on him full unlimited Etherean powers."

"Yes, and?" The elf studied him closely.

"And Klushere does not know where that person is, though he has searched for most of his lifetime." He did not add what most people thought in the honesty of their hearts *and surely this person must be a figment of Klushere's imagination.* If twenty years of searching had revealed nothing, the search was either pointless, insane or both.

Al'aran's eyes narrowed. A line of drool was starting to hang from his wizened chin. He walked round behind Delturn and then whispered in his ear, quoting part of an ancient Precept, "The enlightened man will find his that which he seeks, *Beyond*." He expelled sufficient air with the last word, to cause a drool strand to connect with Delturn's cheek. Amazingly, Delturn stayed still, although he could feel his jaw muscles clenching. "You will seek the goal, Beyond, Vomit-stain."

Beyond. Beyond reality. Beyond the realms of the living. Beyond his world. This, one of the most obscure Precepts, spoke of another place. Delturn had always assumed that it simply referred to the Ether in which the Ethereans moved. But Al'aran must mean something more. By his arts and with the aid of the Chosen, Klushere had scoured all of the Ether that was within his grasp. Delturn was sure that had Klushere's quarry been hidden within the Ether, the hunt would have ended long ago. So Beyond must be something else. He waited for Al'aran to explain.

The silence lasted so long that, had it not been for the feeling that Al'aran's eyes were burning holes into the back of Delturn's head, he would have assumed that the aged man had fallen asleep.

Intense pain! His back was on fire and again the tears were in his eyes. Al'aran was shrieking, "How much more time will you waste? Are you planning to leave without any preparations? Are you as empty-headed as you are insolent?" In spite of himself, Delturn sprang up and adopted a stance for combat. Al'aran was brandishing his staff menacingly, his face grim. No doubt a blow from this stick had caused the pain in Delturn's back.

Slowly and viciously Al'aran snarled, "Oh please do boy. How I long to wipe you from history." Delturn formed a strong impression that Al'aran was considerably more powerful than he looked. Wisely, he backed down.

"I am sorry, Grand Preceptor. Habit forces me..."

Al'aran glared for a moment and then he actually smiled. "Perhaps there is hope for you yet then. Now begone. Return to me prepared, in fifteen degrees of the sun." Delturn moved, but Al'aran raised a claw-like hand. "Tell no one. See no one." With that, he turned his back and withdrew into the shadow of the temple.

Being one of the least accomplished of the Ethereans in the service of Belee'al, Delturn found the task of maintaining invisibility—let alone intangibility—very draining. He was a slight man and often felt that he had few reserves of energy. He compensated for this by his religious fervour at cult meetings. In private he was exceptionally committed to his spiritual masters but he never felt that he was particularly gifted at serving them. His development and honing of Etherean skills had been long-winded and painful.

As he walked free of the temple and its heavy influence, the fear of death ebbed. He could now see that he had been selected for an important mission, because of his passion and devotion. No—Belee'al could not kill him. Delturn was too valuable. His heart beat faster for a moment, but this time with pride, not fear. He thought of Klushere and his strange position of honour before Belee'al. Surely that place of honour belonged to a true Etherean, such as Delturn! Perhaps now was a chance to prove his worth.

The temple was well hidden deep within a lush forest area—part of the cultivated conservation reserve northwest of Rebke, Deb's capital. At this time of night he was unlikely to encounter any travellers or nature lovers. Rather than fade to the Ether, he saved his energy for later and set his face towards his home in the west side of Rebke.

It was out of the question to use a vehicle piloted by one of the

Etherean pilots, so Delturn made use of one of Deb's exotic mechanical forms of transport, a rey. He hoisted himself into the centre saddle of the three-wheeled self-propelled contraption that he called his own and began the strange arm gyrations and leg pulsations that were required to move the vehicle forwards. People often asked of the rey, "How do you steer it?" and Delturn would reply with humour, "I don't. I crash often."

Steering a rey is truly an art form and difficult to master. The arms operate the single forward wheel and the brakes. The legs each operate a rear wheel. And so the theory goes that working one leg faster than the other will cause the vehicle to turn. That was the theory. Delturn had often left the road and found himself admiring the local flora and (surprised) fauna somewhat more closely than he had intended. But still it was ten times faster than walking.

By this means he arrived at his home within a few minor degrees of the sun. At that point he became invisible and intangible, to avoid disturbing his family until safe within his chamber. Inspiration forsook him. He had no idea what to pack. He presumed he should not bring more than he could comfortably carry. A weather proof garment, some warm under layers, a few modest preening items (he flinched whilst packing them, sure that Al'aran would disapprove, but equally sure that he would regret leaving them). Instilled in the Ether once more, he explored the victuals stored at home and selected those that he considered to be most compact and nutrient-rich. The fact that they were also the most noxious items in the pantry is an odd coincidence strangely universal throughout the many realms of humans.

He wrote a short note to his parents. He had been called away on business unexpectedly and did not know how long he would be gone. They were not to worry; he had taken a few provisions for the journey and would see them again soon.

Delturn was a mass of contradictions. He hated deceiving his parents but equally he hated disappointing his spiritual masters. His morality clashed with his spirituality and his loyalties were divided repeatedly until the barest sliver remained for each allegiance. The letter contained not one scrap of truth and yet Delturn believed strongly in honesty in his family relationships. And thus do those forever fecund sisters *pride* and *power* give birth to corruption.

Al'aran descended to the lower levels of the temple. Here the air was more to his liking—redolent with age and mystery. He had spent many years here in these catacombs, giving expositions on the Precepts to those most favoured by Belee'al—a few select members of the Central Elect—and training the band of assassins known as the Chosen. Here also, below his living quarters, easily accessed by a directly connecting staircase, were the dungeons of anguish. In Kytone's mind it was right and proper that all those who denied the authority of Belee'al should atone for their heresy. He had no difficulty with the ideas of torture and murder. They were merely part of his dutiful service to his Master—whose every word was to be obeyed without question.

He took the stair now, down to the room reserved for blasphemers. It was illuminated in the dreariest manner imaginable. A sputtering candle-like device in one corner ever threatened to expire and plunge the hapless captive (whomever that might be) into abominable darkness. Al'aran liked the effect. He surveyed the room, checked the manacles, glanced over his simple instruments of pain and clucked to himself distractedly.

"Medok. How I have been looking forward to your company here," he said. The room was empty apart from Al'aran himself, but in his mind he could clearly see the politician Bars Medok in those chains. Trapped, defeated and beyond the reach of the Ethereans. None of that accursed brood could find their way here. Belee'al, the Ultimate Preceptor had seen to that.

He picked up a knife and held it up to the flickering light. Then, spinning round he hurled it in the direction of the manacles. It embedded itself in the wooden panels beyond—but in Al'aran's mind's eye, it had met flesh and been rewarded with a scream.

It will be a pleasant duty, he thought.

5

There are many spheres of existence in the known universe. The physical sphere is well known and observed by all those of us who have the benefit of physical senses. From the wealth of documentation testifying purely to physical phenomena, one could be pardoned for assuming that there is no other existence. This assumption would be far from the truth however.

The spiritual sphere of existence is less well known. There are a few who have learnt to perceive this other dimension and those most adept could tell you that the spiritual realm is almost wholly coextensive with the "reality" we see and feel. Neither realm can exist without the other. Without flesh, man is nothing. Without spirit, man is less than nothing. We rely on our bodies to sustain our spirits, but without the spirit, the body would become as dust.

Those who undertake to dabble in separating body and spirit do so at great risk. Few can be chosen and gifted to exercise control over these two realms. Men rule the mortal, physical world and angels the immortal, spiritual world. There are some men however, who can pass between worlds as they will. Fortunate indeed the man with this skill, honed and perfected. But oh! how open is it to abuse.

We may not challenge the One who dispenses such power. His

concepts of justice and equality are hard to fathom and often elude us. Suffice it to say that in the course of time, in galaxies other than ours, evil and just men alike have found themselves strangely set apart, with understanding, insight and sense beyond the ordinary, physical realm. Such men are the Ethereans. Such men are they, who may at will walk in the shadows, insubstantial as the mists, as elusive as the desert mirage. Such, one may venture to guess, was Jonathan.

Jon was not at all aware of the extent of his strange gift. Since his early teens, he had known that he had a hidden 'muscle', which when flexed, rendered him physically transparent. Beyond that, he had little comprehension of the mysterious other world in which he moved. His parents knew their adopted son was talented, but they gave him no cause to think that he should experiment or learn more about an ability that would, to their way of thinking, lead to him being further ostracised. At least that was their given reason. From overheard conversations, he was inclined to believe there was more to their concern than that. Whatever the cause, he was carefully drilled that he should reveal his secret to no one and that should temptation to practise overcome him, he must always ensure he was in a private place first.

In reality, his parents did not fully understand. They knew he was different; they knew he was special; but they had no clear idea why. Neither had Jon. Early into their friendship, Isobel guessed that there was something different about Jon. She had not probed though, since she felt sure that he would tell all, in his own time. This showed uncanny good sense.

As the months passed, it became clear to the two that their lives would run together for a good while. Their relationship had mischief, infrequent arguments and a deep common understanding; in short, all the ingredients of a love of promise.

Some six months after Jon and Isobel first admitted they were 'going out', the strain of secrecy had become too much for Jon.

Despite the stern admonishment of his parents, Jon felt that he could—and *must*—trust this woman he loved, with the truth.

The academic year was drawing to a close. Jon was in a flurry of final examinations and Isobel was working hard on her business model project. Their increased workload meant that they were spending even more time with each other, if that were possible, quietly studying.

It was a Wednesday night. Jon had hoped to speak to Isobel at the weekend, but her parents had come to visit and that had been more than enough for him to handle. He had buried his need to talk, but it now surfaced once more. The time was hardly appropriate—he had a fuzzy logic control systems exam in the morning and he could not afford a late night. But they would be talking for some time.

He had been staring blankly at a text book for a while. When he looked up, Isobel had already noticed how distracted he was. She was about to ask him how he was doing, but something in his look halted her.

The muscles along his jaw line were working silently and his brow was furrowed. "Izzy, my love—I have something very important to tell you." Her heart froze. Here came the 'let's be friends' speech. Her reaction was to be quite revealing to her, since it made her realise how much more she wanted from their relationship. She did not have time to consider though. He continued, "There's something I've wanted to tell you for a long time. I have been afraid of telling you this, but I know you love me and I can trust you with this." Isobel nodded reassuringly, because Jon had started looking worried and tearful. He was not prone to crying.

"There's no easy way to explain this and no way you'd believe me if I just told you, so I'll show you." He stood up, walked over to a coffee table, picked it up and placed it in the middle of the room. Of all the things he could have done, this oddly was the most reassuring. The cynical, still hurting parts of Isobel's mind and heart could not begin to associate furniture moving with a forthcoming confession of infidelity or murder. She leant back in her chair and started twirling some stray curls with her right index finger, as she often did when concentrating.

Jon was speaking and she caught every word. "This is going to be a little freaky. No—this is going to be totally weird. You'll probably want to run out of the room screaming." Again the troubled look.

"I'm all ears Jon. Is this where you admit you're an alcoholic drag queen and perform your exotic lap dancing routine on the coffee table?" Serious moments always made Isobel jest. Jonathan snorted, but said nothing. Instead he narrowed his eyes and focused on the table. Isobel thought she saw the table levitate, but then realised that was a figment of her imagination. What was not a figment of her imagination was Jon's subsequent slow and deliberate walk *through* the table.

She lowered her voice. "Do that again," she murmured. Jon obliged. He retraced his steps through the furniture and then returned. Finally, he sat down, *in* the coffee table. His waist upwards appeared to be resting on the table top, while disembodied legs could be seen below.

Jon crossed his legs and assumed an apologetic look. Isobel started repeating under her breath, "No way," all the while shaking her head whilst her red locks trembled.

After the twelfth repetition, Jon quietly replied, "*Yes* way. And there's more. Are you ready?"

"Are you joking? This beats the drag act hands down!" Jon smiled. Again he closed his eyes almost completely, but this time, the rest of him followed. It is hard indeed to describe, but a similar effect can be experienced thus: If one were to sit in a darkened room and relax, eyes closing slowly, continuing to look through the narrowing slits; at the point where reality starts to merge with darkness, solidity itself almost seems to fade. This was how Jon appeared to close in upon himself.

When the transition was complete, Isobel blinked at thin air. She leant forward in her chair, but finding that posture no better suited to grasping the impossible, she slumped back again. She grabbed hold of an empty coffee cup next to her and sniffed it for traces of whisky, or hallucinogenic substances. Her nose had unfortunately ceased to work. At least she thought it was still working, but it was as if all of her sensory input had been re-routed to her mouth and the effect was to make her jaw drop, her mouth drool and her eyes bulge alarmingly. It seemed to her that steam was coming from her open mouth, but this was probably another trick of the senses. The mother of all shivers ran the full length of her spine.

Whilst her eyes remained glued to the table, Jon quietly reappeared, back in his chair. They sat in silence for half a minute. When Izzy broke the silence, it was to utter the greatest profundity that the most educated and eloquent of theoretical physicists could have spoken under similar circumstances. "Whoah." That really did sum it up most succinctly.

Her first degree had been in prosthetics and her science background now caused a thousand questions to rush forward. They all clamoured for attention at the front of her mind, crowding each other out, elbowing and jostling for position. Eventually, a little question small in stature but large in implications slipped past the noisy crowd. "Do you do this often?"

Jon was visibly relieved. She had remained in the room somehow, although he had been expecting her to flee. "Not really that often. Perhaps once a week, of a Saturday night before bed, just to remind myself I can. And then maybe in the morning, if I really don't feel like getting up." He looked up at the ceiling.

"I don't get it."

"The thing is, it's a lot less strain to move around, whilst I'm invisible or intangible. It's like my body is gone and I'm lighter than air." That made sense. How many times had Izzy lain in bed snuggled under the covers with bleary morning eyes, fantasising that she was already up and getting washed? How wonderful it would be at such times, to rise effortlessly and wander about, waiting for the body to wake up, but not hampered by its slothfulness. Isobel was simultaneously jealous and in awe.

She questioned him for several hours that night, both of them forgetting their academic duties, as they had a dozen times before. Isobel became more and more surprised, frustrated and incredulous that Jon knew little about the extent of his abilities and had not been inclined to investigate. Did he still need to breathe when he was intangible? He hadn't really noticed. Why didn't he fall through the ground when he lost his physical presence? He didn't know. Could he make his hands pass through his own body? He hadn't tried. How long could he stay invisible? It was no real effort, but he hadn't experimented. Had he ever become invisible in order to eavesdrop on other people's conversations about him? No, that had never occurred to him (although his embarrassed look belied his response). Had he ever become invisible in order to spy on girls? A huge smile and a simple shake of the head. Jon was intensely moral, so she could believe that, at least.

Did he have any other secrets? Not that he could think of. And it was then that Isobel knew. She thought back to her reaction, when she had feared he was about to call off their romance. He was the man she had been waiting and hoping for, even while she was married before.

It would be misleading to report that their subsequent marriage was inevitable. In the long run, it was, but as with most relationships, it suffered fits and starts along the way, especially in the in-law department. Jonathan had great difficulty winning the heart of Izzy's mother, partly because he thought it was necessary to and that ruined his ability to relate to her. Her father was a little distant, but occasionally Jon caught him looking at his daughter with an immensely proud and satisfied eye.

His own parents could do nothing but worry. Bless them—they were good parents, but to worry was their automatic response to all crises and changes of scene. Penelope, Jon's mother was firmly persuaded that Isobel and all of her family would dislike her. Ron, his father, took the view that it was dangerous for his son to associate so closely with anyone—even though it couldn't be helped. He resigned himself to retiring to his garden shed, for a sherry and a few sad shakes of the head. *It will all end in tears*, he regularly thought.

He did not congratulate himself on his prophetic skills, when he later was proved right.

The wedding was a triumph of substance over form. That is to say an outsider would have presumed the occasion to be something of a disaster.

Upon arriving at the church, Isobel was helped from the car by her father Gordon. He bustled her from the back seat and with a tear in his eye, gave her a peck on the cheek as she stood by the open door of the vehicle. He then closed the door on her wedding dress, adding to the immaculate lace a tear and a four inch greasy mark.

The serene bridesmaids flew into a Valkyrian rage, all but boxing the ears of the unfortunate father of the bride as they sought to pin the dress in such a way as to conceal the new defect. Izzy's mother Faith, who had been coping remarkably well until that point, left the bridal party in a quest to find soothing alcoholic beverages. Happily Faith therefore missed the first marathon round of photographs outside the chapel, which culminated in the photographer dropping his camera. The camera flew open expelling its film and twenty tortuous minutes of preening and posing were lost forever.

Four glasses of Bucks Fizz later, a very calm Faith returned to find the photographs beginning again. All parties except for Faith were looking frayed and fractious. Gordon was alternating between muttering apologies to anyone who would listen and culturing upon his cheeks a bright ruby blush fit to complement the bridesmaids' claret dresses. The bridesmaids were simmering and the photographer was exploring a range of vocabulary that he certainly would not be permitted to continue within the walls of the church.

Isobel had decided that of the two options now open to her—crying hysterically and laughing hysterically—the latter would provide scope for better photographs. The photographer, a maudlin type, clearly did not agree and was not prepared to suffer her hilarity in silence. Izzy was already beyond caring however. It was her wedding and she was determined to enjoy it.

Inside the church, there had been several false starts. The organist, a misnamed Mrs Young, who needed inch-thick glasses to overcome her short-sightedness but who was too vain to wear them, had mistakenly taken a thumbs down from the ushers to be her cue to launch into *The Arrival of the Queen of Sheba*. Betty Young took her music very seriously and once started, she became like a sixteen wheel juggernaut, incapable of being deflected from her sixty mile an hour charge down the musical motorway.

After five repetitions of this, the congregation was becoming heartily sick of the first fifteen bars of the piece. The vicar took to standing next to her, rather than in his accustomed position at the front of the church. He was holding a heavy large print *Book of Common Prayer* and brandishing it menacingly in Mrs Young's direction.

The groom was amusing himself by estimating his pulse rate. So far it had peaked at about 130, during the last of the five solo organ recitals. His best man, an athletic former sport science student called Mick, was doing press-ups with his feet on a pew and his hands on the cold quarry tiled floor.

And thus, at the sixth commencement of the entrance music, no one was quite prepared for Isobel's procession down the aisle. When it dawned on the congregation that *this was it*, a spontaneous round of applause rippled around the building. This was all the encouragement Mrs Young required to set her pipes to maximum volume. When Isobel finally arrived at Jonathan's side, they were both wincing.

But when they exchanged looks, eyes twinkling, they knew that it didn't matter. Today they would be married! Fortunately they were able maintain this irrepressible cheerful optimism throughout what would prove to be a very long day.

The celebrations continued much as they had started. The highlight of the reception (other than Mick's speech) was the spontaneous combustion of several of the table decorations. The caterers had laid out candles on each table, wreathed in paper flowers. It had occurred to them neither that the candles would burn quite so low during the four-hour reception, nor that it might have been wise to coat the flowers with a fire retardant spray. One elderly gentlemen presumed it was all part of the display and with great gusto threw the dregs of his brandy over the burning pyre.

As their parents shot off in four different directions, searching for fire extinguishers, Jon and Izzy became helpless with laughter. Taking their lead, the guests together formed the view that they should make the most of the situation. As one, they headed to the bar and the assembled company became ever more relaxed. By seven o'clock a food fight had begun.

Once it became clear that the wedding could not be 'rescued' and turned back into the dignified affair they had anticipated, the parents gave up trying to behave appropriately and became instead thoroughly uninhibited. The Fentons, Jon's parents, forgot their worries for a few hours and even managed some exceedingly energetic dancing with their in-law counterparts late into the night.

As they retired to their hotel room, Jonathan mischievously asked Isobel how the wedding had compared to her previous experience—which had been a very grand 'top hat and tails' affair. Izzy was beyond words. She tried not to, but could not help dissolving into laughter once more. The tears rolled down their faces as they agreed that it had far exceeded their expectations. Exhausted and incapable of anything else, the pair fell asleep giggling.

6

Located within, what on earth would be called the *west* side of Plaedon, is the charming quarter of Hulladon. The people living there are mostly peaceful souls, productive and useful in their community and with commensurately grand residences. Plaedon is just close enough to the capital Rebke, to be of significance to that crowded cacophony of commerce and far enough away to be relatively unsullied by the jostling joy-seekers.

Graye Lovel was one such peaceful soul. Until her recent retirement, she had successfully coordinated offender rehabilitation programmes and taken an active involvement in the retraining processes. Her husband worked within the executive of the Congregation and since her retirement she would occasionally travel with him to the capital. Mostly though she stayed at home, tending her garden. This was by far the safest course of action for her.

Ironically, Graye had never been under threat from her 'pupils' as she called them. In fact she was held in high esteem by almost all who had come within her care. Even those who had not managed to retain all they had learnt and had slipped back into the ways of delinquency, still referred to her as 'Mother' whenever their paths crossed. There was less chance of attack from a pupil than there was of the scrupulous Bars Medok becoming a gambling magnate.

No, Graye's biggest enemy was herself. The danger was heightened whenever she approached the capital and it was for this reason that she stayed away for the most part. Graye was accomplished, respected, a devout follower of Yershowsh and a compulsive gambler.

No one passing her residence, looking at the stately figure tending her precious plants, would guess the passion with which she would pursue her addiction. None could look at her gracefully ageing face and detect the fury of an all-consuming habit. But when Graye Lovel gambled, she lost all vestiges of grace and respectability. Her features would become ever greyer as her eyes became brighter with the chase—the chase that inevitably would end in ruination of one form or another.

Her actions had brought dishonour upon her family, a plague upon her marriage and had as surely stalled her husband's political career, as it had brought about the end of her own. The murky world of gambling was inextricably linked to the world of drugs and alcohol and through excessive consumption of both, Graye's health had suffered too. And yet, she had achieved so much in her life and was so adored by her husband that at the point of each crisis, rescue had come. Plykar Lovel had influence within the Congregation. Deals were done, promises made. So far Graye had avoided ending up on one of her own programmes.

It had been some time since her last binge. She had given assurances to Plyk that he had heard before, but she had been so utterly desolate and remorseful that his heart had melted again. On that occasion Graye's redemption started with the two of them spending nearly 45 degrees of the sun—three hours as Earth would reckon them—in tears together. So far as he was able, the gambling contracts that Graye had entered into, Plykar fulfilled. He resigned himself to the prospect of many more years of employment as a consequence, but he felt this was his duty. He knew that had the circumstances been reversed, his wife would have done as much for him.

Today, Graye's head was clear. She knew who she was; she knew that she served Yershowsh; she knew that her husband needed her. Also her garden needed her and it was here that she found a profound sense of peace.

Neighbours would invariably pass the time of day with Graye as they walked by. This gave her a welcome break from kneeling, tending the soil, but after each conversation, she knelt back down and continued patiently. Sometimes her thoughts turned to her husband, sometimes they turned to prayer to Yershowsh, sometimes she just let her mind wander. But at this moment, her thoughts were with her wayward son.

It was a habitual thought process. In her imagination, she could see several scenarios. In the first, he returned home, penitent and changed and after much remorseful conversation and apologies on both sides, they would be fully reconciled. In another scenario, she saw a desolate man, a shadow of the boy she knew and loved, found barely alive, abandoned by friends and peers. The Lovels would take him back in again and then as a reunited family, the rehabilitation process would begin both for her and for her son.

But the scenario that most troubled Graye was the scenario she most believed in and feared. She tried in vain to shake the thoughts and visions that oppressed her, but time and time again they would return. In apocalyptic style she saw her son rising in infamy and power, pursuing an all-absorbing obsession and being consumed with and consumed by his one goal: to become a true Etherean and to be admired—or feared—by the Etherean Guard.

Anyone watching Graye at this point would have observed a shadow pass over her pensive face. Graye shivered as she lifted tender plants from the ground, although it was not cold. She shook her head briefly and by that physical action also banished the dreams that troubled her. She did not want to dwell on those things. Such thoughts depressed her. And the road that started with depression ended with obsession. Her obsession meant she was no longer able to work in a job she had loved. And so, with her head clear, she chose to move on and think of other things.

Today it was not difficult to replace these thoughts. During this week there had been considerable excitement at the capital, where Plykar worked. In fact she and her husband had talked about little else. Fifteen days ago there had been an assault on the Seat of the Congregation and Bars Medok was taken. Fifteen days of searching had failed to reveal his location. The Congregation was in uproar and the Etherean Guard in a state of panic bordering on hysteria. For the first time in Graye's memory the peace and tranquillity of this planet she loved seemed to be under serious immediate threat of destruction—save that immediately after Bars' abduction there had been a noticeable and incomprehensible dip in the Rebke-side crime rate.

The Guard was held in high esteem by virtually all inhabitants of Deb, charged as it was with the security of the planet. In a world where there are such men as the Ethereans, only Ethereans can hope to maintain order: ordinary mortals have no other defence against them. But here were the Ethereans, apparently helpless, attacked it would seem by their own number. This was serious indeed. Every member of the Congregation—none more so than Hesdar ru Contin—appreciated that an attack on a member so high in the government meant nothing less than anarchy.

In the temple of Belee'al, Klushere was thinking of his mother. Sometimes it pained him to be so close to her, whilst living in a world so far from hers. He thought about all that they had lost, the disappointments and the regrets. He thought bitterly of her past and blamed her for his own shortcomings. If his mother had not been so weak, Klushere would be an Etherean today—possibly even a member of the Etherean Guard. The bitter-sweet irony of this made him smile, in spite of himself.

Do you regret the path you have chosen, my son?

Belee'al was speaking. Klushere had momentarily forgotten the reason for his approach to Belee'al's altar. He knew not whether Belee'al was able to see into his mind, but he was unsurprised that his Lord knew where Klushere's thoughts lay. He responded aloud, "My Lord and Ultimate Preceptor, I do not regret a moment of the journey I have taken. I regret the place that I started from, but I do not regret my destination. My service to you is unwavering."

I am glad of that. You are a valued and faithful son to me. And now you will see the rewards of faithful service.

Klushere knew that praise from Belee'al was rare indeed. Ordinarily he would have been reduced to tears of gratitude by such commendation. At this moment however, every part of his being was straining to hear what Belee'al would say next and this overrode his feelings for the time being.

Where mere human effort achieves naught, Belee'al is able. Tonight my son you will see the gateway to Beyond and the start of the last stage of your journey.

A thousand questions flooded into Klushere's head. He knew better than to interrupt however. He fixed his eyes on the Belee'al icon on top of the altar. It was part statue, part minor obelisk. The base was of a copper-coloured metal, in the shape of a ball, representing the planet Deb. Above this, in rare woods and precious metals, there was a stylised representation of a tall man, with multiple arms and an array of eyes. In one hand, the figure held a sword. This represented Belee'al's authority. In another hand the figure held a lamp, representing Belee'al's knowledge. A third hand clasped a snuffer, indicating that Belee'al held the power to withhold knowledge and extinguish life. And in the fourth hand, there was a miniature gate, showing that Belee'al alone determined the passage into Beyond.

As his eyes rested on the icon, Klushere felt his mind empty and in this way he prepared himself to receive the rest of his master's message.

Before you begin your journey, there is a matter you must attend to. Your mother is proving troublesome to us.

Klushere flinched inwardly. His service to Belee'al was unquestioning and he would obey any direction given to him. He knew that his mother was a Hearer and this made her one of Belee'al's most hated enemies. But Klushere dreaded the day that Belee'al would instruct him to have his mother assassinated.

I am mindful that you still have ties—you do well to overcome these for the most part and your service to me is of such value that I am willing to overlook this weakness. Your mother may live for now. But I must have her distracted again.

With a brief sense of relief, Klushere suggested, "Might I be permitted to despatch a gambler to recruit her once more?"

That will suffice; make it so. Now Bars Medok has proven to be of great assistance to us. He has shown us the way to your goal and for that he shall be rewarded.

Klushere chuckled appreciatively at his Lord's dark humour.

I sent a scout—someone expendable—to lay a trail for you to follow through Beyond. That trail is now complete and you may pursue it. Then you will find that which you seek. You have cleansed yourself and I am greatly pleased.

The trail begins at a shrine hidden between two rocks atop Shy'vash Mountain. Al'aran knows the way to the shrine and will take you there. Now go. Find the one you seek. Bring him to me.

It was against protocol to run from the altar screaming in jubilation. So by a great force of effort, Klushere arose and made the journey from the altar, head bowed in supplication, and left the inner sanctum. He made his way to Al'aran's lair to discuss the matter—he was sure Kytone would share his joy.

The Elders of the Etherean Guard were in conference at the Seat, in a comfortable room reserved for their use. Each was seated on a low stool, with a drinking receptacle at hand which issued forth gentle wisps of steam.

The Elders all wore their ceremonial robes of office, similar in style, but varying widely in colour. Each outfit was set off by a contrasting sash worn from shoulder to hip. It was this sash that indicated their rank amongst the Etherean Guard that they commanded.

Collectively the Elders were persuaded that the current lull in crime was an ominous harbinger; the calm before the storm. This subject was now foremost on their agenda. Ruith ru Contin, Hesdar's sister, was speaking.

"My friends, it is by now clear that what we are facing is a planned attack, probably by renegade Ethereans, upon our government and our ideology. In such extreme circumstances, I feel that we *must* take the extreme measure of calling in those most trusted amongst the pilots. Only then..."

"No!" interrupted Gylan Gorph, the second eldest of those assembled. "Whilst I respect greatly Ruith's opinions on this subject I feel that she is gravely mistaken in thinking that a solution lies with untrained and inexperienced public servants no matter how well-intentioned!" There were a few mutterings around the room. This was a concern that most of the Elders shared. He continued, "We can only take a measured approach to this solution. If we apply to the Congregation for resources, we can commence an accelerated training process that will supply the..."

The next interruption came from Yorgish bayle Prout, the most senior Elder. His gentle tones were both welcome and soothing. His interruption started as a polite cough, but due to the respect the other Elders had for him, this was sufficient to silence them all. He looked out at the Elders through immensely bushy eyebrows. His words, slightly muffled by a beard that like his eyebrows had almost never been trimmed, came slowly.

"We will stall our response to our present troubles if we become entangled in this political debate. Ruith and Gylan as usual see different sides of the same problem. They are both right and we must reconcile the differences."

Jish, the youngest of the Elders—an intense lady, fond of brightly coloured outfits and verbal sparring—was ready to interject but desisted when Yorgish raised his hand. The venerable leader of the Guard continued.

"I feel in part responsible for the situation we find ourselves in. No—I do not need you to rush to my defence," he added, seeing that a couple of his protective colleagues were ready to object, "I lay the charge at my own feet, feeling the benefit of hindsight. Had we been more structured in our recruiting and training processes, we would not be here today.

"But," he raised his voice, "rest assured, this trouble would have come to us sooner or later. I know that we have an ever-vigilant foe who will seize his chance whenever it comes. Now faced with this challenge, we must respond to it and with Yershowsh's help, ensure that nothing of this nature happens again."

By the nods and murmurings, Yorgish could tell that all of his audience were agreed on that, at least. He continued, his voice lower and steadier again. "The Etherean pilots historically have been the Guards' most ready source of assistance in times of emergency, but we will undoubtedly face opposition from the Congregation and the public if we seek to restrict their freedom to travel. I am not so naïve that I believe they will readily agree to this simply because it is good for them!" Wry smiles alighted on several faces and then fluttered away, banished by the gravity of the moment.

"Mek, you hold the lists of pilots—how many would you say have received basic brack and ethics training?"

Mekly Sur, the Elders' administrator looked upward as she calculated. "About fifty of our local pilots are old enough to have been on the training programme before bracarpiums were phased out for non-Guard Ethereans. Farther afield, I would guess at five hundred to a thousand. But most of those," she added, "will be looking to retire and embrace the Ether shortly—not assist in fighting."

Yorgish pressed the point, "Of those fifty, how many could we usefully count on?"

Again, Mek cast her eyes to the low cushioned ceiling. "No more than ten, I would say."

"Ten is a start. Ten would not seriously dent the local transport infrastructure. Ruith, how do you feel your sister would respond to a request for additional personnel at this time?"

Ruith pulled a face, doubling up her wrinkles. "As you know, Yorgish, we do not see eye to eye, Hesdar and I. If the request came from me, I do not think it would be met with much sympathy. The Congregation is stretching its resources anyway, trying to contain the upsurge in gambling recruitment. I could neither persuade her to lend support to the search for Medok, whom most now believe is dead, nor to the defence against the Belee'ans, since few believe or will admit that the cult exists. If Medok were with us," she added with a wistful look, "I am sure that he could secure the resources we need."

Jish spoke up, "But Ruith, you are closer to the Chair than any of us. Surely you will try the petition, at least?"

Ruith's grunt was non-committal. Gylan interjected, "You will be wasting your breath. Hesdar despises you."

Ruith bristled, "Thank you for putting it so delicately Elder Gorph."

Gylan ignored her, "Let me speak to the Congregation. I have some allies there." Yorgish raised his shaggy eyebrows at Gylan's euphemism. "They realise that the Guard needs assistance and I am sure that some bodies can be spared for the now vital task of recruiting. One question immediately presents itself before we begin though—that of the age limit."

This was a much debated topic amongst the Elders. Many felt that the age limit for admittance to the Guard should be kept high, or even increased beyond the now statutory limit of thirty Deban years. This was because young Ethereans often became unstable through lack of maturity—they were unable to handle their powers, honed and perfected by Guard training, responsibly. The powerful Guards could not risk one of their rank becoming hostile.

On the other side of the debate were those who felt that all identified Ethereans should be entered into training and selection processes from the moment of onset—usually around puberty. This view was not favoured by the government. Being responsible for the distribution of all resources on Deb, the Congregation was extremely resistant to requests for resources that were not seen as productive. Over the long term, Deb had been enjoying a time of peace for many years and understandably the Congregation felt that the Guard could be kept to a minimum level.

Whatever debate the Elders had on the subject, they all knew the matter would eventually be decided by the politicians. Jish said what was on many minds, "Let us not start that fruitless discussion. I say go to the Congregation first and seek whatever scraps they will throw us. Then we will be in a position ourselves to decide what ages we can target."

The only Elder who had not spoken in the conference so far, was Garmon Weir. The most contemplative of the Elders, he could always be counted on to focus attention on spiritual matters. He now spoke. "What is Yershowsh saying in all this, I wonder?"

"We have not heard from Yershowsh recently. Is He speaking still?" Yorgish mused.

"We should consult a Hearer," Ruith said, with a nod to Garmon.

Gylan's brow furrowed. "There is only one Hearer in our locality and we all know who that is."

Jish raised her voice, "We cannot go to her! We cannot trust a word she says!"

Yorgish said, "I believe we must guard our feelings for the time being and reserve judgment on anything she might say. Ruith is right. We must consult her. Garmon," he looked across at Weir, "will you visit her on our behalf?"

"I will do so directly."

"Speak to her husband first, at least," Jish said. "Find out her present state of mind."

"That is wise counsel," Garmon assented.

Yorgish brought the meeting to a close, summarising the tasks they had agreed upon. Mek would speak to the ten Etherean pilots she had in mind and she would also contact the Etherean Guard farther afield, to call them to the capital. Gylan would speak to the politicians.

Jish was to assist Yorgish in preparing a report to the Congregation covering the Elders' view of the current crisis. The report was also to be disseminated to the Etherean Guard far and wide.

No one envied Garmon his job for he was to speak to the disgraced Hearer, Graye Lovel.

7

The giant rampaging lizard was so obviously a little Oriental man in a badly fitting rubber suit that the film delighted Isobel even more than usual. The director appeared to be taking it all very seriously, which added greatly to Izzy's mirth. The clock struck three, as she finally lost consciousness, with images before her eyes of trees and houses exploding. The lizard had now acquired death-heat-ray vision—an entirely unforeseen consequence of the military subjecting it to small nuclear explosions.

Izzy dreamt fitfully that night. She was emotionally exhausted from the strain of Jon's accident. To look at Jon, one could hardly tell how serious the incident had been, but three people were killed in the accident and many others were badly injured. It had taken the emergency services the best part of ten hours to clear the motorway. To return home without another human being to talk to, to offload on, had been difficult for Isobel. It was no wonder that she let her brain cruise in neutral whilst she soaked up some late night entertainment.

Yes, perhaps calling this 'entertainment' was stretching the definition.

Her sleep was filled with images of exploding buildings, low budget flashes and sparks and hospital staff wandering through the wreckage. Just at the point where her subconscious started to become bored of the dream, she was awakened by a loud sound of smashing glass.

Isobel never woke well, least of all in the middle of the night. Blearily, she shifted the assortment of blankets and overcoats that she had gathered up for warmth and looked round in the surreal flickering illumination of the muted television to where the nearest clock would be. All she could see was a huge furry rear end.

Moving Mr Spencer out of the way to get a better view of the clock, she could not help noticing that there was a distinct glow coming from the direction of the kitchen. She clearly remembered turning the light off earlier. She was very particular about things like switching lights off and closing drawers when she was finished with them.

The clock was an anniversary gift—a fairly bog-standard quartz item set in a heavy rough-hewn piece of Lake District slate. Jon and Izzy had honeymooned in the Lakes and Izzy's mum had thoughtfully bought the clock for them the following year. Isobel barely noticed that the clock was reading 4.32am. At the moment, it was simply a weapon.

Isobel slipped out from under the mountain of covers, as carefully as she could. Something about the light—and a strange feeling in the air; what was that?—made her particularly cautious. Her temples started to throb.

Holding her breath, she walked silently towards the kitchen. The pneumatic hammer that was her heart threatened to take her breath away, so fiercely did it percuss. There was a light switch for the lounge next to the kitchen door, so bravely, foolishly, she simultaneously flipped the switch and threw open the kitchen door. The door crashed into the kitchen unit behind and rebounded at her.

When Isobel finally managed to overcome the door and entered the kitchen, she found it empty. The door to the fridge was wide upon and a jar of jam lay smashed on the floor below. Evidently the glow had been the light from the fridge.

Without questioning how the jar could have launched itself from the fridge, Isobel exchanged her clock for some kitchen roll and bent down to mop up the mess. As she did so, she heard someone whisper, "*Ek dashet. Murcom forshay bo nittlee.*"

She spun round. She was still alone. "Jon, is that you?" she asked with quavering voice. There was no answer.

More assertively she demanded, "Jon, if you're messing around it's not funny." Still no reply. A shiver went down her spine.

In such circumstances, there is only one thing to do. With her heart in her mouth, Isobel went from room to room, systematically switching on all the lights. Only when she had entered every room, checked every cupboard and wardrobe and found no intruders, did she calm down slightly. She finished in the bedroom. The presence of familiar furnishings in a comfortable room had a further calming effect on her mind. Perhaps, after all, it was time to get into bed properly.

"*Vo nun sawtare—prewset vo saravot ca necher!*" A loud voice had spoken directly into her ear, at some length. She felt the breath. Her entire body tensed and every hair on her body stood on end. Her green eyes darted in all directions around the room. Her shoulders hunched up and she pulled her now crumpled jacket tightly around her. There were no obvious weapons within reach. She picked up the phone, just as the wardrobe doors spontaneously slammed shut and she immediately dropped it again.

The terror was rising. She started to cry with the fear. "J-jon, if that's you, you're going too far. Stop it!" she begged.

The bedroom door started to close, slowly, menacingly. Isobel backed up to the wall. And then, by the door, a figure began to appear. It was not Jon. It was no one she knew. The figure was dressed strangely, wearing some kind of armour and had paint on its face. Had she not been fully convinced that she was awake, the outlandish clothing would have persuaded her that she was still dreaming. But Isobel saw none of it. All she could see, what she could not take her eyes from, was the object that the stranger was holding—an evil-looking double-bladed sword.

A thousand doctors wearing stethoscopes crowded round him. Each of them had found a novel way of exploring different parts of his body. One attempted to insert a catheter in between his toes; another was tugging on Jon's nasal hair with a pair of forceps. They were muttering between themselves, but Jon could not make out what they were saying. A nurse with an echoing voice appeared in seven different places within his vision, saying, "Drink this—you'll feel much better." Except that what she handed to him appeared to be a well-buttered snail shell.

Eventually he had had enough of this and caused himself to vanish—but instead of disappearing completely in a fraction of a second, he was only losing physical presence very gradually. Each of the thousand doctors in loud voices started saying, "He's fading—he's fading."

With a gasp, Jon awoke, drenched in sweat. He groggily looked around the ward. A group of medics of various descriptions were crowded around a bed at the opposite end of the ward, oblivious to Jon's sudden awakening. A heart monitor next to the bed was showing a flat line and the hospital staff members were using a defibrillator in an effort to revive the patient. One particularly stressed doctor was repeating, "He's fading—quickly—clear—now!" There was a loud humming buzz and then the monitor showed a series of erratic blips, which gradually steadied.

As the resurrectee was wheeled away, Jon resolved to himself to leave the building that day. With attention diverted elsewhere, he removed the probes and needles, withdrew to the safety of a bathroom and faded for real.

Like a lot of teenagers, Jon had been cursed with acne. Although not particularly disfiguring on his dark skin, it had nevertheless caused him considerable pain and embarrassment. Shortly after the awakening of his ability to become invisible, he had made an extraordinary discovery. When he lost physical presence, whether this was due to the lower drain on his metabolic energies or not he was unsure, he experienced a distinct improvement in his bespotted condition. Although not prone to experimentation, he used this discovery to his advantage on occasions when he was injured, since it appeared that all injuries, including glandular disorders, healed much more quickly when he became invisible.

As he faded out, Jon experienced the peculiar sensation of separation from his body. He knew it still existed in some sense or other, but he could not feel it. After a period of ten minutes—not too long to arouse concern or provoke enquiry he hoped—he returned to normal. To his great satisfaction, he felt much recovered.

In the morning, the ward sister put up token resistance only, as he discharged himself. She was puzzled by his apparent rapid recovery and thought it prudent to run some more tests. But they needed the bed and so eventually she settled for a stern admonishment to call an ambulance immediately should he experience any untoward symptoms during the course of the day. Jon happily agreed and ordered a taxi. He thought that he would call Isobel's office, once he got home and surprise her. The thought was soured only slightly because he knew she would lecture him about fading out like that.

As the taxi entered the modern housing estate, he longed as ever for the means to buy the traditional detached farmhouse they both dreamed of. *Good things come to them that wait*, he reminded himself. He had plans. Right now he was accumulating experience in diverse fields of engineering, computing and security, but he had a long-term goal that was such a pipe dream he hadn't even mentioned it to Isobel. If he could make it work, the farmhouse would be theirs. But it would take time.

He paid the taxi driver and looked up at his box-like house, before walking the four short metres that was the driveway. *At least it's home*, he thought. It was ten o'clock and the milk was still waiting on the doorstep. That was a little unusual, but the milkman occasionally delivered the milk after both the Fentons had left for work.

As he entered the house, he thought he saw something move in the corner of his eye—in the corner of his *spirit* eye. That was odd. He was dimly aware of the other plain of existence, but he rarely saw anything in that other plain. It was probably nothing.

The first stop was the kitchen, to stash the milk. It looked like Isobel had had an accident and left in a hurry. She had probably overslept, after staying up too late watching the television. There was a jammy wad of kitchen roll on the worktop and some sparkling shards of glass on the floor. Jon could imagine the scene. He smiled to himself as he pictured Isobel flinging open the fridge door—whilst simultaneously flipping on the kettle and popping a slice of bread in the toaster—and a jar of jam flying out of the fridge. She would probably have uttered some uncharacteristic but choice words, before reaching for the cleaning materials.

He made himself some filter coffee to compensate for the diabolical froth he had received in the hospital. Then he made his way upstairs. A fresh change of clothes was much in need. His present outfit sported various spots of congealed blood and other unidentifiable substances. Of course Jon had no idea that his carefully prepared drink would end up on the bedroom floor amid slivers of pottery.

For as he opened the bedroom door, the assault on his senses overrode all his bodily control and the mug fell from his numb hand. His wife was in a heap on the floor, bound to a radiator and gagged and there was fresh blood on her forehead.

8

Delturn had excelled himself. Alone, on a strange planet, with few clues to guide him and no allies to aid him, he had done it!

He had never considered himself to be a detective, but the person he was looking for left such clear footprints in the Ether that he was easy to track. The search was assisted by the fact that in this part of the universe at least, there was apparently only one person capable of leaving an Ether trail. Delturn had initially been taken aback by this, but having seen only one form of footprint in the local Ether, he had come to accept that there were no other Ethereans in this remote place.

He had traversed the new planet for several exhausting days at speed, before he started seeing signs of another Etherean. Once he had narrowed the search down to one small island, he spent a little more time in the physical world. He was again surprised to note that the person he sought seemed to confine himself to one small area of the island.

The transport on this planet was the third thing that had surprised him. With such a paucity of Ethereans, Delturn had assumed that no one would attempt to travel over long distances. He had thought that vehicles would be limited to self-propelled short-distance mechanical devices such as his rey. Admittedly such transportation was in evidence—two-wheeled affairs that looked slow and immensely unstable—but he was shocked by the larger vehicles that thundered across the land at great speeds. He was grateful that he was an Etherean, able to become intangible; otherwise his trip here would have been ended precipitously by a collision with one of these high-speed death traps.

He had run on adrenaline for the first ten days. Spending more time than ever in the Ether had been extremely tiring—but the longer he was instilled there, the more footprints he glimpsed and the less suspicion he aroused. The prints became ever fresher, until he could almost smell his target.

Arranging the accident had been a stroke of genius. From his first day on the planet, Delturn had felt sure that the quickest way to corner his quarry would be by involving him in an accident with several of the incredible high-speed mechanical contraptions. Delturn had a good knowledge of engineering from his home planet and many of the concepts employed there were the same here. Whilst tailing his quarry, it had been no great challenge therefore, to speed on ahead through the Ether, catch the lorry and then to release the giant pipe from its mountings on the trailer.

He had looked upon the resulting mayhem in disbelief. Not because of the carnage he had caused, but because of the strangely passive reaction of the Etherean. He made virtually no attempt to escape into the Ether. At first, Delturn was worried that he might have killed his prey. That would have upset Klushere who wanted the pleasure himself.

Fortunately, the man he was chasing seemed at least partly able to defend himself by Etherean means and had survived relatively intact. Delturn had been most puzzled by the fact though that he had remained inside the vehicle during the entirety of the accident. This indicated that he was either untrained in Etherean ways or he was a half-wit. But at least he was still alive.

The man had been taken to a place of medicine—as if he were an ordinary human!—and this had given Delturn his cue to report back to Al'aran. The wounded man made no effort to recover by means of the Ether. Delturn presumed that he was unaware of the potential of the Ether to heal Ethereans. And so it appeared that his quarry would be stationed in one location for some time whilst he recuperated.

When Delturn returned home having left a clear Ether trail behind him, Al'aran had not been as grateful as Delturn had expected. There was no hero's welcome—no gifts or rewards. Instead, he had found himself locked up in an Enveloped dungeon beside the odious man who, it transpired, had initially revealed to Al'aran where to begin the journey to the other planet. Bars Medok was a sorry sight—torn and bruised and barely recognisable—but Delturn felt no sympathy. He was mortified to be chained alongside such Belee'al-hating human trash.

Al'aran had indicated to Delturn that he might be given another chance to "further atone," but as the door of the cell slammed shut, Delturn abandoned hope.

No more than a day after this, hope was also far from Jonathan's mind as he looked, aghast at his wife's inert body. For a moment he became incapable of action—incapable even of thought. But then it was as if he had suddenly become detached from the situation. His glands accepted their physiological assignment and began injecting into Jon all the correct chemicals and hormones required to enable him to deal with a life-threatening situation. His mind cleared and he recalled the slight impression he'd had before entering the house. There was something in the house, there but invisible. Something moving in the non-physical world! *Duck!*

He made a rapid fade to invisibility as a sword blade materialised next to him. He felt the physical sword swish through his intangible presence. He had vanished just in time.

But there was no time to congratulate himself. The sword that had appeared was borne by a snarling figure that now swung into view before him. The figure stood in the physical realm, in between Jon and his wife, but was clearly able to see Jon's spirit form.

The other man was not moving. He was holding his double-bladed sword extended in front of him, pointing at Jon and he was speaking. Jon could not make out the words—it sounded like a cross between Latin and Portuguese—but the words seemed to bypass the language processing part of his brain and speak directly into his understanding. That was impossible, surely?

If this translation was correct, the man was saying, "I have found you at last! And now you will pay. Oh! how you will pay!" No further words followed—just a lunge. It may be odd to note that Jonathan's first instinct was to remain still. But he was after all both invisible and intangible. A sword couldn't harm him.

But then the hormones did their work again and reason flooded into his brain. This was not an ordinary man. This was someone like Jon. He could follow Jon in the non-physical world. As it occurred to Jon to move, he felt the blade touch his spirit form. The indescribable pain spurred him away, at great speed.

Jon flew through the wall of the bedroom, out into the garden beyond. He was fifteen feet above the ground and still moving. He did not have time to ask himself why he was only moving horizontally, rather than plunging downward. The armoured figure was directly behind him, in determined pursuit. Jon ploughed on through his neighbours' house, extremely embarrassed to intrude on them in this way, but he knew that he had no choice.

The sword was right behind him.

Jon felt himself gaining speed as he tore on, but he did not seem to be able to outstrip his pursuer. *What am I—an I.T. nerd!—going to do?* Jon asked himself. He could hardly defeat a vanishing swordsman by quoting abstract algorithms or principles of cryptography. He needed a weapon!

Jon remembered that his best man and current squash partner Mick was a keen fencer. Perhaps at Mick's house he would be able to find a weapon of substance. But Mick's house was in the opposite direction!

Before it could occur to Jon that he didn't know how to do it, he had already flipped upwards and around, sailing straight over the head of his surprised pursuer. The surprise did not last long, as the man chasing him turned and redoubled his efforts.

Jon headed straight for Mick's house. There was no time politely to circumnavigate the houses that lay in his path. Straight on he flew, through bedrooms, bathrooms, attics and studies. The occupants of those rooms were blissfully ignorant of his passing, but still Jon had to restrain himself from shouting, "Look out!" as on more than one occasion, he passed directly through the bodies of his unwitting hosts.

Although there were houses in his path, he could now 'see' Mick's residence. He knew he was close. He took to zigzagging, barrel rolling and swerving, to try and throw off the warrior behind. Shortly he arrived at the house and charged through the structure of the building towards Mick's weapons cabinet. In a complex manoeuvre that he had never before attempted, Jon dipped his hand into the cabinet, part materialised, touched something that felt like a hilt, extended his influence over the weapon and withdrew it into the spirit world alongside him.

Thus armed and with no idea what to do next, he halted and faced the painted man.

But the man was not there.

Jon looked round in alarm. He rendered himself visible and looked with his physical eyes, but there was no one about. There was an extremely loud sound of heavy breathing, but he dimly realised that he was the source of that sound; then he became invisible again and looked around once more. Nothing. And then an awful thought struck him.

Izzy!

His stomach went numb.

He had left his wife behind. Whether the sensation was real or imagined, he did not know, but Jonathan felt the blood draining from his face. His fingers were tingling and his heart felt like it had stopped. *Run!*

Instinct took over once more and Jon sped forward, still clutching the sword. Without yet knowing how he did it, he gained altitude as he moved onwards. There were no acrobatics this time—he had to return to the house in the least possible time.

Why was it taking so long?

The estate around him had blurred and he was struggling to locate familiar landmarks. Still he moved onwards and then he saw his house in view. His ears were pounding and his stomach was threatening to expel his last hospital meal—Jon felt all of this, even though his body did not technically exist at that moment.

Arriving at last in the upstairs bedroom, Jon's mind and body came to a dead halt together. The carpet was drenched and a red stain was spreading around Isobel. Izzy's body was white and showing no signs of life whatsoever.

The painted figure was holding his double-bladed sword aloft and appeared to be chanting. Jon clearly heard the word, "Belee'al," repeatedly. Then the man drew back his sword and was about to plunge forward with a ritual blow. All of this Jon saw as if in slow motion.

No! This couldn't be happening! As the swordsman took aim, Jon dived through his body, startling him. Jon rendered his hands and arms tangible and picked up the lifeless body with as much care but with as much speed as he could muster.

In a millisecond Izzy was with Jon in the non-physical world and

Jon was racing away with her body. This time, he seemed to be outrunning the warrior. Perhaps this experience was drawing out of him abilities he never knew existed.

As he raced, he concentrated and as he concentrated, he noticed that the physical world started to disappear from his senses. What was this? Had he completely parted company with reality? Without stopping to think, he continued, deeper and deeper, now taking twists and turns and making every effort imaginable to ensure that he could not be followed.

After he had continued in this way for some considerable time, Jon slowed and then stopped. He looked down at the lovely face and then looked away. How could he have let this happen?

"Izzy, Izzy. I'm so sorry." He started to sob quietly. "What have I done?" He held her for a while longer and then with an immense effort, let go of the spirit form that was his beloved wife. "I will come back for you," he promised in a whisper. He turned away, then turned back for one last look, taking in all of her, trying to capture her very essence and store it in his mind and soul. Then with a last gasped, "I will not forget," he departed.

When he returned to his home, with violence and retribution on his mind, the assailant was nowhere to be found. He had tried to retrace his steps, but had not met the man on his journey. It appeared that he had not followed Jonathan. In a numb stupor, Jon returned to full physical presence, changed his clothes, picked up his wallet and quietly left the house.

There were the rows of houses, just as normal. There were the cars on the drives and the young children playing on trikes. There were the elderly neighbours, pottering in the garden. All exactly as normal. The normality oppressed him—he hated it—he had to get away from it!

Without making any effort to think and plan, Jon walked for twenty minutes until he reached the most disreputable parts of his town. There he found a pub and there he spent all of the money that he had brought with him.

Four hours later, when the money had run out, Jon left the pub, went to a cashpoint and barely conscious, withdrew sufficient funds to keep him inebriated for a week. He then returned to the pub and resumed his consumption. No one bothered him. He sat at a table alone and drank—just another lonely, friendless man with no family and no commitments.

How long this might have continued is anybody's guess. Jon was making a valiant attempt to drink himself to death. He may have succeeded, had it not been for the fact that one of Jon's work colleagues appeared at the pub, a little after nine o'clock. He had a scantily-clad lady on each arm and seemed at first embarrassed and then indignant to see Jon there.

"What on earth are you doing here, Fenton?" the colleague, one Tyrone Gregor demanded. "Does Isobel know you're here?"

With difficulty, Jon looked up and his least favourite colleague slowly came into focus. "What did you say?" he slurred.

"Isobel—she's not going to be overjoyed that you've parked yourself in a brothel, is she?" Tyrone was leering and he had begun to enjoy the moment.

Jon looked around, uncomprehending. He did not know where he was or what he was doing. But one word had penetrated into his consciousness. Isobel. His eyes started to water. "Isobel!" he cried aloud. He leant forward on the table and in despair pushed two half-empty glasses away from him. They fell to the floor and smashed, as Jon began to sob loudly.

He dimly became aware that it had gone quiet in the bar. As he looked up, he could see all eyes staring at him. An enormous barman was hoisting his heavy frame out from behind the bar and moving towards Jonathan determinedly. A moment of horror and panic came over Jon, which was precisely what he needed. His senses cleared enough for him to realise that after the death of his wife at the hands of a man who could not be traced, the last place Jon needed to be was somewhere as public and seedy as this establishment.

As the barman approached, Jon fled. He ignored Tyrone, whom he virtually upended on his way out. "She'll find out sooner or later!" the lecherous Gregor called after him.

It was raining and dark outside and Jon was grateful for these two facts. The rain cooled his raging mind somewhat and a desire for sobriety overtook him. He wondered if by losing physical presence, he could quickly overcome the poisonous alcohol in his system. It was worth a try.

Under cover of the darkness, Jon vanished. Immediately waves of nausea washed over him and he struggled against the feeling that he would black out. But that feeling passed and extraordinarily, so did the alcoholic haze.

What now? thought Jonathan to himself. *Now is not the time to grieve—now is the time to plan.* In this moment of clarity, several thoughts came to him. His wife was dead. The body would never be found, but at his house on his bedroom carpet and doubtless soaking through the boards below, there was an incriminating pool of Isobel's blood.

There was a sword missing from the cabinet of his good friend. That fact may already have been discovered. Izzy had not made it to work that day and Jon had discharged himself from the hospital that morning. On any objective view, Jon must have been the last person to see Izzy alive.

If Jon were arrested for her murder—and he must be prime suspect, lack of motive and body notwithstanding—with what story was he supposed to defend himself? That an unknown man wearing strange clothes and with a painted face had literally appeared from nowhere and attacked his wife with a double bladed sword? That the same man had now vanished without trace? That in fact the same man was unlikely to be seen again, since, if Jon's guess was correct, he did not come from the UK?

Jon had watched enough detective films to believe that the police would find it difficult to charge him with murder, in the absence of a body. But in the meantime, he would be under the closest scrutiny. He was sure he would be cut off from Isobel's family, if not his own. Her family knew nothing about Jon's abilities and would certainly not accept Jon's story, given the circumstances.

Jon thought back to the last view he had of his wife. Her body bespattered and her skin deathly pale. Her hands bruised and... *Her hands!* Jon had not noticed before but as he brought back to mind the image of his wife, he could clearly see her hands, with no rings on them. Jon's memory for such things was photographic.

Izzy hardly ever took her rings off—not even to sleep. Where were her rings? This became an obsession in Jon's mind that momentarily overcame all his other thoughts. As quickly as he could, he returned home and began a frantic search.

If Isobel had removed her rings, she would have put them in one of two places: in a little jar in the bathroom, or in a pot on the kitchen window ledge. Her rings were in neither place.

The more he looked, the angrier he became. The angrier he became, the more certain he was that the assassin had taken Isobel's rings. But why? In his fury, Jon became dangerously rational. He could not remain here. He would abandon his life, until he could find some form of justice. He would dedicate himself to hunting down the man who had robbed him of the dearest person in his life and he would... Jonathan preferred not to think about what he would do when he found that man.

It was time to pack. But first, he wrote a brief note to his parents and left it on the bedroom dresser. It read, "Dear Mum and Dad, Izzy has been murdered. I have gone to find the man who did this. I love you. Jon." After writing the note, Jon gathered a few essential items, together with some things that he could not bear to be parted from. Before he left, he carefully withdrew from the top drawer of the dresser an old and rather crumpled letter that he had read many times. He scanned it briefly and then placed it in his top pocket.

With a last look at his marital home, Jon became invisible again and began his search.

9

"I have an unpopular request." Gylan had entered Resar Playne's office without announcing his entrance and was already helping himself to a drink from Rez's impressive selection. Documents and calculation devices were spread across Playne's desk and for a moment she seemed thoroughly disorientated by Gylan.

Recovering her accustomed diplomatic composure, she leant back in her chair and swivelled to face Gylan. "Elder Gorph, a pleasure as always. Please do have a drink." She smiled with one eyebrow raised.

Gylan examined his beaker with satisfaction. "You're very kind, my dear. And if you call me 'Elder Gorph' one more time I shall steal your entire collection." Smiling wickedly, he gestured at the line of exotic bottles with their many coloured and highly potent contents. A slight mist hung over the surface of the liquid in his drinking receptacle and he sniffed at it tentatively.

"Please be careful with that. Add some pordry syrup to it, or the mist will choke you." Resar pointed to one of the syrup bottles on the far end of her drinks cabinet. As Gylan tipped a small quantity of the precious syrup onto his drink, the mist dissipated. He sipped the beverage and a colour came to his cheeks. "Amazing," he murmured.

"Can I help you Gy?" Gylan carried his drink over to Playne's desk, sat on the chair opposite her and leant across in her direction. She had turned to face him and was looking intently at his nose. Gylan, in return was studiously seeking eye contact.

"You must know why I am here, my dear Rez?" he inquired.

"If you call me your 'dear Rez' one more time I shall steal your brack again." She looked briefly from his nose to his eyes. Gylan coloured more from this comment than from the drink and looked away. He coughed slightly. "Pretend I have no idea why you're here," Resar added.

Adopting a less patronising tone, Gylan continued, "The truth is, Minister, the Elders have asked me to approach you on their behalf with a petition for resources. Yorgish and many others feel deeply embarrassed that the Guard appears to be too weak to protect the High Congregation adequately."

Resar picked up an irrelevant piece of paper and scanned it briefly before replying. "I am sure this was nothing more than a brief lapse in security. Hesdar may even come to be grateful for it."

Gylan frowned. Rather than explain further, Resar arose and helped herself to a drink. Gylan did not pursue it—she would say more if it appeared to be relevant. "Be that as it may," he said, "the full contingent of the Guard is ageing and it is indeed worrying that so little time and resources are available for training and for identifying onset. We hear every month stories of families thrown into disarray with no support for their emerging Etherean children. The Guard does what it can, but there are just too few of us." He trailed off and then spoke both their thoughts, "The demand for pilots is ever increasing.

"It is not just the attack on the Seat that concerns us," he continued, "the effects of gambling are draining our resources heavily. The gamblers seem to outnumber us ten to one. Every time we close down a gambling den, five more take their place. We cannot hope to stem the spread of this plague," he spat the word 'plague', "with our limited numbers."

Still mixing liquids, Resar asked, "I thought that crime was down of late. Is it really that bad?"

Gylan rose from his seat adding height to his feelings on the matter. "Rez, it is appalling. Do you not hear the cries from the medics? Gambling addicts are losing limbs in punishment enforcement action daily." This was an exaggeration, but the Elder needed to make his point firmly. "We have not yet caught an enforcer in action. We believe that the gamblers must be using Ethereans to execute their gambling contracts, but of course we have no proof of this—not enough to enable us to identify a culprit against whom we could employ the Enveloping procedure. We are so short on numbers and so tied to other ventures that they easily evade us."

Drink in hand, she turned to face him. "If true, this is worrying. I will speak to some of the other Ministers. Please remember Gylan that there is little I can do to influence the decisions of the Congregation on this matter. But I will do what I can. Perhaps this could be a matter for debate."

"We must not sacrifice security for the sake of pleasure or convenience, Rez." He looked at her steadily.

She set her drink upon her desk and moved towards him until she was only inches away. "How ironic that you would say that." She then took his hands and gently touched the two bracarpium bracelets on both of his wrists. "How ironic." Gylan smiled.

Releasing him, she picked up her drink again and finished it in one gulp. "Goodbye, Elder Gorph." Without a further glance, she sat down to her paperwork. Gylan looked at her for a while, then turned and silently left.

A heavy rain was falling over Rebke. Rather than take an Etherean transport, Garmon Weir flew himself through the Ether to his rendezvous with the Hearer. His meeting with Plykar Lovel had been formal, but positive. Plyk felt that his wife would greatly benefit from a sense of purpose—and nothing could bestow that more certainly than a rally to the aid of the Etherean Guard during a time of crisis. She had always been sympathetic to their efforts and this had been reciprocated in the past. The rehabilitation programmes had often received the support of the Guard.

Whilst in the Ether, Garmon could feel a sense of the rain falling around him, delicately brushing at his spirit. In the Ether of course, he remained dry. All the romance of the rain, with none of the inconvenience. It was a sensation of which he never tired.

He arrived at the Lovel residence and marvelled briefly at Graye's perseverance with her garden, even during the shower. Then he withdrew to a respectful distance, materialised and walked towards her noisily so that she would be aware of his approach. She looked up and brushed some wisps of long grey hair from her face. *Even covered in dirt, she's an elegant woman,* Garmon thought.

"Elder Weir—now what brings you here?" She rose and with a polite nod gestured that Garmon should accompany her to the house. The house occupied less of the plot than it had in former years. Her gambling troubles had resulted in resources being allocated away from the Lovel family and they had lost one room and another had been reduced. It was virtually impossible to transgress privately on Deb. A loss of reasonable productivity during working life meant a loss of state-allocated resources. If that resulted in a home being reshaped, the entire neighbourhood would know of it.

They would have lost more of their home or been relocated to a shabbier district, but Plykar had been able to arrange an extension to his career, in return for effectively 'borrowed' resources. At the same time, it had been agreed that Graye would be granted an early release from the productivity system. Free from the obligations of employment, she was able to concentrate more on her garden. As the house had contracted, so her beloved garden had expanded. This was the one consolation that Graye had received in the whole sorry saga.

"I wish this were merely a social call, Graye," Garmon replied.

Graye turned and smiled with resignation as she opened the door. "The Elders do not call on me socially these days, Garm. But you are welcome." As they walked together along the entrance hallway, Garmon fancied that he saw everywhere evidence of Graye's reform. The house was spacious and decorated in light, airy colours. He sensed a feeling of peace about the homestead and strongly suspected that Graye was once more devoting time to meditation and Hearing as she had in her younger years. This was a good sign.

She motioned to him to be seated on a padded low-standing high-backed stool. These items of furniture known as 'cruts' were popular, but a little awkward to settle on, particularly for the elderly.

Someone who did not know the ways of the Ethereans would have thought Graye insensitive in offering such accommodation to a man of Garmon's years. Graye however was well aware that his accumulated years spent in the Ether gave him the sprightliness of a man half his age. He assumed the slightly cross legged seated pose with ease. Graye quickly cleaned up and then brought through some refreshments for herself and her unexpected guest.

As she took the crut opposite, laying the provisions between them, she enquired, "I suppose you have spoken to Plyk?"

"You are astute as ever Graye. Your husband said that I would probably find you in your garden, in spite of the rain." He chuckled lightly and rubbed a hand across his moistened stubbly face. "Somehow I feel that even were you Etherean, you would still enjoy the dampness and the dirt! Thank you." Graye had passed to him a steaming drink.

Graye nodded. "I am closest to Yershowsh when I tend His garden. It is of Yershowsh you wish to talk." She turned her pale green eyes on her guest and he felt he were being inspected as if he were a young sapling and that Graye was uncertain whether he would be successfully established when committed to the nutrifying earth.

Garmon shifted his position on the crut and grimaced. "I need not have spent my journey worrying about how I would broach the subject with you. It gladdens me to know you are communing again."

Her head cocked on one side, Graye addressed him, "I have never lost a sense of the presence of Yershowsh—not even when in the slovenly pit of my addiction. But you Elder Weir—you have neglected your meditations I think."

Garmon looked uncomfortable and a pink tinge sprung to his cheeks. He was supposed to have come as an authority figure whom Graye would respect and serve. But already she had asserted herself over him with the quiet unassuming manner that had made her so successful in her former job. He coughed and shifted position again. "Madam Hearer," he addressed her formally and respectfully, "Yorgish believes as do the rest of us that we have come to a point of crisis. It is not simply the abduction of Bars Medok, though that was a profound loss. It is also the rising tide of—er," he hesitated to use the word.

"Gambling?" Graye offered with a bemused look. "Saying it will not plunge me headlong into disgrace again Garm."

"Thank you—the rising ride of gambling is of great concern to us. We have never seen it to this degree before. The forfeits become ever more gruesome and the magnates have no hesitation in executing their judgments, it would seem." Weir's brow was furrowed. "Equally worrying is that we see the hand of renegade Ethereans in the execution."

"Plykar has not been alone in voicing to the Congregation the need for more resources for the Guard, I think?"

"Madam, true. There is some support, but opposition aplenty. With Medok taken, apathy and fear—both infernally potent—drain from the Seat all appropriate response. Rather than taking action, I fear they congratulate themselves that they were 'not as foolish as Medok' to be working at the Seat at so late an hour." He shook his head and his Guard's sash slipped from his shoulder. He did not adjust it but continued, "We cannot detect the reason for this apathy, but we fear that there are influences in the Congregation that escape even our notice. Madam?"

Garmon had noticed that Graye appeared to have lost concentration. He paused before prompting her again, "Graye?"

She lowered her eyes from the point on the ceiling where previously they had been fixed. "And you wish me to ask Yershowsh to shed light on this." She gave a light laugh. "Oh how often do we seek clarity for our own ends! He will reveal what He will reveal, Garmon."

"So you have not Heard anything?" Garmon asked, his voice flat.

"On the contrary Elder Weir; I have Heard one message, repeated often, but until now I did not know for whom it was intended. Now I see it was for the Etherean Guard." She leant back and uncrossed her legs, looking elegant even in that pose.

A tension developed in the air. During the course of their conversation, Garmon's confidence in Graye's ability to Hear had been fully restored. He was not about to interrupt her as she revealed what she had Heard.

"Yershowsh says that the Guardian of the Insensate is returning."

"And that was it?" Jish asked, incensed. They had agreed to meet again directly after Garmon's conference with Graye. "Her excesses have sent Lovel addle-minded. We humbled ourselves to enquire of her and in return she offers us children's tales and insults."

The Elders were conferring in a circle in the Ether, at some height above the Seat. It was a favourite location for their nocturnal meetings. If the subject matter bored them, there was plenty to look at and the night prospect over Rebke was glorious. Architects of that great city had designed the layout and the lighting with an uncanny sense of the spectacular view from the air. The six towers that surrounded the Seat of the Congregation, peacefully watching the machinations of the politicians within, presented an imposing sight indeed.

Garmon spoke in defence of Graye, "Whilst I agree Jish that we should treat with caution anything we receive from Madam Lovel, it remains true that even whilst intoxicated she could still Hear more clearly than I when I am sober."

Ruith, with a puzzled air questioned Garmon, "And those were her precise words?"

"There could be no doubt, in her mind or in mine. She claimed to have received this message every day for the last fifteen days. Yes it could be fantasy or wishful thinking, but today I supped with the Graye Lovel whom I have not seen for many years. I have every reason to rely on her account of the message." For Jish's benefit, he added what all the older Elders knew by experience, "Yershowsh says what He says. He does not say what we want to hear."

"Then it must be true," Jish conceded.

"A Guardian is returning," Gylan echoed.

"*The* Guardian," Yorgish corrected. "Mistake not the words."

Automatically all eyes turned to Mekly Sur. "We have no Guardian," she announced simply. "We have not had a Guardian in Jish's lifetime."

"Do I correctly recall the prospect of a Guardian recently?" Ruith asked of Mek.

Mek chuckled, although humour was rare for her. "Not so recent, Elder ru Contin. We had strong hopes more than twenty years ago for the ward of Bars Medok. He showed encouraging signs pre-onset."

Jish asked, "What happened? I know of no child in the Medok household and certainly no Etherean I know of bears the name Medok. Were the signs wrong?"

"The Cull." Gylan answered on Mekly's behalf, with a dark tone.

Yorgish sighed deeply and looked up with sad eyes. "He was a handsome boy. We never knew who his parents were. The Chair at the time asked that he be placed discretely with a childless family within the Congregation's Ministry and asked the Elders to intercede in this matter. The boy bore the same skin tone as Medok and the same eye colour as Medok's wife; the Medoks were bright rising stars, so it was an obvious placement. Since it was the Chair's request, no questions were raised. The Elders were simply to keep watch. Beyond the peculiar position of the Chair in the matter, he also attracted our interest because he showed great signs of awareness of the Ether." With another sigh, Yorgish added, "At the time, we had hoped that he might prove to be our first Guardian for thirty years. And then the Cull happened."

The Cull. It evoked in all of the Elders' memories scenes of anguish and misery. Many pre-onset children, all of whom had been identified by the Guard as potential Ethereans, were systematically killed by an unknown and untraced assassin. The response of the Etherean Guard had been strong, but totally inconclusive. No culprit was identified, although all agreed it must have been a rogue Etherean. When the Cull ended, hundreds of families were left with no child and no answers.

Yorgish alone had his suspicions both of the reason for the attacks and the likely culprit. At the time he was junior amongst the Elders, but he had not entrusted his suspicions to the senior Elders, since he did not know how many Ethereans might be implicated. He had embarked on a search on his own account and had spent many degrees of the sun on his own time, searching. But the trail had grown ever colder as he grew ever more frustrated. He had harshly considered this to be a failure on his part and had resolved to be wholeheartedly committed to the pursuit of justice ever since.

Yorgish's devotion to his career as an Elder was by way of compensation in his own mind, to the many parents he felt he had failed. As time had marched on, he forgave himself, but he never abandoned his commitment to the cause. In recent years he had developed a resigned, sombre attitude. He could not understand why the other Elders wished to have him as their head, but he took on the role with the humility and dignity that the preceding years had engendered in him.

Gylan asked with his accustomed directness, "So this Guardian is not dead then?"

Jish spoke first, "Is this what we are to believe? Are we, fresh from the hunt for Medok, to begin another fruitless search for a green cloud?"

"Green cloud," Yorgish mumbled. "New one." Aloud he said, "Garmon—your view?"

Garmon lifted his head, which had been bowed previously and said, "Yershowsh said that the Guardian will return. Not that we will search for him and find him. When he does return..."

"...or *she*," Ruith offered.

Garmon coughed, "When the Guardian does return, we will not need to seek. The Guardian, whether an escapee from the Cull or a former Guardian long ago thought deceased, will be revealed. I do not believe any search is warranted or needed."

"So we wait?" Jish asked.

"So we prepare," Yorgish replied.

10

The letter that Jon considered to be one of his most precious possessions read as follows:

Dear Sir and Madam,

May I first make my most humble apologies for intruding upon you. You do not know me and must certainly be suspicious of an unsolicited approach from a stranger—the more so when you read on. I only beg that you read to the end, suspend disbelief for a moment at least and grant me a little of your precious time.

You apprehend that this letter is tending towards a request of some form. This is correct, but the request is not in respect of currency or other units of trade. You do not know me yet but I hope that you may take at face value for now my assurance that my intentions are honourable; I seek no gain from you; I abhor all conduct that amounts to taking advantage of another being.

This is a hard letter for me to write. I find it cumbersome conveying my thoughts and feelings in your language and some of the subject matter will doubtless be strange and alien to you. Nevertheless, I shall persevere—you will understand why.

I am not from your country, nor acquainted with all your customs, but in the time that I have presumed to observe you, I have concluded this: truly you are sensitive, caring and very moral people. I would go so far as to say that you are to my eyes outstanding among your peers in this regard. I know I can trust you. To my request then!

My burden is my blessing; my sadness is my succour. It has been given to me to act as guardian to a young boy; to carry him out of peril and to seek a place of safety. For many cycles of your moon I have striven to secure his well-being for now and for the future. Whilst he was at one time at risk of abduction and possibly worse, I believe that we have at last taken sufficient paths and detours to ensure that he can never be found by those who sought to harm him. I have learnt your language and customs and in turn taught them to the boy. All that remains is for me to place the child in a family.

I did not feel equal to the task of protecting him; by the grace of Yershowsh I believe this task is complete. But I know that the task of raising him is completely beyond my wit and so I must look to others.

I would ask you seriously to consider adopting and raising this boy as your own. In outward appearance he would seem to all eyes to be of the same race as you—you should not experience too many uncomfortable questions. I am sure that whatever formalities may be required in your country to legitimise such a venture, we will be able to complete these together.

Far from wishing to be a burden to you, I will do my utmost to ensure that, should you accept this charge, you are supported fully. I only ask that you meet with us so that we can discuss this further.

Where have we come from? That is a hard question to answer. I am sure you will understand though that we are refugees. We cannot return to our homeland—grave danger awaits us there. But the boy cannot hope to thrive in my care—and thrive he must! His growth and maturing is more important than anything else and I will do whatever I can to secure a safe life and fruitful education for him.

Please join me on this venture. I know the boy to be true and faithful and he will be as open and honest with you as if he were your own son. It is without question that he would love and respect you and regard you as true parents—I truly believe you could not wish for a better son. If there is any space at all for him in your lives, I beg you to allow him entrance.

I will follow this letter with a visit, two sunrises hence. I hope that you will have had time to consider this matter carefully. If you would grant me an audience, I will gladly answer your questions to the best of my abilities.

Your humble servant,

The signature was unreadable—the only part of the letter clearly written in another language using a different alphabet. Jon had read this letter at least once for every year of his life, for it contained the only evidence he carried from his childhood of his unusual origins. He would never willingly be parted from it.

At various times in his life Jon had hoped to meet the author of this letter, whom he now only vaguely remembered. He often wondered if he would ever be able to visit his place of birth, wherever that may be. He guessed that he was originally from an Arabic or Oriental country, judging purely by the signature on his letter.

Jon wished that now as an adult he were able to question in detail the writer of the letter—his original guardian. But the Fentons had long ago lost contact with that man. They believed he was still in existence, for they continued to receive payments into their bank account from the same source, long after Jonathan had left home and become able to support himself. The fact that they could not except by incurring some expense contact the donor and return his payments caused them some embarrassment. From the date that Jon finished university, on their bank's advice, they transferred the payments directly into a separate account, in the hope that one day they would be able to return them to Jon's benefactor.

As Jon left his home he wondered when, if ever, he would see it again. He looked up at the clean bright white double glazing, the even and uniformly coloured brickwork and the monotonous grey roof tiles and thought to himself what a truly dull house it was. Now that Izzy was gone, there was nothing left to brighten the place.

These thoughts caused him to weep afresh. As he passed some of his neighbours in their gardens, they stared at him, but this being England, no one sought to intrude upon him and ask him what was the matter. That suited Jon.

He wasn't clear about where he was going. At the moment he was just wandering, hoping that inspiration would hit him. He tried to keep his thoughts away from Isobel for the moment, but his mind persistently rebelled against this resolve.

A sound gradually encroached upon his consciousness. It was an aeroplane, passing overhead thirty thousand feet away from him, he guessed. He stopped at the end of his cul-de-sac and looked up at the plane for a moment. It was strange to him to realise that he now had time simply to stop and stare. Perhaps this was why, he thought, his elderly neighbours looked at him and Isobel for long periods of time, without any sign that they were aware they were staring. They had more time; the stare did not really signify anything.

He let his eyes drift out of focus, as he gazed upward. His spiritual eyes must have similarly relaxed at this point, because he caught a glimpse of something that he could not identify or explain. A lady and her dog crossed the road to avoid him, but Jon was oblivious—he was trying to bring into focus the thing he had just noticed.

It was an impression, almost like an indentation in the non-physical world. He felt his spiritual eyes adjusting and as they did, the indentation took the form of a man. He could not explain how this was so, but the form resembled the man that had attacked Isobel and chased Jon.

His heart leapt and perspiration sprang to his brow. Now he had seen this, he did not want to lose it. He was concentrating so hard that he stepped out into the road to see better, not realising where he was going. A paper-boy on his bicycle swerved to avoid him, cursing loudly. Jon heard not a word.

He tried focusing away from the indentation and back to it. He found that he could bring it into view at will. With his confidence thus raised, he tried looking elsewhere. As he looked in the spiritual realm, he could see more of the imprints and he noticed too that another impression was visible. It was Jon himself. *These must be footprints*, he thought.

These must be footprints.

The thought sunk in. If there were footprints, he could follow them. If he could follow them, he could find the man that had taken the life of his wife. *You will be careful Jon?* he heard the voice of his wife say—it was an accustomed phrase. *I will*, Jon rejoined. If there was the slightest chance he could catch this man unawares, Jon would take it.

At this point, it would have been wise for Jon to postpone his pursuit, to prepare for the task he set himself. He knew nothing of combat, nothing of the Ether—he did not even have a name for that nebulous non-place. His Etherean powers were untried and untested, beyond the simplest of Etherean skills: invisibility, intangibility and now flight. He was intent upon pursuing someone who was clearly his better in all these respects, but none of this occurred to Jon. So set was he on his mission that had his wife reappeared to him, living again, it is doubtful whether Jon would have delayed his quest one moment.

Having seen the footprints Jon knew that his mission had purpose and a chance—however slim—of success. He looked around him briefly—for a moment he was alone. He faded to invisibility and opened his spiritual eyes fully, for the first time in his life.

He could not believe what he saw! This was a new place!

Indescribable shapes and colours filled his vision, overlaid on top of the physical world he knew. And upon, through and around these shapes he saw impressions of himself everywhere. During the chase, he had been leaving footprints everywhere, oblivious to the effect.

He tried moving forward whilst looking backward. A trail followed him, gradually fading until it reached apparent stability. He exulted in this discovery. He tried various forms of motion, through the horizontal and vertical planes and found that it came to him easily. As he did this, he trailed his hands beside him and noted the gentle ripples that spread outwards wherever they touched the spirit world. He laughed—and in this place even sounds were different. His laugh seemed more musical, more resonant. Having heard the effect, he laughed again, faking it like a child with an echo, enjoying the sound.

A happy memory sprung into his head—Isobel asking him if he had ever experimented with his abilities. He could not understand why he had never tried this before. With a growing sense of wonder and excitement, he dived and weaved through physical and spiritual objects. He shouted and whispered and passed his hands through everything.

With a sudden boyish interest, he tried plunging downwards into the earth below him. To his great surprise, the earth opened up and received him readily. As he shot through soil, rocks and substrata, the magnitude of all he was experiencing played heavily on his mind. What was he? *Who* was he? Why could he do all this? What was his purpose? It was a true awakening to another reality.

Jon can be pardoned for forgetting his troubles for a moment. It is not so unusual after all, that someone who one might expect to be grieving, is instead making new discoveries and experiencing new sensations. Not that Isobel ever held him back—on the contrary, she often expressed incredulity that Jon lacked the interest to explore his abilities. No, Jon had always harboured a desire to be normal, a desire to be seen to be normal. And this all stemmed from a determination to protect those he loved. In the loss of Isobel, Jon experienced an epiphany and few can wonder that an extreme emotional experience may have some advantageous effects as well as some disadvantageous.

It was therefore some hours that passed before Jon became aware of time. Here in the spiritual world, time took on a different meaning in any event. There was no pressure on Jon to achieve any task, no body clock ticking, telling him to retire. Although it was past midnight and the hours of dawn were near, Jon felt no need of sleep and no sense of fatigue oppressed him.

Eventually, Jon recalled his self-imposed mission. He berated himself harshly for indulging his whim and feeling an sense of panic, he returned to where he had first seen the footprint of his assailant. The tracks were still there, he noted with relief. With new determination, fuelled by misplaced confidence in his expanding abilities, Jon now followed these tracks.

He kept one eye, as it were, on the physical world and one on the spiritual world. The tracks continued across country for many miles. When he came to the shores of the British Isles, hovering above them at a height fifty metres or more, he was not surprised to see that the tracks continued onward and outward. He had fully believed that the man was not from his country. Quite how far away the man originated, he was yet to discover.

The sun was beginning to rise across the Channel. He was heading, he supposed, in the direction of southern France. He had barely left his country before, but to be leaving now in such a strange and exciting manner struck him in no way as odd, so focused was he on the footprints before him. A moderate breeze whipped up the waves below him, occasionally sending spray upwards. Once or twice, he casually dangled his foot into the physical world and let the spray splash his shoe.

He passed a small boat below. Jon wondered what the crew might think if they could see him soaring overhead. How would they report their sighting? Would they be taken seriously? Unlikely, Jon thought.

This would not happen however, since Jon was invisible to the normal human eye, nor did he wish to risk any part of his journey by letting himself be seen. Within a matter of hours he was sure he would become a notorious wanted man and soon enough people would be fancying that they saw him in bars, airports and cinemas up and down the country.

So this was France. He looked away from the trail for a moment to take in some of the sights. He was amazed at how French everything and everyone looked. Even the cats looked French.

His flight over France was uneventful. He touched down at one point and noted that the trail was concentrated around a certain restaurant. He presumed that the man he was trailing had looked for provisions here. The trail picked up again and continued about 50 metres consistently above ground.

Jonathan wondered where the trail would take him. He became curious about his final destination and thinking he may be able to predict this, he flew directly upwards for a moment. As he climbed higher and higher, he could see more of the planet opening up below him. He travelled through some wispy clouds until ultimately he arrived at the height where he imagined planes would fly. He then looked down.

Had he been in his physical body, he would have gasped. As it was, he just stared in awe and wonder at the vista spread out below, not breathing, for here, as he was discovering, he had no need of breath. He could make out the outline of many countries he recognised, through the thin cloud below. To the north-west he could see parts of the United Kingdom, although most of that was under cloud, unsurprisingly. The Mediterranean sea was below and if he traced an imaginary line straight from his home in England, through his journey so far and projected it onward, it continued to Italy, beyond to Greece and after that, presumably to Egypt or Saudi Arabia. He wished that Isobel were with him to enjoy this journey.

After he returned to ground level, Jon resumed his course and stayed on task. He picked up speed and the lands over which he passed became of less interest to him. He marvelled briefly at the Alps, before he flew down the length of Italy. By this stage, it was well into the afternoon, but Jon still felt neither hungry nor tired. For Jon, the demands of being invisible were much less than those of being physical. Again, he wondered why he had never tried this before. If he had had time to enjoy the view, he would have appreciated for the first time how much more there was to the world than the small part with which he was acquainted.

The trail took a slightly more easterly direction as he left the southern coast of Italy. About 350 miles later, the trail became more concentrated. This seemed to indicate that the warrior had slowed down considerably. Jon had sufficient time to assemble his thoughts as the island came into view, to realise that he was about to land on Crete.

He had travelled around half the length of the island, when the trail stopped. This was an unwelcome development indeed. It had not previously occurred to him that the man might become completely physical, but now Jon appreciated that if that had happened, he would have no trail to follow.

Jon risked materialising, hoping that news of the death of his wife would not have travelled this far in this time. He knew insufficient about such things to realise that no native of Crete would have heard of him or would ever hear of him. Although he was safe, he was cautious.

The smell of sage hung thickly in the evening air. In the distance he could hear the clanking of goats' bells and the murmur of traffic. He was standing in a field of dry grass, next to a treacherous-looking rough gravel road that lead upward into the mountains. It was warm and the sky was cloudless. Had Jonathan arrived a few hours earlier, it would have been far too hot for the clothes he was wearing and the rucksack he was carrying. But now, he was quite comfortable as the day drew to a close.

His stomach grumbled loudly, alerting him to the fact that he had a body and it required sustenance. Jon wondered what he should do about this. There seemed to be a town a short walk away. Jon decided that he would pay a visit in the hope that a solution to his hunger would present itself.

He took a look around him, committing the area to memory, both in the physical and in the spiritual dimension. He noted the last impression made by the man he pursued and carefully marked out in his mind the likely routes from that point. Then he headed into town.

The sign at the end of this road heralded in Greek and English, his entry into Elounda, clearly a popular tourist spot. He was on the main road, flanked by three types of building only: souvenir shops, holiday apartments and tavernas. Although Jonathan had not come there to sight-see, he couldn't help becoming absorbed by the sights and sounds around him—the very white and very square buildings; the croaking calls of cockerels. On every second doorstep, men sat playing backgammon and drinking raki or ouzo. In between rolls, they all held a small glass in one hand and worry beads in the other.

The women were in evidence too, but more by the sounds of their voices than by their visible activity. It seemed to Jon to be an idyllic sector of paradise. No one appeared to be rushing. All the banter he witnessed was animated, but somehow effortless and accustomed.

He stopped to watch a particularly vigorous game being played by two swarthy, bushy-moustached Cretans. A couple of other gentlemen stood nearby, but whether they were cheering or heckling, Jon could not make out. The game drew to a close and the loser slammed down his glass in ire, firing Greek at his opponent like a machine gun. The two spectators slapped the loser on the shoulders and round the face, as he rose from the table. Then, as if they were one gestalt entity, they all turned in unison to look at Jonathan.

The seated man spoke, nodding upwards slightly. "Kali sfera. You play?"

"Er..." Jon had not expected anyone to notice him and preferred to remain entirely anonymous. But it transpired that the words, "You play?" were not a question but a command, since he was immediately ushered into the seat, despite his protestations.

"Is easy. You learn fast."

"Uh, I have played before," Jon offered.

"Good then. You beat me, you eat at my taverna yes?" He was refilling his shot glass from an unmarked bottle.

"Sounds good to me," Jon replied with a timid smile. "And what if I lose?"

His opponent scowled darkly and drew his finger across his throat. "Then I kill you, yes?" There was a long pause as he and Jon locked eyes for a moment. Then, simultaneously once more, the four men burst out into hearty laughter. The three men standing all slapped Jon heavily on the shoulders and head and one of them indicated in broken English that Yannis was a great comedian, yes? Then, as if on cue, they all reached into hidden pockets and lit particularly foul-smelling cigarettes.

As Jonathan looked up uncertainly at the smokers, Yannis reached across with a fresh glass, full of a colourless liquid. As Jon turned back, he set this glass down before Jon with a display of almost paternal pride.

"This my own raki. No better in the whole of Kriti. You try?" Again, Jon noted that this was a directive rather than a request. With a certain amount of trepidation, he picked up the tiny glass and sipped at its contents.

Jon fancied he could hear his innards sizzling, as the liquid made its molten way down to his stomach. His cheeks flushed and had he been able to breathe, he would have coughed violently. But the innocent looking substance had stolen his air. The sizzling sound was in fact Jon's gasp, as the fire water did its work.

Aware that four intense pairs of brown eyes were fixed on him, Jon felt he ought to make some comment. "That's," he croaked, "that's very good." The words came out slowly and painfully. After another short pause, the men started laughing again—deep belly laughs. One of them laughed so hard he started to cry and another seemed in danger of vomiting. Fearing that his masculinity would be called into question, Jon steeled himself and knocked back the rest of his drink. Better prepared this time, he managed to carry it off without looking too nauseous. This elicited a good natured cheer from his new friends. The ritual of bonding over, the game began.

A wiry, withdrawn, wraith-like acquaintance at university had first introduced Jon to the game. They were supposed to be working on an assignment together, but the acquaintance Samuel was not terribly committed to his coursework. After the first game, Jon was entranced. They met together regularly after that, simply to play backgammon. They had little to say to each other and no real quality of friendship; after university ended, no effort was made to remain in contact. But right now, Jon was grateful to Samuel for his coaching.

One thing that took Jon aback was the speed at which Yannis played. Jon barely had time to register the numbers rolled before Yannis had made his move and the dice were back in his shaker. Jon in comparison must have seemed very ponderous.

The first game was a complete disaster from Jon's perspective. Several of his blots were sent back to the start and with an early lead established he could see there was no way he was going to catch up with the man from Crete. Once the game was over, Yannis graciously suggested, "Best of three." Jon conceded, knowing that no other option was being offered and he had little to lose. He hoped that the threat to kill him was merely Mediterranean humour, but he did not fear an attack from ordinary physical beings anyway.

The second game was far more satisfactory. He lost the nerves he had felt in the first game, after the third glass of raki found its way into his system. Jon couldn't feel his toes, but that did not seem terribly important.

He rolled no less than three double-sixes during that game and felt that he hardly deserved the victory when it came. With the games level, they began their final clash. Jon could not help noticing that several more onlookers had appeared, drawn by the unusual spectacle of this blue-eyed, dark-skinned Westerner playing backgammon with a local—and holding his own. Perhaps not holding his drink, though.

Jon became more excitable in the third game and his hosts laughed longer and louder the quicker his speech became and the more animated he was. In his peripheral vision Jon detected bets being placed. The game itself was entirely free of gambling—except for the prospect of dinner or death at the hands of Yannis. The doubling cube was nowhere in sight and Jon suspected that however friendly they were towards him, he wasn't anywhere near close enough to their inner circle to be allowed a fully competitive game involving the use of the cube.

The third game lasted longer than the others put together. Each man played a more risky strategy than before and both felt the frustration as open blots were hit and sent back to the start. Eventually it was Jon who was victorious, but Yannis did not seem at all surprised or fazed by this. Jon thought that maybe he had planned it all along, but as he was bustled into the neighbouring taverna, there was no doubting the hospitality of the locals, or the sincerity of the offer of dinner.

After the evening Jon could never recall what it was he had been offered to eat. He remembered that there was a lot of it and that it was strongly flavoured with herbs. The clearest memory was of many of the locals sitting at his table, talking to him rapidly in Greek, not caring whether or not he could understand, simply happy that a tourist was eating in their favourite restaurant. An English couple was eating there too, but they did not receive a fraction of the attention with which Jon was honoured. Had Jon been able to speak Greek, he still would not have heard the truth from Yannis's lips—that Jon reminded him of a military colleague lost decades earlier in fighting and that he was overcome with a fit of sentiment that forced him to give the biggest display of hospitality he could muster, in honour of his deceased friend.

The courtesy extended to a night's stay in a clean bed, which Jon gratefully accepted. And so he spent his first night apart from his wife in a foreign land and a strange bed. He reached out for Isobel many times in the night and finding her missing wept repeatedly into his pillow. He nevertheless did manage some sleep and eventually awoke feeling somewhat refreshed.

That morning, Jon was sent on his way with a fresh loaf of bread and a watermelon. Jon bade an emotional farewell to Yannis, who promised him, "Next year, I beat you. *Then*, I kill you!"

11

Another glorious sunrise presented itself to Martin Plowright as he looked out across the waters towards the island of Gomera. He loved walking along the beach front early in the morning, barefoot in the sand. His wife was starting breakfast for their guests, but she was content to allow her husband a few moments of solitude before the rigours of the day.

Gomera was shrouded in mist but to the north of the island Martin could just make out the shape of an airliner on its final approach to Tenerife. This was probably one of the smaller, more select airlines. They tended to add a sense of exclusivity to the flight by approaching Tenerife from the south-west and banking right until the airport came into view. This afforded the passengers a lingering view of the volcano through the starboard windows.

Martin picked up a stone and skimmed it on the calm waters. It skipped four times before finally nose-diving into the sea. Martin counted off the hops in Spanish, under his breath, "Uno, dos, trés, quattro..." He felt mildly irritated with his performance and tried again. The second stone fell after only two hops, so he gave up for the day. He put on his beach shoes and made for his scooter, which was parked on the road between two hotels that overlooked the beach.

Within minutes he was back at the apartment block in Playa de las Americas that he managed with his wife, Elena.

"Hola Lena," he called as he entered the kitchen. Elena was hard at work by the oven, but looked relaxed and content as usual. She offered her cheek for a kiss, as Martin approached from behind. He complied and then moved to the sink.

"There is a señor 'ere to see you Martin," she told him, as he washed his hands. "I tell him you talk after tables is laid." Despite fifteen years together although she had learnt a lot of English from Martin, the grammar of the language remained something of a mystery to her. She nevertheless insisted on communicating in English, the language of tourism.

Martin set out the tables for breakfast and then made his way to their small lounge, where the stranger was waiting. He knew immediately that it was bad news when he saw that the man was wearing a dark suit. He rose as Martin entered. Martin extended a hand and introduced himself, "Martin Plowright. Can I offer you a drink Mr...?"

"Edwards. No drink, thank you."

Martin smiled and gestured to the sofa. "What can I do for you?" he asked, as they sat down. Mr Edwards sat stiffly well back on the sofa, whilst Martin sat on the edge of an easy chair opposite the sofa.

"I have been sent here by my employers, Briggs and Kendal." Martin stiffened. "Some time ago you left instructions with them that should they have any messages for you concerning a certain matter," Mr Edwards paused, head down and peered up at Martin seriously through frowning eyebrows, "such messages were to be conveyed in person, not by telephone nor by other electronic means."

Martin arose, closed both doors into the room and stood looking at nothing for a while. Mr Edwards waited patiently. His meter was running and he did not care how long this interview lasted. If Mr Plowright wanted to look at nothing for a week, that was fine by Mr

Edwards.

Eventually Martin turned towards Edwards. "Please continue."

Mr Edwards looked down at his lapels for a moment and brushed away a non-existent speck of dust. "My message is this:" he said, looking up, "Several days ago, Jonathan Fenton went missing."

Mr Edwards had concluded the meeting a few moments after that revelation. There had been little else to tell. The private detective firm, Briggs & Kendal, had begun a search immediately the disappearance of Jonathan was discovered. Their sources had not turned up anything more than the police had found. Both Jonathan and his wife were missing. The matrimonial home was bespattered with vast quantities of blood, which proved to be Isobel's. One of Jonathan's shirts had traces of blood on it too—his own—but the age of the blood suggested that it had been shed during an earlier road traffic accident, not subsequently. Judging by the amount of blood to be found at the house, Isobel was believed dead and Jonathan was indeed the prime suspect.

Jonathan's friend, Mick, had been obliged to answer some searching questions after he had reported to the police the fact that a rapier had mysteriously vanished from a locked weapons cabinet; Mick was not entirely in the clear.

Jonathan's note to his parents had been the subject of some considerable interest. His parents maintained that their son was a man of integrity, and the note must therefore mean exactly what it said. The police were inclined to take it to be an amateurish attempt at redirecting blame for a murder. Everyone who knew Jon however supported his parents' view.

The last confirmed sighting of Jonathan was at the end of his road. He was alone and staring up at the sky. There was a lot about this case that puzzled the police.

Martin did not know many of the people involved and he did not have access to all of the information within the grasp of the police, but already he was much closer to solving the mystery than they were. He kept quiet about this until breakfast was finished and cleared away and the guests directed onwards to other more diverting occupations, but then he responded at last to his wife's curious glances.

"Lena, something has happened to Jonathan Fenton. No one knows where he is and the police are looking for him."

Elena threw her hands up to her hair and pulled it out sideways to the left and to the right. She started repeating the *Hail Mary*, under her breath. In short, she empathised fully with her husband, who was stressed and extremely concerned. "You must go then—you must pack—go go!" she said, with feeling.

Martin hesitated, "But the guests..."

"I get Josie to 'elp," referring to their daughter, "we be okay. You go!" She started flapping her hands at him, as if she could waft him away by that means.

Martin was touched by her strength of feeling—he had told her all about Jonathan and she almost felt as though the boy were part of her own family. He pulled Elena to him and hugged her for a long time, burying his face in her dense brown hair, breathing in a mixture of perfume and cooking smells. After a few minutes in this embrace, Elena pushed Martin away, sniffing heavily. She wiped her face with her apron and then rushed upstairs to their apartment to throw together some clothes for Martin's journey. It was a journey that they had anticipated for many years, though not under quite these circumstances. Elena knew exactly what Martin would need.

After making a few telephone calls to set into place contingency plans for his absence, Martin went upstairs to the bedroom where Elena was finishing off. She was backing out of a deep fitted wardrobe, the original contents of which were scattered about her feet.

With a flourish she produced two gleaming metal bracelets. She had polished them with her multi-purpose apron and, after nearly fifteen years, hidden beneath piles of clothes, their metallic grey splendour was displayed once more. She presented these precious artefacts to her husband.

Martin took the bracelets and looked at them with almost the same amount of awe he had experienced when he first received them, as a young man. He turned them over in his hands, feeling the weight and solidity of them. He examined and marvelled at the design on the surface. The design was not carved—it was much more ingenious than that.

With outstretched arms, he brought the two bracelets together rapidly. Rather than a metallic click, there was more of a slurping sound, as the bracelets melded together. In an instant, Martin held in his hands a five foot tubular pole. With a smile on his bronzed and weathered face, he tried a few rapid manoeuvres with the staff and relished the sound as the pole swished through the air at speed.

Then, carefully, he brought the pole to rest. He stroked it in a particular manner and again the slurping sound could be heard, as the substance of the rod flowed back into two gleaming metallic bracelets, now locked around his wrists.

"Be careful, Martin," Elena said, tears in her eyes.

Martin smiled and there was a fire in his eyes that his wife had not seen for many years. "Don't worry Lena! I have my brack—what can possibly go wrong?" He gave her a reassuring squeeze.

She looked at him worriedly. "Promise you return?"

"I promise. Say goodbye to Josie for me." They hugged once more and then Martin vanished. He knew exactly where he needed to go next. Instilled in the Ether, he made a bee-line for a little town thousands of miles away; a town called Elounda.

12

Had Jonathan arrived in Elounda a few days later, coinciding with Martin, he might have been spared an extremely unpleasant experience. Or both he and Martin might have fallen into disaster together and hope for Deb lost for centuries. There was nothing fated or inevitable about the events that followed, but it was most fortunate for the Etherean Guard and for the residents of Deb, that Jonathan's journey began when it did. Jonathan's misfortunes were not to be in vain—not by any means. It is not always obvious why disaster befalls the just, but at least at times, it can be for the ultimate good.

Cretans specialise in a modern-day manna. Their bread can be utterly heavenly on the day it is baked but rank the next. Chewing thoughtfully on the delicious and still fresh bread he had been plied with, Jonathan arrived back at the site on the treacherous mountain road. It is so often of great value to approach a problem after a night's sleep, with fresh eyes in one's head and delicious food in one's hand. As he looked at the final footprint of the foreign assassin, Jon saw something that he had not noticed before. It was so much a part of the scenery on this island that it could easily be overlooked.

The last footprint in the spiritual realm, was directly adjacent to a wall in the physical realm. And placed atop this wall was a small enclosed shrine. The shrine contained some photographs, a tiny posy of flowers, a jar of oil, a miniature bible and a lighted candle, protected from the elements by the small glass doors fronting the shrine.

Jonathan looked at this tribute to a person lost in a road accident as if it were a cryptic crossword. Surely if he looked at it for long enough from various different angles, the meaning or the solution would appear in his mind as his subconscious chewed it over. He imagined he could feel the bio-electricity firing in all directions in the neural network of his brain.

The more he studied the shrine the more Jon became convinced that it held a clue to the next part of his journey. He entered the spiritual realm, keeping both worlds in view. As he looked at the overlap between the two worlds, he noticed that the footprint seemed to continue and disappear into the shrine. It was not as if the attacker had become visible—it was as if he had left this part of reality entirely by moving *through* the shrine.

Jon became visible again and sat down on a dusty boulder to finish the loaf of bread. He withdrew the watermelon from his pack and a fancy took him. He wondered if he could extract juice from the melon without breaking its surface.

He rendered his face intangible, as he had instinctively rendered his head intangible to protect it during the crash and as in a similar way he had materialised just his hand in order to retrieve the sword from Mick's cabinet. He then pushed his invisible lips into the watermelon, beyond the skin, deep into the flesh. And then he materialised slightly and sucked.

He was rewarded with some degree of success. He had a peculiar feeling of the molecules of his body mingling with the molecules of the fruit. Whilst in that position, he thought with alarm, *What if our molecules get muddled up? What if I end up part man, part melon?* Had he received the tuition given to Ethereans on Deb, he would have known that questions such as this need not have troubled him. His molecules were safe. He withdrew from the watermelon, feeling somewhat refreshed and was relieved to find that his face was still all his own.

And then, an unbidden thought dropped into his consciousness. *The shrine is a doorway.*

Revelation turned into motivation. Without wishing to lose another second, he leapt up, grabbed his bag, scattering breadcrumbs in all directions and lunged at the shrine becoming invisible as he did so. As he met the place where the shrine was, he felt his entire person become compressed into virtually nothing. There was a pause during which he wondered if he had ceased to exist. And then he mused ironically, *What would Descartes think of that?* This pause was followed by a noise like a sonic boom. Immediately afterwards, he found himself fully visible, hurtling out from a tiny building hidden amongst mountainous rocks and tumbling into some plants that resembled heather.

Wherever he was, it was night time. *Night time, but not on earth.* He looked up at the sky and his entire body shuddered as he counted no less than three moons. Where was he? *A long way from earth,* he thought to himself.

Unobserved by Jonathan, Al'aran chuckled to himself with glee as he saw Jonathan emerge from the mountain shrine. Everything was proceeding as Belee'al had foreseen. He left his hidden vantage point and hurried back to the temple to await the arrival of his guest.

Jonathan picked himself up off the floor where he had landed and marvelled as he looked around. The land was illuminated brightly by the satellites orbiting the planet. The vegetation was sparse here and the temperature was much lower than it had been on Crete. But then he had left Crete at nine o'clock in the morning, local time. Here—wherever 'here' was—it was night time.

It was too cold for Jonathan to remain dressed as he was. Rather than pull some warmer clothes from his pack though, he took the easier option and simply became invisible again. As he did, he reeled from the images that hit his spirit eyes. There were footprints *everywhere*. He could see many different forms—this planet must be full of people like himself. He shuddered again, invisible though he was. Was this 'home?'

It took him some time to become used to the additional data now available to his spiritual vision. He had only just started to use these senses and he was experiencing information overload. How would he find the one footprint amongst the many?

Don't be dazzled, Jon, he told himself. With an effort, he relaxed and concentrated. Having followed the painted warrior's footprints for thousands of miles, he was sure he would recognise them here, if indeed they were here. And as he relaxed, it came into view: A fresh footprint leading into the valley below him. The trail was clear, so he followed it, more cautiously than before.

The path took him down the mountain that he had arrived upon and into an extensive forest. The forest was dense and the moonlight barely penetrated the canopy overhead. This was not a problem however, since Jon was not following physical clues and did not require physical light. The spiritual realm is bathed in its own nebulous illumination. As he proceeded, now accustomed to following the footprints, his mind drifted again, back to the horrendous encounter at his home.

Jonathan's mind habitually tried to solve problems. It was the way he was made and he always refused to take any credit for the fact. His thoughts turned to the words that had been spoken by the assailant. *By the alien*, he thought. Somehow he had understood what the creature had said to him. But he had not recognised the language.

He replayed the sounds in his head. Why could he understand them? How could he translate those sounds into his own language?

There were creatures flying here, in the dark. Strange noises came to him from the physical world. The trees were familiar and yet different and the smells were alien and yet close to what he might expect to smell in an English wood in autumn. He told himself not to become entranced by the views in this new world into which had arrived, but it was difficult to be restrained when he thought again, this must be where he originated. Maybe here he would rediscover a part of his childhood that he had previously forgotten.

He was lost in thoughts of this nature, when he arrived at the temple.

The footprints ended outside the temple door. It was a curious building, apparently in the middle of nowhere. But this was an alien place, Jon reminded himself and he should not expect any direct correlation between the behaviour of people here and the behaviour he was used to on earth. Could this be the house of Izzy's assassin?

The building was overgrown with vine-like plants and mosses and ferns, but its essential form was still identifiable. From the size of the door pillars and the elaborate but obscured carving, Jon guessed that the building had a religious significance. Jon estimated that it was possibly only two or three times the size of his house on earth.

The vegetation was parted at the entrance to the temple and evidently the building was still in use, in spite of its aged and crumbling appearance. With great trepidation, he kept his spiritual and physical eyes wide open and entered. He was completely unaware that as he entered, a mysterious spiritual force caused him to become entirely visible.

Looking forward into the gloom then, he had no opportunity to see the sword behind him before its hilt pummelled the back of his head and he fell to the ground unconscious.

Deb's politicians prided themselves on their decision-making process. So pleased were they with their methods, so assured of being beyond reproach, that they willingly took the risk of making their main discussion meetings public events. Any person without employment at the time of this discussion could attend and view these debates from the large galleries overlooking the Seat's principal debating chamber. Those that could not physically attend were able to follow the proceedings by way of the planet-wide newscast system.

The High Congregation had such a vast quantity of matters under its oversight that each matter being discussed must be allotted a precise amount of time in the agenda. Before any motion could be carried or even proposed, the Agenda Committee would determine what should be discussed and for how long and what should be the default outcome for any motion that expended its time slot before the Congregation could arrive at a decision.

The Agenda Committee was nominally under the governance of the Congregation, but undoubtedly it was an exceedingly powerful committee and had much scope for manipulation—for good or ill. This part of the planet's political system, more than any other, was dependant on a high standard of ethics.

The members of the Committee could be replaced at any time by the Congregation. Indeed it had been necessary in the past for the High Congregation to intervene in the proceedings of the Agenda Committee, where there had been evidence of abuse of power. Where intervention had been necessary however, this was only after a certain amount of damage had already been done by the less scrupulous Committee members.

It was customary for at least one member of the Etherean Guard's Elders to sit on the Agenda Committee. Mekly Sur had been an obvious choice and the Committee owed much to her innate organisational gifts. In their turn, the Guard owed much to Mek's presence on the Committee and her ability to keep Etherean issues before the Congregation. Today, for example, buoyed by encouraging noises from Resar Playne's direction, she had ensured that the Congregation would debate the question of resources for Etherean recruitment. She had also managed to persuade the Agenda Committee that the debate would require no less than three time slots. She was determined that the Elders would have an answer by the end of the day.

At the start of the debating sessions, the members of the Congregation chose the motions and matters that they would front. The triple time slot allocation allowed up to four members of the Congregation to front the resource allocation issue. It remained to be seen what angle each minister would take before the matter was released for the entire Congregation's comment and ultimate vote.

Yorgish and Gylan checked the agenda in the morning and noted that their debate was placed immediately after lunch. That was perfect from the Elders' point of view. The members would be refreshed and would have benefited from spending time considering the matter prior to the afternoon session. Gylan was delighted to note that Resar Playne herself was one of the four fronting the issue. When the afternoon session started, all the Elders made their way to the front row of the gallery for the best view of the speakers' platform.

As they waited for the Congregation to return, some of the elders adjusted their sashes or fiddled nervously. Even Yorgish and Garmon were apprehensive, which was rare for the others to see.

The Chair, Hesdar ru Contin, with her retinue of aides led the procession of politicians into the chamber. She resumed her seat to the right of the speakers' platform. Yorgish had been disappointed that Hesdar was not fronting the issue, but Ruith was not at all surprised. What little respect Ruith had for Hesdar had evaporated after the stabilising influence of Bars Medok was removed.

The central debating chamber at the Seat was a large round room. Comfortable and luxuriously carved and engraved benches were set in concentric circles around the room, with spacious curved desks before them. The circles were broken in places to form aisles and a large gap at one end of the chamber provided space for the raised thrones of the

Chair and Director of the Congregation and the accompanying seating of the members of their retinue. The speakers' platform stood between the thrones.

The chamber's structure included many cunningly contrived arches and curves overhead, designed to provide the optimum acoustic setting for discussions. Every minister could be heard clearly in all quarters of the room without the need to project his or her voice significantly.

Above the chamber was the gallery, forming a complete circle around the room. The seating here was more modest and no desks were provided. It was still true to say however that the seating accommodation for the viewers was amongst the most comfortable on all of Deb.

When all the members of the Congregation had filed in, the chamber's entrance doors were closed and flanked by members of the security corps. The Etherean Guard also had a small presence there, apart from the Elders, but they preferred to remain out of view. Hesdar rose to commence the session.

"Esteemed ministers, ladies and gentlemen, honoured Elders," she gestured up to the gallery, "the afternoon session is now begun. May we be guided by Yershowsh as we speak, listen and vote." Hesdar tucked her several robes behind her, as she sat.

Ti'par ru Masal, the new Director of the High Congregation after Bars Medok's abduction, announced the first item in a booming voice. "The next issue before us this session is the question of allocation of extensive resources to the Etherean Guard. The Elders have requested assistance in order that they might commence an intense recruitment and training campaign." Yorgish objected inwardly to the words of exaggeration: 'extensive' and 'intense'.

"The first speaker for this issue," Ti'par continued, "is Jowl Ruban." He clapped his hands together and sat down, as Jowl made her way to the speakers' platform.

"Esteemed ministers," she began, "we are given to understand that the Guard is in peril. We have experienced an unprovoked attack upon our government and in spite of the best efforts of our protectors, we find ourselves robbed of our most gifted and respected speaker." Many members indicated their support of this statement, by slapping their issue-portfolios repeatedly on the desks before them. Whether they loved Bars or hated him, showing solidarity at this time cost them nothing and gained the approval of the watching and listening public. Bars had been held in high esteem by the majority of the civilians on Deb.

Jowl emoted further, "May we not lose any of the ground gained these last few years by deviating to the left or right from the course set before us, championed by those such as Medok." She looked sternly around the chamber. "Medok knew the value of the Etherean Guard both in our economy and our security and he was not afraid to speak even in the face of considerable opposition, when he recognised their needs."

The nervous Elders began to relax as they warmed to the flow of Jowl's words. "And so today they come to us, expressing their requirements and we, charged with the guardianship of the resources on Deb, must consider carefully how we respond to the request."

Jowl held up her papers, "You will see in your portfolio a summary of their demands." Garmon jumped at this word and looked at Yorgish in horror. Yorgish's eyes narrowed as Jowl spoke on and he ran his hands contemplatively through his beard. "I will not trouble you with a detailed account of these. I would however draw you to the reasoning given below the summary. I quote point 3, 'The Elders require resources to assist in a further search for Bars Medok, in the absence of any evidence of his death,' and point 5, 'It is the intention of the Elders to begin a detailed and careful investigation into the activities of the Belee'al cult. It is the considered opinion of the Elders that when the location of the cult's headquarters is discovered, there also will Bars Medok be found.'" Jowl set down her portfolio on the podium before her and looked out at the members, adopting an expression of regret.

"The Elders have my full respect. If such a cult exists and if it makes its business the assassination of respected politicians, then clearly it is dangerous and should be eliminated." She paused thoughtfully. "It is my recollection though that three days ago with great reluctance we resolved to allocate resources away from the search for the late Director." Looking up at the Elders, she said, "No one can doubt the dedication with which the Guard as well as our regular security corps have searched for Bars, living or dead. He was sadly not found. I believe that our resolution to end the active search was the right one. It is time for us to gird ourselves and move on. We should not reopen that debate."

The Elders were relaxed no longer. Clearly Jowl Ruban was not minded to support them, as they had initially supposed. There were three members yet to speak however. Yorgish prayed that Jowl would do little damage to their cause. She went on, "Yes, the Guard may well be in peril." She smiled, in a way that Yorgish interpreted to be condescending. "The Guard is perhaps a casualty of its own success! We have enjoyed many years of peace and prosperity on Deb and a fact that we regrettably overlook all too often is that we owe this largely to the efforts of the Guard. They have served the people well and deserve our praise."

During the last few comments, ripples of approval had flowed around the chamber and as Ruban paused, a wave of applause broke out. Many of the members rose to their feet, turned and looked up to the gallery where the Elders were seated, as they clapped. In some embarrassment, the Elders acknowledged the thanks.

As the applause died down, Jowl recommenced, "I for one see that we have entered a period of plenty when, rather than stepping up its efforts, the Etherean Guard should rightly be taking the opportunity to enjoy a well-earned rest." She lowered her voice. "My friends, what little unrest we now face is relatively minor. We have established a security corps that is able to provide all the protection our people need—after all there is so little now that they need to be protected from, thanks to the success of the Guard! The attack on Medok was a one-off—an anomaly. We have not had such an occurrence for many years and it has not been repeated since. In fact, since that black day, we have experienced an unprecedented season of peace. In any event and with all due respect to the Guard, the Guard's presence or absence appeared to have little bearing on the final outcome.

"I am not so naïve as to think that we will never need the services of the Guard again. I am sure that one day we may face corrupt Ethereans who seek once more to use their advantage against their brothers and sisters. Until that day, I say maintain a small, select core from the Guard. If circumstances ever require, they would no doubt be able to train a new Guard to face that challenge. In the meantime, we should seriously apply ourselves to this question: Since, like all men, the Guard comprises one of the resources that we are to manage, how should we now allocate this resource?

"We are all acutely aware of the increasing demands on our infrastructure. As we reap the rewards of successful government we must also face its ongoing challenges. Our population has increased, as has our need to feed that population. We have ever more need of transport and it is here that the Ethereans have truly come into their own.

"Surely it is not right for such a wonderful gift to be employed solely for warlike purposes?" Several of the Elders gasped and Jish started to turn red and splutter in outrage. "Surely now in a time of comparative peace, the Ethereans can shoulder the mundane burdens of life, hand in hand with their brethren. Surely now we can forge our future together!"

Garmon heard none of what Jowl had left to say. He had started praying earnestly under his breath. The other Elders became preoccupied with their thoughts. They had experienced the climax of Jowl's speech and now as she wound down, each of the Elders were lost in other considerations. But when Jowl returned to her seat and the next speaker was called, all became alert once more.

Ti'par announced Resar Playne and Gylan gave Yorgish a reassuring smile.

Gylan had never made any attempt to hide his admiration for this woman. Rez, on the other hand struggled with her feelings for Elder Gylan. Were he not in such a position of responsibility, she would have had less difficulty. Resar prided herself on her independence and believed herself largely free of prejudice. Since Gylan was an Elder in the Etherean Guard and matters of the Guard were regularly debated in the Congregation, Resar intentionally placed distance between herself and Gylan, in order to prevent others from judging her opinions to be tainted by association.

In two respects she was wrong. Firstly, Rez was wrong in believing herself to be free of prejudice and secondly she was wrong in thinking that her fellow ministers could believe that her judgment was untainted. Her feelings for Elder Gorph were known more plainly to her colleagues than they were to her. None of the ministers doubted that she would speak in support of the Ethereans. Thus was her testimony weakened. And for what? She won neither in the arena of politics nor in the arena of love.

Nevertheless, Resar gave a compelling argument on behalf of the Elders. And she dealt with the points that Jowl had conveniently overlooked from the Elders' petition for resources. Resar had looked up at the Elders and cocking one eyebrow she scolded them for the size of the print on their petition.

"Whilst I share Jowl's respect for the Elders, I judge that their wisdom is lacking when it comes to choosing a typesetter. Why,

Minister Ruban was simply unable to read some of the points on your petition, so small was the print! For her benefit and for the sake of my other esteemed friends, may I report to you what you may, understandably, not be able to read for yourselves.

"Point 1 of the summary, 'We the Elders must recognise our shortcomings, not the least of which is the fact that we are all growing older. We have a great concern that unless a systematic programme of recruitment and assessment begins, the Guard will find itself with a generation gap and dwindling members.'

"Point 2, 'Whilst there are many known Ethereans in active service in the community, we are painfully aware of how few have been afforded the chance of a full rounded education in all matters Etherean. The simple truth is that were we to experience any concerted attack that required our services of defence, we would be unable to respond in a reasonable time. Resources are desperately required to redress the balance. To our shame it took the loss of a valued Minister and friend for us to realise this.'

"Item 3, Minister Ruban has dealt with. Item 4 reads, 'The Elders have received ever more evidence, physical and spiritual, that a group of Ethereans exists whose views and ethics directly oppose those of the Guard and those of our government. We have reason to believe this group is associated to an ancient religion, that of Belee'al. Further we believe the group to be cultic, dangerous and highly motivated. To what ends, we can only guess.'" Resar did not consider it necessary to expand on those words.

Minister Playne, encumbered by her thirst for the illusion, at least, of independence, did not continue much longer. She had however said exactly what the Elders would have said, given the opportunity. Their petition was included in the ministers' issue-portfolio, but this did not mean that it would be read. Rez had given the outline of their concerns and Yorgish believed that those concerns should speak for themselves. The Guard's problem and its solution were now plainly before the Congregation, he thought. It mattered not what the next two speakers would say—if the Congregation voted against the Elders, they would regroup and pursue another strategy.

In fact, in spite of Yorgish's optimism, it mattered a great deal what the next two ministers were to say. Yorgish could not have guessed quite how much it would matter. The first speaker of the two was to have only a little bearing on the issue, speaking mainly it appeared for his own entertainment. A somewhat pompous individual, he evidently enjoyed the effect of his sonorous voice resonating from the sculptured ceiling. His speeches were considered useful by the other Ministers, since it afforded them ample opportunity to think about other things. The thrust of his message was in support of the Guard, but this support was weakened and counteracted by his laborious delivery.

The final speaker however had many forceful and relevant comments to make and held the attention of all those assembled. His points were pertinent, but not at all to the liking of the Elders. In fact this speaker was to deal a significant blow not only to the issue at hand, but against Ethereans in general.

13

His legs and wrists were manacled and his body was held in tension between those four points. He could not move to stretch or adjust position. The cold hard floor beneath him was unforgiving. The wood behind him was rough and splintered.

This room was hell's antechamber.

Only one of his eyes was opening—the other was bloody and gummed up. He was unsure how long he had been here. It could have been a minute or a lifetime. Just one minute of torture at *their* hands could eradicate all knowledge of a former life.

He dimly remembered that he was Jonathan Fenton. He was special. Yes! A revelation! He could become invisible; slip off those manacles.

But he couldn't remember how to. A gift that had come to him without training or explanation, had suddenly left him. He wasn't sure whether he had ever possessed a special ability, or if it had all been a fantasy created by a mind in torment, as a means of escape.

The only light in this forsaken place flickered unsteadily. With every ounce of remaining mental energy, he prayed that it would not go out. At least in the gloom, he could tell when *they* were coming. He would go mad otherwise, waiting for the next episode of cruel punishment.

A groaning from the other side of the room startled him. There was no one else. Only him and *them*. The groaning must be another method of extracting screams from him. He would satisfy *them* quickly. He took a deep breath and prepared to scream in the way that pleased *them* best.

"Please don't!" It was spoken in the new language, that Jon had lately discovered he dimly remembered. Strange word. *They* didn't say, 'please.' *They* never said, 'please.' *They* said, "We have come. Prepare yourself." *They* said, "Eat. We do not want you dead yet." *They* said, "Does this hurt? Good."

On no account did *they* say, "Please."

Perhaps this was a new way of sporting with him. He turned to find the source of the voice that had spoken, but before his head was able to turn much, his body began spasming.

He remembered that he didn't use to spasm like this. That must have been a blissful, happy time! He clenched his teeth as wave after wave of shuddering wrenches buffeted and tossed him like a rag doll. He could not suppress the fit—that would be more painful still. He endured it.

When the tremors subsided, the voice spoke again. "Over here."

Cautiously, he turned to his right. There in the darkness he could see another form. It was a man. He was not stretched out like Jonathan, but he was in chains nevertheless. Jon was not alone.

The man spoke. He said, "I am," then some words that Jon could not translate, although they sounded like, "Bars meddock." The stranger continued, "What is your name?" Bars must be his name. *What is my name?* Jon wondered vaguely. He had forgotten again.

Jon turned away from the man. He troubled Jon—made him recall something from long ago—a journey? A quest? He did not want to remember. Lying as best he could, facing away from Bars, Jon tried to sleep.

He awoke to the sound of sobbing. The sobbing was mixed with words. It was Bars again. What did he want from Jonathan? He was saying, "Please tell me who you are! Did you come to rescue me? Please tell me who you are." Then he started sobbing again. Jon wished that the noise would stop. He thought it was time for some action.

"Stop your noise I can't bear it!" he snapped. Bars stopped for a moment. Jonathan felt relieved. He relaxed somewhat and turned to face Bars, as far as he could. The shape before him resolved into a human being. A beaten and battered human being. That made him a comrade. The comrade was about to speak.

"You do not speak like one from Rebke-side." Jonathan did not know what he meant by this. "But you do not speak like one from Norvesh-side either." This was more of a monologue than a conversation. "Not Rebke-side, not Norvesh-side. Where then?" He gasped. "No no—it cannot be, it cannot be."

With difficulty Jonathan found the words in this unfamiliar language to say, "Not from this planet."

Under his breath, Bars began repeating, "Not from this planet, not from this planet—no no—that's what you think you see. Ha ha!"

The conversation took Jonathan's mind away from his pain and he was about to try and ask what Bars meant, when they were interrupted by a loud snore. It came from beyond Bars. He shrieked, "Aah! No they don't torture you, posh boy, you sleep well enough, they leave you alone they do, want you in one piece but what for what for that's the question." Then he shrieked again and turned back to Jonathan.

"I'm not mad you know. They hurt me..." he began sobbing again, softly.

There was a pause where neither of the conscious men spoke. They listened to the hateful regular snores of the other captive and to the sounds of small creatures scurrying around. Occasionally one of the creatures would come over to Jon to investigate him. He had woken from a half-sleep once, finding a rodent-like creature, with glowing yellow eyes and a stumpy tail, licking an open wound on his leg. He thrashed around then, to shake off the creature. In fear it had run out of sight.

He had not seen one touch him since, but he had felt them.

A new noise came. It was a voice. It was coming from the man Bars. But this time it was slow and even and clear. "Chankwar?" The word sent electrical sparks into the deepest recesses of Jon's memory. The word meant something. "Chankwar? Have you come? Have you learnt? Are you yet living only to die here?"

Jon looked again at Bars, who was staring back at him intently—no trace of madness now. "That word, 'Chankwar,'" Jon asked, "I know it—what does it mean?"

A smile barely recognisable as such broke on the wounded face of the comrade. "Why Chankwar, it is your name." Still smiling, Bars began to weep.

Jon could feel no pain now—he was fully focused on the next words that Bars might say. "You know me?" he asked.

Bars sniffed and nodded. Jon gratefully noted that this scrap of body language seemed to correspond to the meaning he was used to. "I know you," Bars said. "You were to be an Etherean!" A flicker of emotion crossed his face. Jon did not know the word, 'Etherean,' but he could recognise the emotion as pride. 'Etherean,' must be a good thing.

Without warning or reason, a feeling of desolation struck Jon. He now took his turn to weep. "I should be able to break free but I can't. Izzy would know what to do Izzy Izzy Izzy..."

"Then you *have* learnt, but here it helps you none," Bars said. "This place is a prison for body and spirit. You are trapped as fully as am I."

Their conversation continued no longer. Someone had entered the prison. It was one of *them. They* had come for Jon.

How long he screamed for he did not know. It was some time after *they* left before he was able even to think; speech would take longer. He was hoarse from screaming in agony and his captors had not seen fit to minister to his thirst.

Bars did not rush to talk to Jon and for that Jon was grateful. Bars must already know what it felt like and how it robbed you of mind and voice.

Eventually, Jon was able to turn to face Bars. "Why do they do this?" he asked.

Bars snorted and looked down. "Because they are evil. Because they enjoy it. Because they wish to purge the good from us. Because they have no reason. Because they know no other way. Because their parents did not love them." He looked up at Jonathan. "I have no reasons." Then he laughed, loud and long.

"Yershowsh!" Bars said, "I see you moving men like pawns, playing your games with us. You bring Chankwar here to me, but how do we leave alive, tell me that!"

Jonathan again found that he was labouring in an effort to understand his comrade. But whilst he laboured with his mind and his memory, a calm voice spoke into his brain, *In the chains that bind will you find your freedom.* Jon looked round for the source of this voice.

"What do you mean?" Jon asked.

"Do you not know Yershowsh?" Bars replied.

Jon shook his head violently, ignoring the pain and said, "No—not that—'In the chains that bind will you find your freedom,' you said." Had he been able to point, he would have thrust a finger at Bars.

Bars sighed. "Voices torment my mind. I think I will go mad. Maybe I am mad already."

Jon shook his head again. "I heard a quiet voice—it was peace. Mad men hear no peace. Was it the other one?" He nodded his head in the direction of the person beyond Bars.

Bars frowned. "Delturn spoke not. You heard a peaceful voice?" Then in a low voice, "Yershowsh—the boy Hears too?" Aloud he said, "Chankwar, you must listen and respond to that voice."

A higher-pitched voice spoke from beyond Bars, "Such words will get you killed, you scab witted old man."

"I am already dead, Delturn." Bars replied simply.

Jonathan had switched off. Clearly Bars was raving. Jon was not surprised—he felt sure that less than ten percent of the words leaving his own mouth were coherent. How long had he been here, he wondered again. Was this his lot in life?

Unbidden, the calming voice replayed in his memory. There was something about it that was familiar—it reminded him of a time when he stood at a shrine somewhere. "The shrine is a doorway," he said aloud and laughed. "The chains that bind..." he tailed off.

He looked round at the solid, unyielding chains and down at his solid, unyielding body. *There's no way out for me.* Wearily, he pushed at one of the manacles that held him taut. His hand slid through it in the direction of the wall a short distance and then his body jerked him back into tension again.

His hand had passed through the manacle. *What? Could this really be a way out?* He had no time to consider this further, because his tormentors returned once more. *Why so soon?*

The visit had, thankfully, been to provide food. It could hardly be dignified with the word, 'food,' however. It was foul in taste, texture and smell, but it passed Jonathan's withered lips and somehow made its way down to his belly, where it lay, barely digestible. Just enough to keep him alive until the next session.

Whilst *they* were feeding him lumps of non-food, held out to him on a stick, Jonathan had thought over the puzzle of the chains. If his way out was through the chains, how could he break free? He could not spread outwards in all four directions and he was already under so much strain that he had no flexibility left to push in any one direction at once.

As usual the tormentors left long before Jonathan was able to eat his fill.

With the desperation of a man whose need to survive has surfaced above his rational thought and fear of pain, Jon now tried to break loose. He concentrated on the hand he had first tried and found that he could still slide it, partially in non-physical form, along his chain.

As his arm snapped back into the manacle again, he screamed out, "Of what use is that though?" And directly, the calm voice came again: *When you have reached the end of your abilities, there will I meet you.*

A chill in his spine mingling with his pain, Jon tried again. He pushed and stretched and forced his wrist along the chain—not caring if any damage was done to his innards. Sweat broke out on his forehead and the sores on his face cracked and opened, but still he continued stretching. He was taking rapid shallow breaths now as he tried harder and harder to break loose.

And then, at the point where for the fifth time he thought *I can stretch no more!* his hand flipped sideways and outwards from the chain. He clutched the free arm to his chest, groaning and hyperventilating and passed out.

He awoke to the sound of the familiar word, "Chankwar, Chankwar, awake!" He tried to reply, but could only cough. "Chankwar—you must keep going; you must hurry!" It was Bars, speaking firmly and reassuringly.

Jon almost panicked. How long had he been unconscious? How could he have risked *them* finding him here—discovering the weakness in his bondages and finding a surer means of securing him?

The process was much easier with one limb unencumbered. It

worked for the three remaining shackles and shortly Jon arose, a free man again. From his standing position, he looked down upon Bars and Delturn.

"Impossible," Delturn was saying. "Everything below ground level here, including the room and the chains—*everything* is Enveloped. No man—not even an Etherean—can break free."

"And yet here he stands," Bars said and laughed. A rich tone had entered his voice. "What have you been called in your life, Chankwar?"

"Jonathan," he replied.

"Don A'Thon," Bars repeated.

"No, *Jonathan*," he emphasised the sounds.

"Jonathan?" Bars suggested.

"Good, yes!"

Bars smiled again and held out a chained hand, saying, "Well then, Jonathan—do you think you could find a way to release me, impossible though Delturn claims it to be?"

Jon managed a grin and forced confidence that he did not yet feel, "Perhaps you are not dead, after all Bars Medok."

14

The Elders were in shock. They had assembled promptly for their evening conference at the comfortable uncluttered home of Yorgish, but had sat in silence for five degrees of the sun—twenty minutes—without breathing a word of greeting to one another. They could not talk. Garmon at least was using the opportunity to meditate and commune with Yershowsh.

Jish, dressed more sombrely than usual in a grey flowing wrap, spoke first, slowly and deliberately. "We cannot allow the Etherean Guard to be dictated to by politicians. There is too much at stake."

The other Elders looked at her, without interrupting.

She continued, buoyed by the fact she had not been rebuffed. "I respect our political system and I hold Hesdar in high esteem, notwithstanding the issues she and Ruith have. But I do not think that we can accept the proposed restrictions. There must come a point when we as Elders decide what is best for those in our care: this is after all *our* commission, not the politicians'."

Ruith looked wearily at Jish. "I cannot deny that Hesdar made a valiant attempt to stop the rot in that debate. How differently would events have flowed though, had Bars been present."

"This rot would have defied even Bars' attempts to cure it, I think," Mekly offered. "Did you not observe the organised resistance in numerous quarters of the Congregation? Six figures opposed to us, each surrounded by lapdogs and yes-men? And where was *our* organised support?" Mek pounded the desk before her—an uncharacteristic gesture.

"Perhaps we should have directly approached and recruited the pilots and bypassed the Congregation altogether," Gylan said with resignation. He noted Ruith's look of surprise and quickly added, "Any assistance would be better than this."

And how right he was.

Dayle Rother, up until now a fringe member of the Congregation, had proven to be a persuasive, powerful speaker. Amongst the Elders, there could be no doubting where his allegiances lay. They knew that such an attack against the rule of justice and order, such an attack as spearheaded by this man, must stem from a dark and evil source.

And yet it was couched in such reasonable, peaceful terms. Rother was armed with a myriad array of statistics concerning the usefulness of Ethereans to the global infrastructure and their complete redundancy in matters of security. He argued that the regular security corps were more than able to contain the small amounts of crime on Deb—mostly associated to gambling. Of course since all agreed that gambling was the head and tail of all things criminal, it was not difficult to persuade the Congregation that he was right in focussing on the gambling problem. Every member of the High Congregation had a friend, relative or acquaintance whose life had been adversely affected, directly or indirectly, by the activities of the gambling community.

Rother produced reams of evidence that the majority of the gamblers were small-time criminals. The rumours of forfeits were greatly exaggerated. Admittedly, he conceded, there had been a few isolated incidents, but he had found no real cause to think that the problem was widespread or common.

No one in the chamber had been able to contest this. It seemed that no hospital anywhere had a record of treating someone suffering from the execution of a gambling forfeit. Having personally spoken to staff within hospital administration departments of several hospitals, Dayle Rother had to conclude that these forfeits were little more than myth and legend.

In terms of global security, there was not much left to occupy the Guard. In terms of labour, there was plenty that they and the other Ethereans could usefully turn their hands to. He saw no reason why the Ethereans' additional freakish ability should lead to them receiving preferential treatment above other citizens of Deb. Long ago, Hearers had lost their privileges and society was none the worse for this—indeed many Hearers had become extremely useful citizens in fields unrelated to their special gift. Why should it not be so for Ethereans?

Dayle had gone on to offer a dazzling range of suggestions for the Guards' occupation. The Elders had been taken aback by this—many of the suggestions were inventive and highly credible. It seemed that there was so much work for the Ethereans there was little excuse for them to waste time meditating whilst waiting for some petty scuffle or insignificant theft to occur.

Having thus undermined the Etherean Guard, he shattered any final resistance by hinting that he also had good reason to believe that Bars' disappearance was in fact manufactured and executed by dissident members of the Guard. So subtly did he introduce this theme, that barely a minister noticed what Dayle was saying before that minister was already fully persuaded of the truth of this allegation. Indeed how else could it be explained that the Guard 'could not find' Bars? They had unlimited access to the entire planet and the Ether around it. There must be some collusion somewhere.

When Jish had realised what Rother was saying, she leapt to her feet and began hurling invectives and rebuttals at the bemused minister. None of the stunned Elders had attempted to stop her.

Ti'par ru Masal with a look of fear and horror on his face, had nervously requested that the Elder come to order and when this had achieved nothing, had in a stronger voice called for the assistance of security. Jish had become incensed by this, but fortunately a warning glance from Yorgish had prevented an escalation of the conflict. Jish had left the chamber in disgust, but returned shortly by means of the Ether. Yorgish saw her re-entrance and had smiled in her direction, realising that Jish was taking the best approach to prevent her feelings from further interrupting the debate. So far as the Elders were aware, none of the Congregation was an Etherean, therefore no one would hear her subsequent inevitable angry outbursts.

During the discussion part of the session, several proposals were tabled, all of them detrimental to the Elders' cause. All but the most radical of those proposals were voted in. And so the Elders had to face the fact that the resources for the Etherean Guard were quite suddenly to be phased out and eventually withdrawn. Ethereans on the whole, would no longer have the same liberty to choose how they should be employed. They were to come under the same assessment and assignment system that applied to the rest of society.

On the face of it, these decisions had all the trappings of equity and justice. What the decisions lacked was the benefit of the wisdom and insight available to the select few—the Etherean Guard—whose role it had been over many decades to protect the very people who now undermined them.

When the session was over and before any Elder had opportunity to speak, Yorgish had taken the rare step of issuing an order to the rest of the Elders. He said, "None of you is to discuss this. We must all spend time now in meditation—something which to our shame all but Garmon neglect. I make this order and place myself under its restraint along with the rest of you. We will meet at my residence, fifteen degrees of the sun after nightfall. Until then, think, pray and remain in seclusion. Now go."

With that, Yorgish had turned on his spiritual heel and sped away. The remaining Elders stared at one another in silence for a moment. Then, without a further word, they had scattered, each to his or her own favoured place of solitude.

Now, at their meeting in Yorgish's large study, the Elders were even more concerned than they had been earlier. Without exception, all of the Elders had a strong commitment to the welfare of society. They saw it as their role, for better or worse, to protect these people from attack and at times, to protect them from themselves. For two centuries the Etherean Guard had been able to accomplish this as a recognised organisation within ordered civilisation. How it should come about that the tide could turn so rapidly against them, they knew not.

But Garmon was starting to understand and Yorgish was not far behind him.

In a strength of feeling that could only be expressed physically, Garmon stood upright, rapidly pushing his chair away from him. "Have we been foolish and blind? Have we completely overlooked the machinations of our enemy?"

Garmon tended not to speak at length, but his posture indicated that he was settling in for a speech. The Elders looked at him with considerable interest. Yorgish's fingers were firmly entwined in his beard.

"Mek has hit upon the very thing we have missed. How unfortunate it is for us that we have not kept a closer eye upon the day-to-day activities of the High Congregation! We now see evidence of organisation—conspiracy even—against the standards that we hold dear; against our notion of righteousness and justice itself. For how long must this canker have been developing? And we saw it not!" He shook his head sadly and paused, still standing.

Ruith spoke into the gap, "We have no idea of the extent of this resistance. Our enemy has been well hidden and we should not berate ourselves for that. Clearly those that oppose us have more influence than we could have accounted for, but all is not yet lost."

"No, Ruith!" Garmon shouted, provoking a stunned reaction in his colleague. "We must not try to shake off our accountability. Don't we believe that nothing is hidden from Yershowsh? Were we true to Him, who knows what He might have revealed to our clouded Insensate minds!"

Gylan gave Garmon a sharp look. "And yet He *has* revealed something of great import; you now remind me." He leaned forward on the table. He could see that the other Elders had followed his train of thought. Garmon sat down, quiet once more.

"You're right, Gy," Mekly said, nodding, "the Guardian of the Insensate is returning—that is what Lovel Heard and none of us now doubts that she Heard correct. We know in our own hearts that she Heard true."

In frustration, Yorgish exclaimed, "Well where is he then?"

Had Yorgish known the location of the Guardian, had he known the immediate peril facing the Guardian, he would have doubtless ordered the Elders into battle against the Belee'an threat without further deliberation. In a time of stress and anxiety, impulsive action often leads to rapid results. Whether those results are ideal, however, is another matter. To quash the few Belee'ans guarding Jon, would have made the remaining Belee'ans more alert and cautious and could have rendered impossible more thorough action against this menace.

We are not always given as much knowledge as we *think* we need.

It is true to say that Jonathan, the unwitting Guardian, was at that time in grave danger and he would certainly have appreciated the assistance of the Guard. Ultimately the assistance he was to receive was far more timely and of greater value than the assistance he would have chosen.

Having freed himself, it became apparent that he could not use his gift to release Bars and Delturn. If he were to free them, it would require the use of a key. Bars had told Jonathan simply to escape, to save himself and if at all possible bring help. Jon was adamant that if it were within his power, he would ensure that Bars and Delturn would escape with him. Delturn had remained quiet during this discussion.

Bars reluctantly conceded that he had no choice but to accept that Jonathan was going to attempt to rescue him single-handed. Jonathan was the one who was free. Bars was not in a position to give orders to the freed captive.

For his part, Jon was driven by the principles drilled into him by his parents. If he saw a person in need and if it was within his power to help, he felt that it was immoral for him to turn away. At all times, he was to put his own comfort last. The wisdom of this is of course questionable, at least taken to this extreme. Nonetheless, Jon had decided that he had a chance of rescuing his fellow prisoners and therefore he could not ignore that chance.

In a hushed voice Bars had explained to Jonathan that he did not know Delturn and could not give any indication whether or not Delturn was a person that Jon should consider freeing. Jon saw the matter in black and white however. Delturn was imprisoned by the same vicious people who had captured and tortured Jon and Bars. Delturn too must be rescued.

With his heart in his mouth and his one good eye opened wide, Jonathan approached the door to their cell. Taking a deep breath, he pushed against it. It stoutly resisted his attempt to open it. Was it locked? His spirits sank slightly.

Taking a more careful look at the door, Jon saw that set into the wood, was a slatted handle. This might explain why it could not be pushed. Hope rising again, he inserted his swollen hand into the groove, obtained a purchase on the handle and pulled.

The door swung freely towards him. It was not locked! He turned and glanced at the watchful prisoners, gave them a 'thumbs up,' which elicited completely blank looks and exited the room.

He came to a spiral staircase, leading upwards. Since there were no alternatives, he climbed this carefully and with much trepidation. All the while he was looking for a hook or a shelf upon which a key might be placed.

He counted twenty-five steps, before his head knocked against the ceiling. He could barely see where he was going now—there was very little light in the stairwell. Feeling above his head, he concluded that he must have come upon a trapdoor to the room above. What might lie before him in that room, he had no idea.

He stilled his breathing and trying to ignore his pounding heart, listened intently for several minutes. Once he was reasonably sure that the only sounds he could detect were being made by the scurrying rodents, he gingerly pushed against the trapdoor. It took an immense effort and he had few reserves of strength, but the door lifted upwards, revealing a much brighter room.

Grunting somewhat from the exertion, he emerged into this room, his one good eye winking in the brightness. Making sure that he made as little sound as possible, he rested the trapdoor against a pillar behind it that appeared to be part of the room's structure. Having done this, he started to scan round the room. And then, without warning, he found himself looking into the devastatingly frightening face of Al'aran Kytone.

What manner of sound passed his lips Jon could never remember. He felt sure that it had been at the least, a loud gasp. But he suspected that it had in fact been more like a shriek. He knew the face of his primary torturer only too well.

But the figure had not stirred. After waiting for what seemed an age, to see how the malevolent dwarf would react, Jon dared to approach him and look more closely. He now realised that the vision of his one open eye was clouded by beatings. On closer inspection, Al'aran proved to be sleeping soundly with his eyes closed, sat on a bench, leaning against a padded wall.

Two inches to the right of this padding was a hook.

And on that hook there was a single key.

15

It was with trembling hands that Jon now inserted the key he had found into Bars Medok's manacles. Mercifully the key unlocked the restraints and Jon was able to help Bars rise to his feet. He saw for the first time that despite his beatings and the pain inflicted upon him, Bars was a man with natural authority and stately bearing. As Jon turned to help Delturn, Bars grasped one of his hands firmly.

"Chankwar, Chankwar—the man! Jonathan, I am glad to be in your presence; the joy this brings to me banishes all of the torment of this accursed place!" He laughed loudly and Jon lifted his free hand to his lips in alarm. Bars fell silent again, but did not release Jon's hand.

He continued speaking, repeating his concerns about Delturn, "I do not know this man Delturn. He has not been punished and tortured as you and I have been." More quietly he said, "I am not persuaded that we may trust him or that we should take him with us."

Jon looked at Bars steadily with his one open eye. Still struggling with the language he reiterated, "He is imprisoned with us. I know neither of you. I must release both of you or neither of you."

Bars released Jon's hand and smiled. "You speak with simple truth Jonathan, Chankwar."

Delturn had not managed to catch the content of their

conversation, but was relieved to see that Jonathan intended to release him too. "Thank you, thank you," he said, "You will not regret this. I alone can show you the way out of here."

Bars looked at Delturn sharply. "You know this place, Delturn?"

Delturn chuckled nervously. "Oh yes—I know many of the levels of this maze," he exaggerated. "Many years have I been in the service of Belee'al, but those days are over." The last word he said with passion.

Bars cocked a blood-encrusted eyebrow, immediately wincing and observed, "Belee'al, you say? Then the cult is truly active. Many questions have I to ask you."

Jonathan interjected with urgency, "Later! We must go!" Then gesturing to Delturn, he indicated that their new comrade should lead them.

Delturn was physically trembling. He knew only too well the power of Belee'al—he had heard of many followers who had been insufficiently devout and had paid the ultimate price for this. It was a price that he had personally expected to pay many days ago. Belee'al was rarely merciful. If he were caught escaping, Delturn's temporary reprieve would be ended swiftly and permanently.

It had occurred to him though that he could bend these events to his significant advantage. He had not formed a plan, but as they ascended the stair together, he was turning over possibilities in his mind.

One option that he seriously considered was abandoning his faith entirely. If Belee'al was finished with Delturn well then Delturn was finished with Belee'al. But he had served Belee'al since his late childhood and he enjoyed the Belee'an life and could not relinquish this easily.

As they cautiously tiptoed through Al'aran's chamber, Delturn considered whether on the other hand, he may find favour with

Belee'al by accompanying these two men into the heart of the Etherean Guard—for he was sure that the Guard would want to question Medok following his escape. There, Delturn may acquire knowledge that would be of great service to his former masters.

Neither option was free from drawbacks. And so as they emerged into the catacombs below the temple, Delturn decided to improvise, for the time being.

The paths were dimly lit and Jon thought that it would be easiest to proceed invisibly. As they assembled cautiously at an intersection of paths, he quietly communicated his thoughts to the other two.

"Bars says that I am an," he experimented with the unfamiliar word, "Etherean." Delturn of course already knew this, but attempted to look at first surprised and then understanding.

"In that event," Delturn said, "as soon as we are free of the Enveloping, we should continue in the Ether. Perhaps Bars can make his way alone?"

Jon did not understand what Delturn meant, but on an impulse, he took the shoulders of both men and faded, taking the other men with him. Through the Ether, Delturn looked at Jonathan and gasped. Jonathan however was preoccupied with Bars, who had started flailing his arms looking greatly alarmed.

Jonathan released Bars' shoulder and Bars returned to the physical world, breathing heavily. Jon and Delturn followed shortly, Delturn still looking at Jonathan with amazement in his eyes.

Bars turned his pale face towards Jonathan and asked, "Was that the Ether?"

Jon nodded, knowing that Bars would understand this body language.

"It is a good idea, but I wish you had warned me!" Bars smiled, held out his hand to Jonathan and continued, "Let us leave this place."

Jon took Bars hand and then turned to Delturn, who gingerly held out one hand towards Jon. Grasping these two hands, Jonathan returned once more to the Ether, invisible and intangible and took the most direct route to the surface.

As they passed through the structure of the building, Jon noticed Bars' reactions—it was as if he were a blind man. There was no indication that Bars whilst in the Ether could see either the spiritual or the physical world. *How much I am learning!* Jon thought, ironically.

On the journey to the forest floor, Jon felt his strength returning. He was dimly aware of his physical body and he could almost feel his wounded eye healing, along with the rest of his body.

They had arrived at a point to the rear of the temple, on the opposite side to the entrance. It was difficult to tell through the thick canopy overhead, but judging from the temperature and the sounds of creatures—*animals and birds, perhaps,* Jon thought—it was late afternoon.

He left the Ether, relinquishing the hands of his fellow escapees. Delturn looked around warily, but Bars simply looked down at his body, his arms and legs, in amazement.

"I am whole!" he said.

Jonathan smiled and patted the shoulder of this man whom he already liked. "That is the effect of the Ether."

Bars shook his head and frowned at Jon. "But I am not Etherean—I cannot be restored in the Ether."

Jon shrugged and pulled his rags about him. "We should leave this place."

"Follow me," Delturn said.

But they had not travelled four paces, when they heard a mighty bellowing roar. Delturn turned white and sank to his knees in terror. The other men looked at him in concern. Through trembling lips, Delturn said, "That is Preceptor Klushere. We have been discovered already."

"Jonathan, Delturn, we must go!" Bars said with urgency. He was pulling Delturn off the ground, but Delturn seemed to have lost the use of his legs.

Delturn was moaning and quietly saying, "If he finds me with you, he'll kill me... I don't want to die..." Bars looked across at Jon, infuriated and then gave Delturn a backhanded swipe across the cheek. That had the desired effect. Restored to his senses, Delturn leapt to his feet, ready to flee.

Bars now turned to Jonathan and asked him, "Can you take us away from here at speed?"

Jon felt extremely unsure of the answer to that, but told himself, *Now is not the time for a crisis of confidence.* Rather than waste time with words, he took Delturn's hand and Bars' elbow and entered the Ether. He could not have known that this was a mistake.

Jon felt a surge as if a tidal wave were heading towards him. He turned in the Ether to locate the source of this energy, to see coming towards them the man he now most feared and hated—his wife's killer, one of his tormentors. He stood transfixed, Bars blinking blindly, Delturn cowering behind him.

And then reason rushed to his aid and he took off, speeding away from the pursuer as fast as he could. He did not know whether having two bodies—or were they spirits?—in tow would slow him down, but he knew that he had no choice other than to flee. His previous experiences and his time in torment had been more than enough to persuade him of the folly of trying to fight this man.

Strangely, as he faced away from the pursuer whose name he now knew to be Klushere, he could feel Klushere's progress behind him. The surge continued unabated. And Jon felt no indication that he was outrunning that surge.

Twists and turns now seemed irrelevant; there are no obstacles in the Ether and swerving would only slow him down. He was sure that Klushere would take the most direct path towards Jonathan. And so he fled in a straight line, not knowing where this path would lead.

How long this chase might continue Jon could not say. He was not tiring, but he had no reason to believe that Klushere would tire either. And he was sure that Klushere was gradually gaining on him. *What an introduction to my home planet*, he thought miserably.

Yes Klushere was indeed gaining. That sword was at the ready. Jon could feel the imprint of the sword, through the Ether and he feared that any confrontation would be ended swiftly. At last he was starting to recognise his own lack of experience.

And then, at the point where Jonathan thought that defeat was inevitable and he should simply turn and face the attacker, a miracle occurred.

To his right, there was a second surge and there came an unearthly searing cry made all the more eerie by the strange effect of the Ether upon sounds. And then, another figure entered the fray, brandishing a long staff, heading past Jonathan towards Klushere. It was this new figure who was whooping and as he held out his weapon in front of him, Jon had no doubt whose side he was on. Jon could only turn and observe, part in amazement, part in curiosity.

Klushere halted in horror as the man approached him. Then, the fight began.

Jonathan had never had the opportunity to witness a fight within the Ether and he could not help but be fascinated as he watched now. It was an amazing spectacle.

The speed at which the two combatants moved was mind-boggling. Both men, Klushere and the newcomer, were clearly adept with their weapons. Klushere flipped his sword, attacking now with one blade, then with the other, then with both simultaneously. It seemed as though the Ether was full of flashing swords.

But similarly, the opponent was well able to keep up with the thrust and parry of Klushere's weapon. The pole spun, intercepting rapid swipes of the sword from all directions. Jon could not believe that any material whether in the Ether or out of it, could withstand the repeated pounding of Klushere's blade, but there appeared to be no sign of damage to the stranger's staff.

As the fight continued, at incredible speed, the combatants drew closer to Jon and his comrades. But Jon was rooted to the spot and could not have moved if he wanted to. Delturn seemed to be similarly encumbered, his face bearing a look of morbid fascination, contrasting with Jon's attentive wonder. Bars remained relaxed and at peace, unaware of the events taking place around him. All he knew was that he was still alive and this must mean that their escape was a success, thus far.

Jon wondered whether he should lend some assistance, to tip the apparently even balance in favour of his champion. But he knew that there was little value in him entering the fray. He was simply not competent in battle.

And then—a lucky strike from Klushere's blade caught his opponent off-guard, entering the man's body. But the man seemed unaffected.

Jonathan puzzled over this before he realised that he had witnessed the stranger exit the Ether and the blade, still in the Ether, had passed through him harmlessly. The stranger adopted a new strategy immediately after this—Klushere was slow to notice what had happened and assumed he had connected. In his moment of triumph, he overlooked the pole as it swung round from one side, connecting firmly with his head.

Klushere reeled from the blow. Jon heard a reverberating thud from the impact. The opponent moved in swiftly to make the most of his advantage, but Klushere took to the defensive, parrying the attack with lightning sweeps of his sword, the flats of the twin blades meeting the pole and deflecting the intended critical hits.

Within a short time Klushere had recovered his composure and he returned to the attack with renewed vigour. His movements became a blur, barely matched in speed by the other man and Jon braced himself to run again. But then so rapidly that Jon could only afterwards, playing back the memory, deduce what had happened, one end of the stranger's staff flowed into a new shape, becoming hook-like. On his next attack, he took the hook low towards Klushere's legs. It was a risky move, leaving his shoulders exposed and Klushere was there with his sword—but with a deft flick, the hook connected with Klushere's ankles, pulling him off balance. Immediately the stranger whipped round the other end of the staff, striking Klushere in the sternum and Klushere came crashing down. And down he continued, plummeting into the ground, with the opponent in hot pursuit.

They entered the earth together, Klushere looking more or less inert, the stranger focused and ready to end this battle. Jon strained his Ether sense to follow the action, but for some reason he found that he could not detect what was happening below the surface. Just as he was considering following, the stranger emerged, alone. He was showing signs of exhaustion, even though he was still within the Ether.

The stranger held out the staff with both his hands and flicked his wrists. Instantly the pole transformed into two bracelets, wrapping themselves round his wrists. Whilst this was happening, he approached Jon's party.

Jon was astounded when the man addressed him in English, smiling as he did so, "Hello Jonathan. I lost your friend, I'm afraid—he was not as immobilised as I had thought and disappeared shortly after reaching the ground. We should leave this place quickly and consult with the Elders."

Bemused that *another* stranger should apparently know him, Jonathan looked at the English-speaking gentleman, quizzically.

Missing the reason for Jon's puzzlement and with his mind still on the skirmish the man continued, "That was not a true Etherean—at least not a fully adept Etherean. He was tiring very early—did you see? Lucky for me! I am not as flexible as I once was." He chuckled slightly.

Jon studied the weather-worn, bronzed face before him and felt a glimmer of recognition. "Uncle Martin?" he asked.

"Of course—did you not remember me? Has it been so long?" Martin cocked his head on one side. "Yes I suppose it has been. But you are unmistakeable." He approached Jon to hug him, but Jon was constrained by the fact that he was still holding on to Bars and Delturn, to keep them in the Ether.

It was then that Martin took more notice of the two with Jon. "And who is this with you in the Ether—but no, don't tell me—even in Ether form, there is no mistaking Bars Medok." Tears, an incongruous reminder of physical life, sprang to Martin's eyes. "And your other companion?"

Jon looked at Delturn, who was still cowering somewhat. "This is Delturn and he and Bars were with me in my captivity."

Martin raised his eyebrows and then said, in the new language that Jon was relearning apace, "Let us visit the Elders; we have much to discuss." He looked around himself and took a deep breath. "How I have missed Deb's Ether!" He smiled once more and then gestured to Jonathan to follow him. Jon duly complied.

16

Neevairy Ewtoe loved her job. Not her day job. Not the job imposed on her by the state. No, it was at night, when she was free, that she came into her own.

Neev saw herself as a problem-solver. Her nocturnal employers had a problem: they needed more recruits; Neev was the solution. Nature had endowed her with great perceptiveness. She found it easy to read people. Having read them, she was then able to manipulate them. In many ways she thought of herself as a politician. It was her duty to persuade someone to take a course of action and to persuade so skilfully that the other person felt that he alone had conceived and resolved to pursue this course.

On Earth, Neevairy would have made a successful salesperson. Deb knows no such employment however. Neev was obliged to find other ways of exercising her talents.

It helped that she was, amongst her peers, an outstandingly beautiful woman. Certainly this was of assistance when she sought to recruit men. Very few men were a challenge. Sometimes this disappointed Neev; other times she exulted in her power.

Like roughly sixty percent of Debans, Neev was dark skinned and green-eyed. But her skin was so much glossier, her eyes so much more intense than those of the majority. Her face was classically shaped—slightly more round than heart-shaped. Her lips were full and strongly contrasted with her skin. Her cheekbones were fine and her nose dainty. Her hair, which was long and straight, fell over her shoulders and down to her waist. There were few men who would not rate her figure as 'perfect'.

But Neevairy's charm was not confined solely to the men of Deb. She bore herself with an unaffected air. She never gave the impression that she knew how attractive she was—indeed she gave the strong impression that she considered herself quite plain in comparison to other women. This was invariably disarming.

If her target were female, she dressed down, to avoid attracting too much male attention. The last thing that would assist her cause would be if her target were incited to jealous hatred of her, for example if that target's partner were to pay too much attention to Neev.

It helped that she came across as genuine, kind and pleasant. She was always interested in the things that interested her targets. Tonight, for example, she was an avid fan of plants and produce of the ground.

This assignment would be a challenge. She had been warned by her employers that the target would be extremely resistant to any open invitation. She would have to be surreptitious, devious and highly persuasive, whilst keeping her intentions closely guarded. Truly it was a delight to Neevairy to work under such conditions. The greater the challenge, the greater the satisfaction that came with success.

Plykar Lovel would be late home tonight. His department was heavily involved in the Etherean reassignment project. Until this point, Ethereans had been largely immune from the government's absolute control. But now all Ethereans were to be assignable resources. The majority of Ethereans would no longer have the option of entry into the Guard at the expense of the state.

It was a huge task, requiring the creation of a new department within the Resource Allocation Unit. Plykar was responsible for creating the new sub-unit that was to specialise in Etherean assignment. The High Congregation had made it clear that this project was urgent, so Plyk and many of his colleagues were working long hours. For Plyk, this meant the opportunity to 'buy back' some of his life. He had extended his retirement age previously; he was now able to reduce this by working beyond the state requirement.

Graye wished with all her heart that she could work again, so that her husband could be released from his additional obligations. But the Congregation would not permit her to take up her chosen profession, or any other employment. Tonight, as she spent the evening alone, she regretted again the errors that had brought her family to this position.

She was working in the part of the house devoted as a nursery for her seedlings and young plants. It was a small room, but she loved the smell of it—the warm pungent aroma of the compost and the heady scent of the myriad preparations that she used to nurture her growing plants. The sound of someone winding the door-rattle interrupted her reverie.

She moved through the house to the reception door, wiping her hands on her smock as she went. Graye was not expecting company, but had always been accustomed to receiving unannounced visitors. It had been a hazard of her job.

Graye slid the door open and looked out on a worried-looking young lady. She was shabbily dressed and bore a haunted look that marred her youthful beauty. The woman looked as though she were about to collapse.

Without waiting for the formality of introductions, Graye ushered her visitor into her home, making clucking motherly noises. She settled the lady on a crut, not allowing the visitor to engage in communication until she at least had a warming drink in her hands. When Graye return to the room, bearing drinks and viands, her guest perked up and looked eagerly but shyly at the provisions.

Graye set the tray down on the floor and drew up a crut close to the young woman. She wanted to be within reach so that she could give the waif a reassuring pat or squeeze if it seemed appropriate.

Her guest gingerly took some food and drink and at length became more animated. At this point Graye considered it safe to pursue a conversation.

"Welcome to my home, Debanika. My name is Graye. I would dare to say that you have the appearance of someone in trouble or distress. My resources are at your disposal." Graye judged that greeting the young woman of Deb—the Debanika—in this formal manner, would help to create a more objective, professional atmosphere in which her guest could talk of her troubles, if she were so inclined.

The visitor looked timidly at Graye across a bowl of victuals and responded, "Madam Lovel, I knew that I had come to the right place. You have such a reputation for kindness and acceptance and," she broke off in a strangled sob. Graye smiled encouragingly and the girl continued, "My name is Neev and I am in terrible trouble."

"Well you eat and drink and refresh yourself Neev and then if you wish to, you can tell me about this trouble. If I can help you, I certainly shall. Excuse me a moment." Graye left the room and then returned with some clothing that she judged to be the right size for her guest. She offered it to Neev, saying, "My chamber is to the right—please will you take these and make yourself comfortable? No, please, it would make me happy."

At first reluctantly and then gratefully the girl took the offered clothes and nervously slid open the door to Graye's chamber. Graye watched the door for some time once it slid shut after her.

At Yorgish's house, the Elders were once more in conference. It was the day after the meeting in which they had resolved to defy the

Congregation. They had much to arrange. Up to this point, the meeting had been running to plan. It was not going to continue proceeding normally, however.

The more it became apparent that the Congregation intended to restrict the freedom of the Guard, the more the Elders had been forced to reach the conclusion that anarchic action may become inevitable. Out of all the Etherean Guard, the Elders were selected from those who held the strongest views about the role of Ethereans in peacekeeping. They were fiercely devoted to a charge that they believed was laid upon them not by men but by Yershowsh the Creator Himself.

What the Congregation proposed threatened seriously to hamper the Guard's ability to fulfil this charge. The Guard was to be reduced to twenty percent of its present strength, at a time when the Elders believed that their numbers were already dangerously low. The Elders were advised that they should plan for their own retirement. The Congregation intended to involve itself in the selection of Elders in the future. It was perhaps this imposition more than any other that concerned the Elders. Much as they believed in the monarchic democracy that pervaded Deb, they believed even more that politicians were too indebted to the electorate to be sufficiently impartial when it came to matters of planetary security.

The Elders believed that their ultimate mandate came from Yershowsh. Therefore if the will of Yershowsh conflicted with the will of the Congregation or the public, it was Yershowsh they would obey.

Graye Lovel featured prominently in their discussions. They had no difficulty in agreeing that now, more than ever, it was essential for them to know what Yershowsh was saying. True Hearers were far rarer than Ethereans and the only Hearer to whom they had immediate access was Lovel.

On the one hand the Elders did not want to begin depending too heavily on someone with a history such as Graye's; on the other hand Graye was by far the closest Hearer and she also had a flawless past record when it came to Hearing accurately and consistently. A complicating factor to be sure, was that Graye's husband worked for the Congregation. But under the present circumstances the Elders had to conclude that Graye's assistance would be essential. They did not want to risk defying the High Congregation unless they were certain this was sanctioned by Yershowsh.

The Elders were in the process of discussing the extent of their proposed rebellion and the practical implications of this, when four figures burst from the Ether into their meeting. Of these men, they could immediately recognise but one. That man's arrival caused an incredible stir, but stood next to him was another whose presence they would shortly find yet more stirring.

At the sight of Bars Medok, Ruith ru Contin leapt from her crut and let her body flow intangibly through the low desk before her. Breathless she stood before Bars for a moment and then she grasped him by the elbows impulsively and buried her face in his neck.

Bars looked over Ruith's shoulder at Yorgish, a man whom Bars respected more than any other on Deb and smiled at him. Yorgish's expression, displayed mainly in his eyes, was all joy and relief. With a smile obscured by his prodigious beard, he said, "Minister Medok, you are welcome."

As Ruith released him, Bars cocked his head on one side and replied, "'Minister,' you say? Then am I already displaced as Director?"

Jish, who had recovered quickly from the reappearance of the supposedly late Bars Medok, snorted. "In the short time that you have been gone, the *High* Congregation has changed beyond all recognition." She emphasised the word 'High' with contempt. "Forgive me Minister—your face is a welcome sight indeed, but you will not be pleased to hear what has transpired in your absence." Jish bowed slightly and then left the meeting room to obtain refreshments for the guests.

Yorgish, like the other Elders, now turned his attention to the other three men standing before him. His eyes widened when he looked at Jonathan, but he spoke next to Martin. "Dear me, is this Rohan of the Guard?" He looked at Gylan for confirmation, as Martin beamed back at them.

Gylan looked puzzled and then incredulous, "It can only be him. We were of equal rank when he left on a secret mission that all believed took his life. How could I forget the face of the supreme linguist and warrior who persistently bested me in brack combat without breaking into a sweat?" As Ruith returned to her crut, Gylan arose and seized Martin by the elbows. A hint of a tear came to his eye. "Ro, it has been too long."

Martin nodded. "Nineteen years as they are reckoned on my adopted planet. Twenty years by Deb time." He reached up and placed his hand round the back of Gylan's head. "It is good to see you Gy. And an Elder now!" He gestured at Gylan's sash of office.

During these moments, Garmon had not for one instant taken his eyes off Jonathan. He studied him closely, noting his body language, the poor state of his clothing and the evidence of recent flight. Garmon had observed Ethereans for many years. He thought that he knew by sight at least all the adult Ethereans on Deb. He did not recognise Jonathan. That could only mean one thing.

Whilst the rest of the Elders were starting to talk amongst themselves and fire questions at Bars and Martin (who had been known on Deb as Rohan ru Porvish), Garmon approached Jonathan, smiled to him, said something in Deban which Jonathan could not understand and then removed his bracarpium bracelets and forcibly placed them into Jon's hands. Jon returned Garmon's intense look, not at all comprehending the significance of what Garmon had just done.

This interchange had not escaped Mekly's notice, nor Jish's as she now stood in the doorway of the room. In silence, each of them with trembling hands repeated the same strange ceremony, approaching Jonathan, removing their bracks and giving them to him.

Jon was now holding six of these strange items of jewellery, feeling increasingly overwhelmed. It was not simply that he was amongst strangers: all of the events of the last few days were strange and alien to him, as were the sights, sounds and smells that he now experienced. He was in a state of cultural shock and since he had escaped the dungeon, nothing had made much sense to him.

The remaining Elders became less engrossed in their conversations and inquisitions as they noticed what Garmon, Mekly and Jish had done. And then in a strange gargling shriek, Ruith voiced the thought that now occurred to all of them, "The Guardian!"

Yorgish looked for confirmation from Garmon, whose opinion he most respected on spiritual matters such as these. "There can be no doubt, Yorgish," Garmon said. "He has the aura; he has all the identifying marks. This is our lost Guardian."

Upon hearing this, Yorgish turned to Jonathan. "Guardian of the Insensate, we have been waiting for you—you cannot know with what anticipation! We have much to discuss. My bracarpium belongs to you." He clicked his wrists together and again Jon marvelled as these metal objects unformed and reformed. He received the two additional bracelets as graciously as he could, but it was becoming difficult to hold them all.

"What is your name?" Gylan asked.

At least Jonathan could interpret these words. "I am Jonathan. Jonathan Fenton. But I think I was once called Chankwar."

Gylan cocked his head at Yorgish. "Yonuffen?"

"Jonathan," Mekly corrected. "But this name, Chankwar—that is familiar."

"As it should be," Yorgish said in an authoritative tone. "You and I were younger Elders in those days. You too Garmon. But how could we forget the strange circumstances under which Bars and Floom Medok came to acquire an adopted son, Chankwar."

Jonathan, who had followed most of this, now looked at Bars. Bars was looking back at him, in tearful admiration. And then Jonathan reached out to his father, leant his head on his shoulder and began to sob heartily.

In the house of Graye Lovel, matters were similarly emotional, albeit for different reasons. When Neev could at last be coaxed into revealing her problems, Graye had discovered that here before her was a scared fellow gambling addict. Neev told Graye that she knew Graye had worked in the past with people involved in the gambling community. She begged Graye now to come to her aid. Graye did not think it appropriate to mention to Neev that Graye struggled with the same violent addiction.

Neev explained that she had upset some influential figures in the gambling community. She had lost at a critical game of ti'alor and had fled the gambling den before forfeits could be finalised. She knew that it would only be a matter of time before an enforcer caught up with her and removed one of her limbs—or worse.

During this conversation, Neev had brought out of her carry-sack a ti'alor board. She explained to Graye that she had devised a strong ti'alor strategy and had been extremely successful with it. But she had made the mistake of playing once, when under the influence of serj, one of the stimulant drugs often available in gambling dens and whilst on a high she had forgotten to follow the fail-safe elements of her ti'alor strategy.

Neevairy had lost and she had lost impressively. The stake had been a specified quantity of building material and after gambling away all of her own, she had then gambled with her parent's allocation. She had done this often before, she told Graye and she had always clawed back all her losses, once her fellow gamblers had become overconfident and incautious. But on this occasion, she had been unable to recover what she had gambled. Her parents, who lived in a state of luxury, not knowing that this was courtesy of their daughter's illicit winnings, were now to be reduced to life in a shack, unless Neev could win again.

Having lost so badly and having had nothing left to stake, she had fled, before the building material transfer forms were signed. She was now a marked woman and she knew that the enforcers would catch up with her sooner or later. It was only a matter of time.

Whilst Graye had been listening to this story, she had not noticed that her pulse had quickened and her breathing had become shallow. She was fascinated with Neev's description of a virtually foolproof method of maintaining a respectable—but more importantly, consistent—winning streak. To her ears it did indeed sound as though the system was reliable and guaranteed success to anyone who kept her wits about her.

Temptation stood before her—but not for her own purposes. She had devoted much of her life to helping others. Surely now she could use her experience in the gambling world, to win back for someone in need all that she had lost. Graye overlooked the fact that the gamblers to whom Neev had lost would certainly not entertain gambling with anyone associated to her.

Another point that Graye did not consider was the fact that the only way for her to restore Neev's losses, would be to deprive someone else, unconnected with Neev's disgrace. With the best motives at the forefront of her mind and her worst motives hidden even from herself, in the darkest depths of her heart, Graye agreed to do what she could to help Neev.

17

It had been a hectic two days since Jonathan first burst into the Elders' lives. The Elders had decided not to make public the news of Bars' reappearance. Medok agreed this to be a wise course of action, since there were suspicions that some members of the High Congregation were implicated in his abduction. After Floom and Bars Medok were reunited, it was subsequently arranged that they would travel incognito to a holiday residence on the Norvesh side of Deb. There they would stay until the Elders deemed it appropriate for them to return.

Once established in their retreat, they would be joined by Jonathan, Garmon and a bracarpium master from the Guard. The Elders had no difficulty agreeing that Jon's Etherean training must be a priority—even though Jon was still below the legal age limit for Guard training. Initially Martin had been eager to take responsibility for Jonathan's combat training. To be involved in training a Guardian! It was too good an opportunity to miss. But the Elders had not offered him the chance to train Jon; only to accompany him.

Martin had to concede that their decision was the right one. He was out of practice with his bracarpium. He hated to admit it, but the fight with Klushere had been much too close for comfort—closer than it should have been if Klushere truly were not an Etherean. Far better it would be for Jon's training to be left in the capable hands of a younger warrior, one up to date with current training and combat methods.

Having accepted this decision, Martin recalled the life that he had so easily overlooked upon his return to his home planet. Excited though he was to see old friends, desperate though he was to catch up on all the developments since he left Deb nineteen years ago, he was even more concerned to return home to his wife. He was missing her and Martin knew that she would be worrying for him.

Reluctantly then, Martin left the Elders and his dear 'nephew' after tutoring Jon as rapidly as possible in some key Deban words and phrases and returned to Earth. Many promises of visits were exchanged. Mekly in particular was keen to see this strange planet that Martin spoke of. The prospect of visiting a new world lit her up in a way the Elders had not seen before. Before that could happen though, she had more pressing matters to deal with. Quite a few Ethereans had responded to her request to come to Rebke. Hers was the task of organising teams as the Elders decided how best to pursue their silent rebellion. She was also responsible for selecting the two people whom she felt would best be suited to begin Jonathan's training.

The Elders were spending much time in conference with Delturn, who was proving to be an endless source of information. The only thing that he had pleaded ignorance of was Belee'al's plans for Jon. He told the Elders that the Belee'ans had mastered the art of Enveloping and were far superior in this respect to any of the Etherean Guard. Indeed a large network of underground passages was Enveloped and thus rendered impervious to Etherean powers. Delturn omitted to mention that whilst within those very Enveloped passages, once free of the dungeon, Jonathan had shrugged off the Enveloping effect as if it were nothing.

It would seem, according to Delturn, that the Belee'ans had a vast web of supporters from all strata of Deban society. Unfortunately Delturn was unable to give names, since it would appear that secrecy was maintained even amongst the Belee'ans themselves. Delturn explained that this secrecy was specifically designed to make it impossible for one Belee'an to betray another.

Even as he told these half-truths, Delturn could not decide whether he was attempting to sabotage the Elders' efforts to thwart the Belee'ans, or if he simply sought to protect himself from Belee'an reprisals. Whatever the case, he felt that he had earned the trust of the Elders in a short space of time and he was sure that he could use this fact to his advantage, in time.

When they were not engaged interrogating Delturn, the Elders were questioning Jon. They took the questioning slowly, particularly once Jon had told them of the recent loss of his wife. The Elders marvelled at how well Jon was coping with the many strange turns that his life had taken recently—but they did not know the horrors that oppressed Jonathan when he tried to sleep. In his dreams, his memories of the school bully Ashley and the gnarled Belee'an Grand Preceptor Al'aran merged into one long ordeal of bitterness, bigotry and brutality.

On both sides, all were keen to discover how Jon fitted into the current circumstances on Deb. Jon was overwhelmed by the discovery that the Elders considered him to be an Etherean par excellence—a 'Guardian'—the more so when they recounted the history of the Guardians of the Insensate and the solemn charge that Yershowsh placed upon the shoulders of the Guardians. This implied that he was part of some grand plan—the plan of Yershowsh.

His mind spun ever quicker the more they told him and after a day and a half of this, it became clear that nothing productive could be achieved by further questioning or instruction. Preparations were made for his departure with his new mentors, the Elder Garmon Weir who would be responsible for his spiritual education and an Etherean brack expert called Ulsa.

For Floom Medok, the last two days had been unsettling, traumatic, but ultimately joyous. Soon after Medok's arrival at the Elders' conference, Ruith had visited the Medoks' home, requesting that Floom urgently attend to receive important news concerning her husband. She had not gone so far as to enter mourning, but she had come to believe that her husband was lost forever. She did not therefore expect to receive any further news. Accompanied by Ruith, she had arrived at Yorgish's home fraught and emotional.

In this state, she had been reunited with her husband. When Bars was brought before her she had screamed briefly and then smothered her husband with tearful kisses. Neither she nor her husband were given to public displays of affection, but under these circumstances, none could feel embarrassed by their uncharacteristic behaviour.

When Jonathan's presence was announced, Floom had screamed again and demanded intoxicating beverages. She curled up with her husband at the opposite end of the room to Jonathan, occasionally plucking up the courage to sneak a glance at her long-lost adopted son. Each time she looked and saw that he was still there, she clapped a hand to her face, gasped and buried her head in her husband's chest again.

Jonathan was nonplussed by this. He did not have a strong recollection of his Deban adoptive parents. He could not empathise with their emotions. When he had clutched at his father Bars previously, it had been as much because of the natural fatherly presence that Bars bore, as because of the relationship between them. As he sat opposite his parents, not quite knowing where to look, he hoped that he would have an opportunity in a less formal setting, to become re-acquainted.

Now, many miles away from that scene, Floom had begun to

regain her accustomed calm. She was a sturdy soul—as indeed the spouse of any politician must be. Furthermore, she was now able to fall into her time-honoured role of hostess, as she prepared their holiday home for the arrival of their son and the two other guests.

Few residents of Deb own a second home. In fact the very concept of ownership is quite different from that experienced on Earth. Land and property are simply resources to be allocated by the executive agencies that work for the High Congregation. But members of the Congregation are awarded special privileges and in Bars' case, one such privilege was a retreat home, far away from the capital, where he and his family could relax and recharge.

The home was built on a tiny plateau on the side of a mountain north of Norvesh, Deb's second largest city and Rebke's antipodean counterpart. Other than by an extremely challenging and arduous climb, it could only be reached by Etherean means. The Medoks were somewhat dependant on the local Etherean pilots whilst at their holiday home, but otherwise the seclusion and tranquillity of the place suited them perfectly.

Flowing rapidly by the front of the home was a rivulet, on its frantic flight to join the streams of Norvesh at the foot of the mountain. The Medoks found the noise of the running water soothing—as soon as they heard it they started to unwind. It had been wise to allow the delay before Jonathan joined them at the retreat; they were once more settled in their relationship and they were ready to greet their adopted son as he arrived.

Jonathan, Garmon and the bracarpium master Ulsa Grabe arrived shortly after dusk—the customary time at which Rebke-side Debans take a late dinner. Garmon announced their arrival by noisily winding the door-rattle. It would have been rude simply to materialise within the building.

Bars answered the door, extending both arms to the three visitors in turn. They exchanged greetings and Ulsa, who had been heavily involved in the search for Bars commented, "It is like seeing a ghost!" And then, chuckling she added, "And I do not believe in ghosts." Bars smiled graciously in return. Divine aromas floated down the hallway and Jonathan, who had experienced little of the pleasant side of Deban cookery, showed a keen interest indeed in those enticing smells.

Floom came out to greet them and insisted that before they ate, the guests should settle themselves in their quarters, unpacking what they had brought with them. On Jon's part, he had little to do. Of the items that he had brought with him from Earth, nothing remained—not even the precious letter, although that seemed relatively insignificant now. The Elders had promised to secure some clothing and other necessities for Jon and would send them along shortly.

So Jon looked around his room, exploring the storage arrangements and puzzling over the unusual mechanisms by which the various compartments opened. When there was nothing more to see within the room, he sat on the bed and gazed out of the window. The bed was low, but mercifully at least as comfortable as similar Earthly arrangements.

Jon did not know it, but of the three guest rooms at the home, the Medoks had given Jon the best room. His room looked out onto the stream and he could trace its path up and down the mountain. In the morning, when it was lighter, he would be able to see down to the bottom of the mountain and marvel at the city that lay far below him.

Floom found him leaning against the wall, gazing out in the semi-darkness. She could not be aware of this, but he was also sizing up the Ether, noting that there was little evidence of Etherean footprints here. Floom gently touched Jon's elbow and he then became aware of her presence in the room with him.

"Are you ready to eat, Jonathan Fenton?" Floom inquired.

Jon looked at her steadily for a moment and then took her hand and said, "I should like it if you would call me Chankwar."

Floom smiled, then sniffed. She coughed a little to cover over the mist that had sprung to her eyes and then turned, indicating that Jon should follow her to the source of the gorgeous aroma that would be his first formal Deban dinner.

Training began in earnest the following morning. Although Garmon had felt, perhaps rightly, that the spiritual aspects of Jon's training were the most important, he had reluctantly agreed that the brack training was an urgent priority. Then knew not when Jon would next have to defend himself.

This suited Jon. He was fascinated by the bracarpium weapon—especially the technology behind it. His enthusiasm for the training was to some extent assisted and magnified by the fact that Ulsa Grabe, the three times worldwide bracarpium tournament champion, was very easy on the eye.

She wore close-cropped hair and an authoritative demeanour. Jon probably would have felt shy of her but for the fact that she had a calm, businesslike manner and was clearly at ease with herself.

Ulsa had not intended to make reference to the brack in the first session, but Jon was so evidently amazed by the weapon, that she felt it appropriate to change her plans slightly. She reminded herself that here was a man who had seen little of such things. Although she was accustomed to the use and operation of the brack, she could understand its mysterious appeal to an off-worlder.

Jon could not entirely follow the explanation; some of the words that Ulsa used were entirely beyond his ken. But as far as he could understand, the bracarpium bracelets were made of a curious alloy of a base metal and a liquid element that the Debans called 'ebullene'. This alloy was exceptionally strong, but when an electrical charge flowed over the alloy, the molecular structure reformed itself in predictable ways. Debans had learnt to exploit this behaviour, by embedding miniaturised electrical controllers and self-charging power sources within the alloy. Ebullene was a very rare material, but fortunately for the Etherean Guard, the High Congregation had agreed that this resource should be used primarily for production of the traditional bracarpium weapons that were now the trademark of the Guard.

With a feeling of wonder, Jon received his brack. Ulsa explained that this weapon would, excepting accidents, remain with him for the rest of his life. She caused the bracelets to flow around his wrists and told Jon to start becoming used to the weight of them. She took pains to impress upon him that he should only remove them if he needed to use them. On no other account should the weapon leave his wrists.

The brief introduction over, Ulsa then looked at Jon sternly and said, "Now, this is your first lesson: Catch me."

Jon was about to ask for clarification, but only managed to say, "Wha...?" Ulsa had already vanished and Jon then realised that his training had begun.

The chase through the Ether was an eye-opener, but by this stage Jonathan had become accustomed to experiencing strange new revelations. When Ulsa had faded to the Ether, Jon had thought, *Provided she's not faster than me, this should be easy.* But how wrong he was.

Jon's first problem as he followed his mentor into the Ether was that there was no sign of her. Not a trace. No footprint, no echoes, nothing. *How can I chase something I can't see?* Jon wondered.

And then he remembered the surge he had felt, warning him of Klushere's presence. He must have other Ether-senses at his disposal. Although he could not at that moment see Ulsa, he realised he could feel the Ether's response to her. But the feeling was faint—was she already so far away?

Jon headed for the source of that feeling, with all the speed he could muster. He seemed to be making some progress, because the feeling became gradually more intense. Jon was halfway around the planet when finally, he was able to see Ulsa Grabe. And then it became apparent why he had been able to catch up with her. She wasn't moving—in fact she was waiting for him.

When Ulsa came into view, he heard a distant call from her. "You'll never catch me that way!" And then she laughed.

Irritated, Jon tried to move even more quickly towards her—his speed seemed to surprise her. He was almost upon her before she had time to move and then... But what was this?

As he neared Ulsa and reached his hands out towards her, she had stretched her entire Ether presence out, upwards and away from Jon. It was as though instantly, rather than one discrete form, she had become several slender and impossibly long threads of herself. And as Jon's hand was about to brush the end of the strands, they snapped away like elastic, far more quickly than Jon could follow.

If Jon had eyebrows in his Ether form, they were raised high. "Wow," he said aloud. He did not have time to ponder this novelty, since he was interrupted by a new surge coming towards him rapidly; in advance of the surge, he could hear an Ether voice in crescendo saying, "Outgetoutgetoutoftheway!"

He moved just in time; an Etherean was charging straight at him. After Jon had dodged, that Etherean kept on going. He was not chasing Jonathan. Jon looked after him, puzzled. The man's hands were missing. He looked again and could see that the hands of this man were mostly in the physical realm, holding a bar and around this bar there was a huge cage—like the carriage of a train. And in that carriage there were some thirty people. So that must be one of the Etherean transports he had heard about.

Whilst he was musing about this, temporarily distracted from his task, he felt a pair of hands clasp about his neck and a voice whisper in his ear, "Swish—and you're dead. A moment's lapse of concentration can be fatal." Standing calmly behind him was his mentor Ulsa, who had appeared from nowhere.

She had not removed her hands. Jon felt a little uncomfortable. "Do you know how many times I have wished I were dead?" he asked bitterly, looking over his shoulder.

Ethereans do not blush whilst in the Ether. But Ulsa rapidly removed her hands and conveyed by her body language that she was embarrassed and flustered. Jon could feel her blushing even though there was no visual evidence of this. The Elders had ensured that Ulsa knew of Jon's recent history.

In truth Jon had given little thought to his own death. It was an unnecessary overreaction provoked by the bruising Ulsa was inflicting upon his ego. Aware that he was being unfair, Jon in turn was embarrassed. He turned the subject away from himself. "How did you do that... thing?" He lacked the Deban language to describe how Ulsa had extended her Ether form so dramatically.

Ulsa smiled, more impish than businesslike. "To find out, catch me!" And with that, she threaded her way away from him again.

This will be a long session, Jon thought.

18

Al'aran was in a foul mood. He was happiest when he was angry. The Central Elect were nervous simply because of his presence. But the nerves of the Elect were further threatened and frayed as they learned of Al'aran's vitriolic and violent disposition. Amongst them, only Klushere who had a personal acquaintance with the Grand Preceptor, was relatively at ease.

He had summoned them into his dark chamber. The Elect did not consider this to be a fortuitous invitation. Al'aran's personal chamber? They would rather swim in the city's sewer systems with heavy weights about their ankles and carnivorous rodents chewing at their ears.

Not only were Al'aran's lodgings dank, dismal and depressing, but when Al'aran was in a mood such as this, he was prone to fierce physical outbursts against everything and everyone in the room. Since the room was Enveloped, preventing retreat to the Ether, and since they dared not resist him, the Central Elect bore his wrath physically, flinching as little as possible.

If Grand Preceptor Kytone wished to work out his anger on their hides, this was doubtless for their ultimate betterment. Forbearance would stand them in good stead with Belee'al and it was right for them to bring their bodies into subjection. They knew that they should not be too reliant on the Ether. Their immediate superior Klushere, reminded them of that often.

Al'aran was in mid-rant, when he stopped before Sivian. He seemed suddenly thoughtful. "You. You're a fine fellow—devoted to your masters—ever honouring to Belee'al." Sivian nodded nervously. "You have the mark of an accomplished Etherean about you," he looked slyly at Klushere, the only non-Etherean in the room, "surely *you* have located our missing Minister and the boy?"

Sivian took a breath and then stoically replied, "No, my Lord, I regret that I have not."

"No? But you are so young, so adept, so *powerful*." Al'aran came near and attempted a close approximation of an ingratiating smile. "But you know at least where Medok was heading, before his disappeared?"

Sivian looked down at the ground and just managed to say, "No, Grand Preceptor."

Al'aran lifted his staff up so that the handle rested under his withered chin. Sivian was looking down at him. "Kneel down boy," Kytone said to Sivian. Sivian complied.

Next Al'aran moved to Jerud. She bore a respectful, apologetic look. "My daughter," he said, almost happily. "I believe you have news for me of the blaspheming Lovel woman?"

"Y-yes, my Lord. I am pleased to report that we have all but neutralised her. I am expecting word of her descent into decay imminently."

"Good, good. I want you to be there when it happens," Al'aran cooed. He then thrust his staff firmly into Jerud's stomach, causing her to gasp and double up. With her ear now within range of his mouth, he bellowed into it, "BEAT THAT KNEELING WRETCH FOR ME!" His untrimmed eyebrows tickled Jerud's cheek as she arose, taking the proffered staff.

In dismay she looked at the staff, at Klushere and then at Sivian. She knew that there was no point in attempting to avoid the duty placed before her now and certainly no merit in holding back with her blows. As she moved towards the sorry Sivian, she turned to Al'aran for guidance, "How many times, Grand Preceptor?"

Al'aran charged at her, head down and knocked her off her feet. She fell backwards over Sivian and cracked her head on the floor. Whilst she was lying there, Al'aran seized her by her tunic, thrusting his stick into her hands again. "UNTIL I SAY 'STOP,'" he screamed. Then he pulled her back to her feet—a remarkable achievement for such a decrepit old man half her size.

Wincing from the knock to her head, but in no doubt about what would happen if she delayed to ask another question, she set to Sivian's punishment, whilst the other disciples watched in horror. Klushere, a little removed from these proceedings, looked on with the air of one who had previously knelt in Sivian's place.

During the beating, Al'aran sauntered over to Klushere, his easy motion belying his age. He looked at his disciple, the only person on the planet for whom he felt anything approaching warmth. "I have an idea that may help us deal with at least two of our irritations simultaneously," he said, with a cunning smile.

When Plykar Lovel returned home he was to discover his wife in conference with a stunningly attractive, unpretentiously attired young woman. Graye introduced him to Neevairy Ewtoe and by the little that Graye said, Plykar deduced that here was another waif in need of assistance. She would probably stay with them that night and maybe even for some time to come. Plyk could not imagine what kind of trouble could have befallen one so beautiful.

After they had all retired for the night and whilst Graye was untangling her wind-blown hair, she told her husband Neev's story. Plyk expressed concern that Neev was a gambler, but Graye's response was, "And what better path to redemption for me than to aid someone who has failed where I also have failed? Surely this must be the will of Yershowsh."

"Really? Is it?" Plyk asked.

Graye confessed that she had not sought an answer from Yershowsh and she had not Heard anything specifically about Neev, other than an internal voice urging her to be cautious. But she *was* being cautious and she would turn to Hearing in the morning. There hadn't been time before.

In fact Graye gulped inwardly when she realised that she had completely overlooked the possibility that this was a situation in which Hearing would be wise. She scolded herself for the oversight and then repeated her assurances to her husband. She did not want him to worry.

"You know that I find it hard not to worry Graye. Especially when gambling is involved—no matter how indirectly." Graye looked crestfallen, but Plyk then approached her and gave her a reassuring hug from behind, kissing her on the top of her head. "I trust you though," he said, partly in an effort to convince himself that he did indeed trust his addict wife.

As if sensing his inner turmoil, Graye made every effort that night to demonstrate to her husband that she was clean. One area of their marriage had particularly suffered when Graye was gambling; not so tonight. For Graye took care to prove to her husband, that she was free of the curse. By the end of the second proof, Plyk was convinced. He felt pleased with himself afterwards that he had managed not to bring the lovely Neev to mind at the crucial moment. He did love his wife.

In the morning, the three occupants of the house took breakfast together, talking about uncontroversial subjects such as the health of Graye's seedlings—Graye was gratified by Neev's keen interest—and the imminent qualifying rounds of the Rebke brack tournament.

Plykar was adamant that no matter what changes there may be to the Etherean way of life, the tournaments would continue.

After breakfast, Plykar lovingly kissed his wife goodbye, not knowing that this would be the last time he would see her for a long while.

When Plykar had left, Graye excused herself, indicating that she had some paperwork to attend to. She invited Neev to amuse herself in their modest library in the meantime.

Graye's intention was to use the time to meditate and if possible, Hear. Neev seemed amenable and less afraid of imminent reprisals than she had been yesterday.

Unfortunately Neev's calmness was only temporary. Graye had not been in her study long, when Neev entered, tearful and breathless. She expressed concern to Graye that if she did not face up to the gamblers soon, they may instead seek to exact revenge against her parents—who were totally innocent in the matter.

Although she had not meditated for as long as she wished, Graye was starting to believe that it was Yershowsh's will for her to attempt to help this poor young girl. So she reached out to Neev and squeezed her shoulder, saying, "Do not be afraid, Debanika. Collect your things and we will go."

Neev looked at Graye shyly through her tears and mouthed a heart-felt "thank you." She then rushed to her room to pack the few belongings that she was carrying with her. As she packed, Neev started to consider and celebrate her success thus far.

The Lovel woman was turning. Neev saw the hunger in her eyes. She had seen it a thousand times before. These reformed gamblers were all alike. Prey on their weaknesses and they would soon return to their oft-trodden paths of delinquency.

Ironically, Neevairy had no interest in gambling herself. For sure, some of the resources acquired by the gambling magnates assisted Neev in maintaining a luxurious lifestyle, but even if that lifestyle were threatened, she would not herself turn to gambling for enrichment. She would far rather seek a more human solution to her needs. Why gamble for resources when she could use her skills to obtain those resources in a far less risky manner?

Plykar Lovel had been a problem. As soon as Graye's husband had returned home, Neev noticed that Plyk was attracted to Neev. Of course her dowdy clothing had been taken from her and she had been obliged to don the more elegant clothes offered by her generous hostess. With Neev resplendent in tasteful garb, the husband had required careful handling. Whilst Plyk was present, Neev had adopted a subtly more childlike persona. It would not be a problem if Plyk related to her as a father. What she did not want was for him to relate to her as a lover.

This strategy had been successful. As far as Neevairy could tell, her hosts had enjoyed each other's company last night and not a thought had been given to their ever-alert guest. Their preoccupation had given Neev the opportunity to send a report to her masters. The gamblers would ensure that someone took care of Neev's regular state-assigned employment for as long as it took for her to land her catch.

She entered the hallway with the pride of a successful fisherman. How could she fail? Neev was both fisherman and bait.

Resar Playne was stressed. There were two items on her desk. The cause and the cure.

She had already read Ti'par and Hesdar's joint statement, the cause of her stress. She had taken the wise precaution of pouring herself a powerful cocktail of nerve-deadening liquid chemicals—her stress cure—before making any attempt to read it through again.

She had seen very little of Elder Gorph in recent days. It was inevitable that he and the Elders would be extremely preoccupied following the devastating début of Dayle Rother and his hijacking of the Etherean Guard resource debate. But the report before her shed new light on Gylan's absence.

It was not difficult to believe the allegations contained within that report. Resar could well imagine that the Elders, seeing their power being stripped away, would decide to take matters into their own hands. Who could blame them? They believed that they had a divinely ordained responsibility for the protection of the planet. They were bound to consider that their standing mandate overrode any decision of the High Congregation.

No, she was not entirely surprised and certainly not shocked by the suggestion within the report that the Elders were spearheading a rebellion. What shocked Rez and made her reach for means of inebriation, was the conclusion contained within the ru Masal/ru Contin document.

"This Government will not tolerate insurrection in any form, from any source. Whilst not wishing to lose sight of the people's indebtedness to the Etherean Guard, we must never abdicate our primary responsibility for their protection and well-being. It is a fundamental tenet of our democracy that the High Congregation must be the highest authority on Deb. We conclude from the compelling evidence before us that the Elders do not respect and submit in full to that authority." So the report read.

It had been circulated to all ministers early that morning. Apparently Hesdar and Ti'par had worked on the document all night, together with countless other aides and executives. When Resar had entered her office, the bound report awaited her on her desk.

Rez's ministerial portfolio did not specifically include any matters Etherean. She had been thus insulated from the major overhaul of the resource system so far as Ethereans were concerned. Nevertheless, she was aware of the changes and whilst reading through the report, she had not been surprised to learn of the Elders' reaction to those changes. What had surprised her was the fact that someone within the

High Congregation was not only aware of their reaction but must also have damning evidence of it.

The Eldership had never been obliged to report to the High Congregation; a peaceful co-operation existed between the two entities. Sometimes ministers would be invited to attend Eldership meetings; oftentimes Elders would attend the Congregation's debating sessions. A flow of information passed between the two. But the Elders certainly would have guarded this kind of information closely. Resar could not imagine from whence sprang the leak. It was not as if Ethereans could be spied on without their knowledge. They were always too aware of the spiritual and physical presences around them.

And yet, clearly there had been a leak. And Hesdar ru Contin had been dismayed to learn of the Elders' position, so strongly did she believe in the monarchic democracy upon which Deb's politics were founded. Resar doubted not that Ti'par, who was less pro-Etherean than Hesdar, would have played heavily on this evidence of rebellion. The report she now perused was the result.

But the conclusion! That was deeply concerning to Rez. Without reference to the rest of the High Congregation, Hesdar had decided that immediate action was required. The report strongly argued that the actions of the Elders, no matter how well-intentioned, were unlawful and demanded that sanctions and penalties be imposed. Furthermore, given the peculiar position of Ethereans and their advantage over their fellows, these penalties should be imposed without delay.

The purpose of the report was not to solicit the views of ministers—it was to advise them what action was to be taken. Indeed the High Congregation may already have despatched Ethereans to take the Elders into custody.

She had to get word to Yorgish urgently.

19

As she and Graye waited at Plaedon Central's station, Neev explained with embarrassment that she had gambled away her year's travel allowance. Graye laughed lightly and said, "That is the least of your concerns my dear. I rarely travel and have plenty of my allowance to spare. I am sure the pilot will accept credits from me on your behalf."

Graye was trying her utmost to be relaxed. It was difficult when so many people passing through the station recognised her. She pleaded inwardly that no one would ask her where she was going. She knew she could not answer that question.

At the same time, Graye tried to exude calm. Her young friend was displaying advanced anxiety and expressing the desire for it all to be over. Just as Graye wondered for the twenty-seventh time whether she was doing the right thing, the carriage descended into their bay and it was time to board.

Graye was not entirely enamoured with Etherean transportation. Even though she had grown up and lived with this as the sole means of rapid commuting on Deb and despite the fact that she had always been in contact with Ethereans, it still seemed to her a very unnatural way to travel.

It is a shame that she felt this way, since it truly is a remarkable means of traversing the planet. There are no delays and no pre-flight checks. There need be no concern of mechanical failure since, apart from the windows that open, the carriage has no moving parts. The only noise generated by the vehicle is wind noise, but in the well-insulated carriages, that can hardly be heard. It is a profoundly relaxing way to travel, once one becomes used to the speed at which the carriage accelerates. That part can be quite breathtaking.

On a long flight, to the Norvesh-side of the planet for example, the craft would soar high above the planet's surface, providing a splendid view of the world below. Until the advent of Etherean transport, such views were the exclusive reserve of those Ethereans with the inclination to fly high and look down upon Deb. But now their non-Etherean brethren could share the wonder. Indeed some Debans would take a flight to Norvesh simply to marvel at the spectacle and then immediately return home.

Neev and Graye were taking a more modest trip to the small city of Contin, south-east of Plaedon. This was large enough to provide gambling opportunities coupled with anonymity and far enough away from Plaedon and Rebke for Graye's comfort. At this stage, much as she respected him, she wanted there to be no risk of her husband discovering what she was about to do.

Neevairy said that she had gambled in Contin before and she was reasonably confident that she would be able to find a suitable den where they could settle. For as long as it took.

During their journey, Graye decided that she needed to explain to Neev that she already had some experience of gambling. She judged this to be prudent since Neev would be reassured if she knew that Graye was not a complete novice. Graye was in fact offering not only to provide the stake for their gambling, but also to participate actively in the process. She particularly wished to try Neev's ti'alor method—but she kept her enthusiasm for this closely guarded.

Their conversation naturally lulled during the short journey. Graye used this opportunity to feign absorption in the scenery whilst actually communing with Yershowsh. *Am I doing the right thing?* she asked, in the quiet of her mind.

I will be with you, came the immediate response.

"I will be with you?" That did not seem to Graye at all likely. She was about to enter one of the most decadent, lawless places on the planet. She could not for a moment envisage that Yershowsh would be found there. No, it must simply be the case that she was projecting her own wishful thinking into the voice that she usually Heard from Yershowsh. She had Heard nothing but her own mind, her own justifications and her own prideful thoughts. On this venture, she would be completely alone.

Graye sighed and then realising the effect this might have on Neev, quickly turned it into a yawn. She focused back on the carriage and her companion and asked, "So where is it that you grew up, Neev?"

Neev seemed pleased to have her mind taken away from their imminent encounter and responded with animation. To the east of Plaedon there is a small cluster of hamlets surrounding a lake. She asked if Graye had ever visited any of the four hamlets.

Graye had occasion to visit three out of the four, during the course of her professional life. Neev told her that she had lived at the fourth hamlet, Masal. Neev spoke with great enthusiasm about her life at the water's edge—how, when she was a child, she would spend a long time in the water, darting about, pretending that she was an Etherean flying through the Ether. This was of course many children's dream.

During this account, their carriage touched down in Contin's station. "We're here," Neev announced brightly. She gathered her small pack of belongings and Graye clutched closely to herself her various luxury credit tokens and property allocation documents.

Together, they made for a certain part of the city where Neev believed a gambling den might be found.

Graye could have spotted the den from any distance. Simply by watching the movement of people, her practised eye could detect the types that would be heading towards gambling quarters. It still amazed her that Ethereans seemed to have such a difficult time locating and closing down gambling dens. But then they didn't have quite the same experience that Graye benefited from.

Neev could not say how long it had been since last she visited this den, but it was still in operation. Graye could feel eyes watching them as the two ladies made their way as discreetly as possible into the target building. They handed over all they were carrying to one of the aides inside, whilst they were quickly but thoroughly body-searched for weapons. All this happened without a word being exchanged. Neev and Graye were professionals. They knew how the system worked.

Their belongings were returned to them after they too had been searched. Graye noticed the usual distasteful twinkle in the eyes of the guards, as they mentally allocated between themselves some of the resources that they expected Graye and Neev to lose.

But not today, thought Graye. Today, she would win and as soon as they had recovered what Neev had lost, they would leave. Graye was not to know that many influential people, including the very person she sought to help, had different ideas.

Graye had chosen not to start with ti'alor. She thought that she would try one of the other games first and possibly lose a little, to avoid attracting too much attention at an early stage. This would actually be harder than it sounded. Every patron of a gambling den would be closely scrutinised and assessed by the management. New gamblers would invariably be shown favour by the house, when playing the lower stake games. The house could always afford to lose at these, so long as the wary new gambler was eventually enticed towards the big tables.

So as Graye set out to lose a few luxury credits here and there, the house also set out to ensure she won. Neev was aware of the strategy on both sides and had to turn away from the game occasionally, for a private smile. She had watched gamblers at work before, during the course of her employment.

In Graye, Neev she saw an experienced and skilful gambler. Indeed, if Graye did not suffer from the fatal compulsion to go for the big win, she could have been extremely successful. That flair together with that destructive compulsion were precisely the characteristics that Neev's employers treasured in a gambler. She could understand why Graye was so valuable to them, at least until her resources were exhausted and they had finished having sport with her.

Graye was showing little sign of her compulsive streak at this stage. They wandered from table to table, around the periphery of the den, playing games here and there and just about breaking even whilst they pursued this strategy.

As time moved on, Graye noted that they were attracting a little more attention from the staff. She and Neev were offered complimentary sachets of serj, for example. This was nothing new or unusual. It was almost always in the interests of the house to provide free stimulant drugs to its clientèle. A happy, exuberant gambler placed larger bets.

Neev was so intent on watching Graye hungrily consume the contents of the sachet that she failed to spot the sachet that Graye dropped under the table. The sachet that Graye consumed contained nothing stronger than sweetener and had been carefully concealed in one of her sleeves, along with several similar sachets. There were certain parts of today's strategy that Graye was not prepared to reveal to Neev. There was something about the way Neev had reacted when Graye revealed that she had experience of gambling. Graye had not found Neev's expression of surprise particularly convincing. She would help Neev as best she could and then leave as quickly as possible.

She may have achieved this aim and her life continued as normal, had it not been for the arrival of Bravish Ha'ware.

As noon approached, Neev and Graye were treated with more and more favour by the house. Graye detected that the management had decided to encourage this gambler and her attractive young friend to move towards one of the larger tables. Graye resisted this for as long as she judged necessary to be in keeping with the behaviour of a fairly novice gambler. She and Neev then started to skirt the ti'alor tables, taking in the action and waiting for a game to finish, in the hope that they may be allowed to participate.

It was customary before a game of ti'alor started, to ensure that all members of the gambling party had sufficient provisions to sustain them through the game. The games could last for quite some time, so the chairs positioned around the table had integral holders for liquid, solid and chemical refreshments. As one game drew to a close and a few gamblers retired, many shaking their heads, the house staff attended upon the new party to ensure that they were properly refreshed. Serj sachets were supplied in abundance. Graye was careful to exchange these for her replacement sachets, when no one was watching.

The parties around this table varied somewhat from the fringe gamblers. Elsewhere around the room, the people had been day trippers and sightseers—mainly happy-go-lucky types looking for some entertainment out of the ordinary. Around the ti'alor table, one could sense that matters were a lot more serious.

Mostly the gamblers played alone. It was unusual to see team players such as Neev and Graye pooling their resources. Graye did not wish to attract any attention by acting in an unusual manner, but she needed Neev with her to remind her of the necessary strategy for this game. Neev was more than happy to let Graye take the lead and for Neev herself to stay on hand for tips and consultation.

Graye made a cautious start to the game. One of the other gamblers, a grizzled, sweaty, bristly pig-like man, barely contained a sneer as he watched Graye lay her small stake for the first game. The house steward, overseeing the game, accepted the bet professionally but a little stiffly. Graye was unperturbed. She knew what she was doing.

Several rounds into the game, it started to occur to the other members of the party that she did indeed know what she was doing. The house and Graye jointly bankrupted the overconfident pig-man, apportioning their winnings according to the level of their stakes. Graye barely suppressed a grin as he left the table, grunting as he went to the administrative bureau to discuss how his losses should be exchanged for resources.

Until that point, Graye had lost small amounts. With this win however, she was significantly ahead. Enough, she judged, to recover at least one room for Neev's parents' home.

Her losses had been carefully managed, according to Neev's strategy. The win had been almost inevitable, as Graye employed the clever technique that Neev had outlined. She marvelled to herself at the success—she had not expected it to be this easy. *That is because I am with you*, a voice said inside her head. It took her by surprise. She didn't think it was her imagination, but she could not believe that it was anything else. She did not have time to ponder this any further though, because at that moment Bravish Ha'ware entered the room.

Graye could not initially see who it was, but judging by the stir created and by the way every member of staff immediately smartened his or her appearance, she knew it must be one of the magnates. She looked with interest. She had never gambled in Contin before, but she wondered if this den might be nominally supervised by someone she had encountered previously.

Every bodily sensation within her ceased when she saw who it was. As the crowd parted slightly, her eyes met his and locked. She knew that her face had paled. She knew that her body language indicated that she was not pleased to see this man. He could tell what she was feeling.

Bravish Ha'ware looked at her and actually smiled. The man who had most catastrophically robbed her of her dignity and self-respect, many years ago, smiled as if he could not have hoped to see anyone whose presence would delight him more. But the delight was commercial and proprietorial, not personal.

Bravish exchanged some comments with his minions and then walked purposefully over to Graye's table. He was accompanied by a woman whose physique and bearing suggested that she was his protector.

Whilst Bravish was crossing the room, Graye indicated to the steward that she wished to settle up and quit the game. Neev gasped and spoke urgently into Graye's ear, saying that she had not won nearly enough to cover Neev's debts as yet.

Do not worry; I will be with you.

And then Graye saw several things, simultaneously. The house steward was refusing to allow Graye to leave the game, claiming that it would infringe some house rule that Graye had never heard of. Three members of staff were approaching the table from different directions, all reaching under their garments as they approached. The woman with Bravish had drawn two slender swords from her sides and was holding them at thigh level, pointing downwards, but in full view of all those in the room. And at her side, Bravish approached, arms outstretched. He was talking.

"Madam Lovel, what an honour it is to see you here. You must join me in my private chamber. There is something I wish to say to you." He was smiling in a way that anyone else would have interpreted as courteous. In the light of their history however, Graye knew that he was mocking her.

"You are too kind," Graye arose and replied formally, "but you must excuse me. I have no wish to confer with you." Turning to Neev, she was about to indicate that they had to leave, but Neev had gone.

And then everything fell into place. She had been taken in.

With determination, Graye stepped away from the table. She stopped in front of Bravish and looking him in the eye said, "You are lower scum than even I had thought possible."

The two swords twitched. Bravish held out his arm across his bodyguard. "Be calm Jerud. Madam Lovel and I are old friends."

Feeling strangely at peace, Graye interjected, "Friends, you say? And so I am to thank you for luring me here I suppose? You have gained nothing Ha'ware. I came for a purpose. I see that purpose was a fraudulent contrivance. I will now leave. You have not ensnared me."

Bravish raised his hands and his eyebrows. "I? No, this was not of my doing my dear. Everything I could possibly want from you, I have already had!" He laid a hand on Graye's shoulder and continued. "But now you really must join me in my chamber. I *insist*."

His insistence was accompanied by a further ominous twitching of Jerud's swords. Still feeling oddly serene, Graye allowed herself to be directed away from the table, into the recesses of the building. Neev was nowhere in sight.

But still reverberating in her mind were the same words, *I will be with you.*

She may have entered Bravish's personal chamber feeling serene and at ease, but her peace had fled. When she entered the chamber, her eyes immediately fell upon a crut, the sole piece of furniture in the room. The crut had additional extensions to either side and above and attached to those extensions were ropes. Upon the seat and back of the chair were bars and pins, protruding from the surface. It did not look like a comfortable place to recline. As Graye was drawn farther into the room, she noticed that there was blood on the chair.

"It is unfortunate that you cast my gifts upon the ground, Graye," Bravish said. He was holding several sachets of serj in his hand. "This would have made things less uncomfortable for you. Open your mouth if you please."

Graye looked at him in bewilderment. To his right, Jerud had raised one of her rapiers and was pointing it at Graye. Her muscles flexed under tension. She raised an eyebrow, cocked her head and pleasantly said, "I do think it would be as well for you to comply, Madam Lovel."

Graye correctly perceived Jerud's meaning and opened her mouth to receive the rag that one of Bravish's aides pushed into it. More rags were then wrapped around her mouth and neck. Her eyes asked a fearful question of Bravish.

At first Bravish pretended not to understand. Then he approached Graye and spoke into her ear, conspiratorially. "We cannot have the patrons disturbed by your screaming."

Graye started to tremble.

20

Jon was exhausted. He would not have thought that being in the Ether all day could use so much energy. It wasn't physical exhaustion so much as mental and spiritual exhaustion. And the irritating part was that although he had managed to emulate Ulsa's thread technique, he had still not been able to catch her.

Ulsa debriefed him after the day's training. They were sitting on ornate padded chairs outside the Medok's holiday home, looking out across the brook. "How has the day been for you, Jonathan?" Ulsa asked.

"I cannot begin to describe in your language how tired I am, Ulsa," Jon replied, wearily. He leant forward and rested his head in his hands, listening to the soothing sound of running water. It was very calming.

Ulsa placed a hand on his back. "I am not surprised. You have attained more in one day than most of my pupils attain in a year. Yorgish said that as a Guardian you would learn quickly."

"Attain?" Jon asked, sitting up. Ulsa quickly removed her hand. "I didn't catch you all day—that was the purpose of the exercise, was it not? What did I attain?"

Ulsa laughed lightly and pulled Jon round by his shoulder to face her. Looking earnestly into his eyes, she said, "Only the most able Ethereans learn to thread. Even then, it takes many cycles of the moons for them to achieve what you grasped so easily." She smiled and shook her head slightly.

Easily? It had not seemed particularly easy to Jon. He had focused and strained and wrenched his mind into contortions, trying to find the key to Ulsa's amazing ability. Knowing that he would not capture his tutor by any other means, he had giving up simply flying after her. Whilst he was trying to recreate the strange thread patterns that she had displayed, she had passed him several times, presumably each time having circled the planet, urging him to keep trying.

No, he would not have described that as 'easy'. He raised his eyebrows and turned back to contemplate the stream.

As they sat there, Garmon came out of the house, carrying a tray of steaming drinks. He quietly offered them to Jon and Ulsa. Ulsa accepted gratefully, whilst Jon took his drink with some trepidation. He had not yet experienced a hot drink on Deb. His taste buds were a long way off becoming used to Deban fare. He rather suspected that any warm drink would constitute one more olfactory assault.

Jon was surprised then when he took the offered cup and felt that it was cold—very cold in fact. He looked at Garmon in surprised inquiry. "Try it," Garmon responded. The corner of his mouth twitched and he glanced at Ulsa, who looked away.

Jon had seen this kind of interplay before. On Earth. When exposing someone to an unaccustomed liquor. He thought that after his Cretan experience, he could probably withstand anything of that nature, so he smiled stoically and a little sarcastically at Garmon and took a gulp.

Well that was tame, he thought. The steam tickled his nose and the liquid felt cool and soothing in his mouth, but he detected no alcoholic kick.

He smiled again at Garmon. Once more, Garmon looked at Ulsa.

Ulsa winked. *Now what does winking mean on Deb?* Jon wondered.

Whilst he was thinking this, his eyes blurred. He noticed that the pathway to his stomach was feeling increasingly warm. That warmth was spreading outwards, radiating from his body, surging back up to his throat, causing him to gasp—causing him to blow steam out of his mouth!

Jon was belching loudly and watching in amazement as vapour left his mouth and dissipated into the air. He looked down at his still steaming cold drink, this time with a trace of awe.

Ulsa was suppressing giggles.

"You learn to control the steam discharge," Garmon said to Jonathan. He was speaking calmly as usual, but his eyes were twinkling. "This drink, which we call rynyn gives energy and restores weary Ethereans. It is cleansing and purifying." He sat down next to Jonathan and faced out towards the brook. Jon watched as Garmon took a long draught of rynyn and then a few seconds later quietly released a trail of steam from his mouth. He sighed, contentedly.

For the first time since his arrival here many days ago, Jon thought, *I love this planet!*

The next morning, Ulsa deemed it appropriate to move onto what Jon understood to be *the good stuff.* They spent thirty degrees of the sun—this was about two hours as far as Jon could tell—looking at the bracarpium controls and practising the movements associated with activating, deactivating and reshaping the weapon. Ulsa took pains to point out that these were the most important things he would learn during his combat training. They went over the movements repeatedly, until Jon felt not only comfortable with the motion but truly bored of it.

Once these patterns were well established, Ulsa then made this brief speech: "Fighting with another Etherean is the most challenging thing you can ever do. There are no rules. All parts of the Ether and reality are available to you and you know that through threading you can be in many places simultaneously. The spreading technique which you will learn later further assists and complicates this for the master of the Ether.

"There are no limits to the speed at which you can move in the Ether. Use this fact to whatever advantage you can. Remember that your main strategy against another Etherean is to tire her out. A tired Etherean will start to return to reality more and more frequently. Out of the Ether and only out of the Ether, can an Etherean be defeated.

"No rules. No tricks. No strategy manuals. You are your own strategy manual. Feel the Ether surge of your opponent. For inspiration and guidance, look to yourself and seek Yershowsh. There is no substitute for experience. Ready your weapon."

And that was all the warning Jon received. Ulsa attacked immediately after this and Jon barely had time to click his wrists together and bring his brack into its pole shape, before his mentor was upon him.

She was still in the physical world and yet she had moved with dazzling speed. She was flourishing her brack and spinning it quicker than Jon could follow. How could he hope to keep up with this?

Before he had time to think, Ulsa had hook-formed one end of her brack, just as Martin had done and upended Jon with a low sweep to his legs. He fell over backwards and Ulsa was upon him, pressing her brack against his neck, pinning him down so that he could barely breathe. She leant close, her face only centimetres away from his. He could feel his ankle throbbing where she had struck it.

"That was a friendly warning," Ulsa said. Friendly! It hadn't felt friendly. She paused, still close to his face. He could feel her breath and sense her smell. Jon parted his lips, felt the pressure ease from his throat and moved his head forward. Ulsa didn't move—she was still on top of him.

Whilst they were staring into each other's eyes, Ulsa paused as if waiting for something, Jon surreptitiously touched the controls on his brack. It separated at the centre and Jon then brought the two resulting short poles to bear against Ulsa's temples.

At least that was what he tried to. But Ulsa was ahead of him. With a gleeful laugh, she back-flipped away from him, using his stomach as a launchpad. His brack poles swished through the air and clanged together against each other. Winded, but determined, Jon instinctively became intangible and leapt off the ground in pursuit. He tried a few flourishes of his own and found himself laughing as he realised this was what Ulsa had done and was why she had appeared to be so fast. He could see her with his physical eyes, but the image was merely a residue of her presence—she had no physical form. This was a glimpse of the unique nuances of Ether combat. The first of many, he supposed.

There are no limits to the speed at which you can move, she had said. Of course. Jon brought both the short poles together, touched the controls of the weapon and they reformed into a single pole, one end shaped as a blade and the other end shaped as a pummel. "I have a friendly warning for you," Jon cried and flew at Ulsa, brack flashing.

It was impossible to describe it as anything other than a battle. When Ulsa first drew Jonathan's blood whilst he flashed briefly through reality, Jon seriously wondered whether this were not another part of an elaborate plan to destroy him. He had tried to avoid Ulsa's blow by moving out of the Ether, parrying her blow with his brack still in the Ether. Once more she had been too fast for him. Just as their bracks were about to clash in the Ether, hers materialised and moved through Jon's. Jon had incorrectly guessed what she was about to do and also materialised. He noticed too late that her pole had transformed to a blade—just as it cut into his shoulder.

He had yelped and grabbed hold of his shoulder, looking at Ulsa in disbelief. Ulsa just laughed at him, saying, "Move back into the

Ether, Debanika!" He did not know that this was an insult and this was probably as well. Recognising that she was not about to finish him off, he moved back into the Ether as suggested and with relief felt his metabolism accelerate as the healing process started apace.

Ulsa was coming for him again, but Jon decided that he needed some thinking time. He exercised his new-found skill and threaded away. He was halfway across the planet before Ulsa had chance to respond. He didn't hear her murmur to herself, "Very good. Very good."

Jon tried a new tactic and redirected himself out through the planet's atmosphere. He proceeded onwards and outwards, until he reached the very edge of the sky. His Ether presence reshaped into his normal form and he turned to try and locate Ulsa. She was nowhere in sight.

Deb looked truly wondrous from this position. He could not identify the land masses or name the oceans, but he could appreciate the panoramic view of this foreign land. He could see the shadowy path of Deb's sun, proceeding across the face of the planet, as it brought morning to the lands below. It was peaceful here.

Use your time wisely, learn quickly—I will have need of you soon. Soothing words spoke into his mind. He knew now they were not his own thoughts, but he did not know where they came from. It was the same voice that he had heard before, at the shrine and in the dungeon. By virtue of those two occasions he knew that he should take heed. He took the message to mean that he should carry on with his training rather than sightsee. Ulsa was still not in view, so he returned through the atmosphere to find her.

Soon, he picked up her footprint and threaded along the path that she had taken. She came into view and as Jon neared her, he unthreaded himself, brack at the ready and struck her with great force on the back of her neck. Surprised and stunned, Ulsa spun out of control, with Jon in victorious pursuit.

It was not long before she righted herself and turned to face her gleeful student. Jon pulled up sharply when he saw the look on her face. Ulsa looked worried, in pain and almost tearful. She held one hand to the back of her neck. *How badly can one be hurt in the Ether?* Jon wondered.

"Are you hurt?" Jon asked, aloud.

Ulsa winced, but then composed herself. Then with an incredulous look on her face she said, "I lost you!"

Jon pulled what he judged to be an exceedingly smug look. It was a mistake. He knew that Ulsa was very experienced, but he did not know that she was the three times brack champion. She held that title for good reason and here was Jon, inciting her to use her skills to the full.

The next hours were a blur. Jon recalled that Ulsa let out a war whoop and charged at him. He tried hard to defend himself, but Ulsa was simply far and away his superior.

As they tussled, in and out of the Ether, Jon received blow after blow and cut after cut. He was switching so rapidly between the two realms, that he was barely having time to heal and his Ether presence was injured and exhausted.

Every time he thought he had had enough, Ulsa would arrogantly ask him if he wanted to surrender, or if he would rather play with the children. Each time she taunted him, he became fired up and ready for more fighting. And each time this happened, Ulsa would toy with him for a while and then deliver yet another of her dizzying blows to his head, chest, or stomach.

But he was not feeling demoralised. Every trick of Ulsa's—every dodge, every feint, every leap and dive became lodged in his mind. Whilst in the Ether he seemed innately to be able to copy those moves and execute them with ease. Yes, he was always one step behind his talented trainer, but he felt that he was making progress. This sense of learning coupled with the message he had heard whilst on the outer edge of the planet's atmosphere, were the things that kept him from throwing in the towel. Of course Ulsa's taunting helped too.

A strange change had come upon Ulsa by the time the party of five assembled to eat together that night. The usually confidant, vivacious bracarpium master became withdrawn and hesitant. Jon was conscious of this and concerned that perhaps Ulsa was embarrassed by the events of the day—either that she had hurt Jon, or that he had hurt her. He decided to make light of his training therefore.

Bars and Floom made eager listeners as Jon recounted how he had fared ill at the hands of his mentor. He laughed off the blows he had received and painted himself in a ridiculous light—as a slow-witted, clumsy learner. Floom was quick to defend Jonathan, telling him that she knew that bracarpium training could be very demanding. She appealed to Ulsa to be more gentle with her adopted son. Though she made this request smilingly, she made it seriously. And Ulsa seemed yet more uncomfortable.

Bars, one of the few non-Ethereans to have been taken into the Ether, was interested to learn more about this other world. His curiosity had been kindled by his blind experience and he hoped that any of the three could describe the Ether to him. Garmon was quiet as ever and Ulsa did not seemed willing to be coaxed into conversation, so Jon took the lead.

He explained that it was as hard to describe the Ether to a non-Etherean as it was to describe sight to a blind man or sounds to a deaf man. He had only been in full possession of his 'Ether eyes' for a few weeks though and as one with a newly acquired sense, he was probably as able as anyone could be, to paint a picture of the Ether for his father.

"It is like there is another world overlaid onto the physical world. It has its own spectrum of colours, its own sounds and its own smells. Just as you can focus between the table before you and the mountain outside, yet not see both clearly at the same time, so it is with the Ether." This was an approximation of the truth, since Jon could not convey a better analogy given his present grasp of the Deban language. But it was fairly close to the truth and Bars indicated that he understood.

"And so I am the short-sighted man, able only to see what is before his nose and not the wider world around me, eh?" Bars chuckled. "Well that may be truer than you think Chankwar." He sighed and looked down at his dinner. Floom reached across and squeezed Bars' elbow.

Jon looked enquiringly at Floom, but before she could explain on her husband's behalf, Garmon spoke. "If anyone has been blind, Madam Medok, it is the Elders of the Etherean Guard. We who have sight beyond sight were so busy looking to the mountain that we missed the table." He paused, holding his audience until Bars looked up once more. "Minister Medok," Garmon said, "it is inconceivable that you could think you were somehow responsible for failing to foresee your abduction. Those charged with protecting you failed in their duty. This was not your responsibility."

Garmon drifted off again, his mind elsewhere and Floom bustled around the table, clearing away the dining carousel and tools.

A formal meal on Deb is different from that on Earth in a few practical ways. Firstly, their technology has developed along different lines from ours. One would not see a knife, a fork and a spoon on a Deban table. The implements they use more closely resemble a pair of tongs and a pair of scissors.

Food is placed directly into a dining carousel, which is made to fit a dining table. Both are circular. Within the carousel there are heaters for the food and several courses will be laid out simultaneously. Once the diners reach a consensus that a course is finished, the carousel is rotated and they move on to the next course. In this way, the chef can sit with the rest of the diners and does not need to rise to attend to the later courses. If any of the courses are intended to be served cold, the heaters are turned off beneath those compartments.

A typical dining carousel has compartments for six courses per diner. The more ornate carousels simply have additional compartments per course, to enable more complex dishes to be served.

As Floom was collecting the removable compartments in order that they may be cleaned, Bars suggested that the party take an excursion down to the local city of Norvesh. Garmon was reluctant to permit Bars to be seen in public, but Bars assured Elder Weir that he had at his disposal various disguises he frequently used when he wished to travel incognito. "Ethereans are not the only ones able to escape detection, you know," he said.

By this time, Jonathan was feeling that he was unable to take in any more new sights, smells, sounds or cultures and so he declined to accompany the party. He was in fact keen to continue his training and preferred the prospect of an early night and an early start. He indicated as much to Garmon and Ulsa.

Garmon considered for a moment and confessed that he admired Jon's stamina. He said that he thought it may be appropriate to spend some time tomorrow concentrating on the spiritual side of Jon's training. Jon was intrigued by this not knowing what Garmon could mean, but he knew that Garmon's guidance was to be respected and so he assented.

Once it became clear that Jon was determined to stay behind, no matter what the rest of the party did, Ulsa became suddenly interested to see the city of Norvesh herself. She had frequently flown over and around it, but never explored it. She had heard of its strange architecture, influenced heavily in its design by the need to accommodate the bi-annual flektor migration and she wished to see it. Jonathan's interest was piqued by this comment, which he did not understand, but he detected in Ulsa a desire to be where Jon was not.

He was not insensitive so he stuck with his decision to remain behind.

It took quite some persuasion to convince Floom that Jon could survive for one degree of the sun let alone ninety on his own, but eventually she accepted Jon's promise to come and find them immediately if he should need them and relaxed a little. And so, shortly after this for the first time since Jon entered the dungeons of Belee'al, he found himself on his own for an evening.

This was useful to Jon for three reasons; firstly he felt the need to chew over and consolidate in his mind the things that he had seen and learnt over the last weeks, since his accident. Secondly, he desperately wanted some space to practice using his brack, without his mentor watching over him. And thirdly, he found that his thoughts were drifting towards Izzy and he believed that he would need some time alone to grieve.

Thus began for Jon, a long night of learning and growing.

21

Resar Playne was too late.

She had scattered aides and clerks in her wake as she ran from the Seat and made for the Congregation's private station. Her Etherean chauffeur took her with all speed to the home of Yorgish bayle Prout, but as she arrived she could already see armed Ethereans guarding the building.

Hesdar had indeed acted quickly. Rez could not imagine by what means the Congregation had persuaded members of the Guard to rise up against their leadership, but clearly the arguments used had been effective. Here were ten Ethereans, bracarpiums at the ready and presumably more inside the building.

Yorgish was under house arrest.

Minister Playne was allowed entry into the building and she found Yorgish alone in his study, sat at his conference table, staring gloomily into an empty cup. Although she could see no one else in the room, she guessed that there would be Ethereans about, watching.

Yorgish did not look up when Resar coughed politely, standing in the doorway to the room. Instead he spoke into his cup and began as if in mid-conversation. "I think maybe the Congregation has a valid point. I may not agree with the reasoning that requires me to vacate my position, but I must conclude that I am too old for this job." He sighed and then said with more force, "Too old and too senile!"

Resar quietly moved round the room and took a seat opposite Yorgish at the table. Yorgish still looked into his cup, playing with an irregularity on the receptacle's surface. "It was the arrival of the Guardian. Made us all giddy. How could I have allowed us to let our defences down? How foolish we were! Imbeciles and children would not have missed what I overlooked in my doddering excitement."

He then took aim and flung the cup from him. It smashed against the wall behind Rez. Although Rez could not see into the Ether, she suspected that Yorgish had aimed the object at one of his Etherean guards. Her suspicion was confirmed in part when she heard Yorgish muttering to himself, "Turncoat!"

Rez did not wish to impose upon a man already clearly depressed, but she felt that she still carried important news of which Yorgish may not be aware. "Elder bayle Prout, I have this morning read something that disturbed me greatly."

Yorgish raised his eyes to meet hers and said gruffly through his beard, "I don't doubt it Minister. You may be assured that what you have read is true. No doubt I am to be tried for Grand Anarchy. I have no defence. The accusation is well founded and if I am to be subject to the laws of men, I will be found guilty and punished accordingly."

Rez chose her words carefully, "Yorgish, I believe I understand your position better than most. But you must be aware of the implications of this?" She gestured around herself, towards where she imagined the guards to be.

Yorgish's eyes narrowed. "Speak it, Minister."

"If you will not defend yourself, judgment will be swift and certain. Only one outcome is possible." She lowered her voice, "Elder bayle Prout, you, along with the other Elders, will be Enveloped."

Underneath the ample beard, she could see his jaw muscles working. Yorgish's eyes reddened and Rez could tell that he was fighting back the emotion. "After all we have fought for and achieved—can you believe it would come to this?" Yorgish looked above and beyond Rez. "Can you believe it Sivian? You who I trained and mentored in your early years in the Guard? How is it that you are now counted amongst those who seek to imprison me—to lock up my spirit forever?"

Yorgish paused. Resar could not help but look over her shoulder. All she could see was an indentation in the wall, where the cup had smashed. She turned back to Yorgish. He seemed to be having a staring competition with the invisible Guard.

Rez watched Yorgish's expression change from one of anger, to one of questioning, to an expression of understanding and then on to horror. She leant forward and whispered, "What is it Yorgish?"

He looked at her with an expression that made the blood freeze in her arteries and said, "Yershowsh—no! They are in the Guard!" He then leant closer to Rez and whispered urgently and quickly in her ear, "*Must* speak with Graye. Then find Medok. Holiday home. Distrust Delturn!" He then leant back rapidly, as an armed Etherean materialised, brack extended between Rez and Yorgish. It was Sivian.

"No secret conferring!" he snapped. Turning to Resar, he said, "Minister, I regret to advise you that I must end this visit. Please leave now."

Resar was a minister for good reason. With a calm head and with plans already forming in her mind, she stood and saluted Yorgish, elbow bent, fist clenched. "I will see you soon," she said and then left. To Sivian, who moved towards her she commented curtly, "I will have no difficulty locating the exit. But thank you."

As she walked away from Yorgish's house towards her waiting transport, there suddenly came from the building an enraged yelling. She instinctively turned to locate the sound and saw all ten Etherean Guards moving swiftly into the house, through the doors, windows and walls. With a growing feeling of dread she told herself, *keep walking*. Her chauffeur looked at her in concern as she entered the vehicle, but she simply said, firmly, "To Hulladon please and quickly."

She had been wrong and she now cursed herself. When Bars Medok was abducted, Resar had seen an opportunity for Hesdar to free herself from dependency on the former Director. Rez had no quarrel with Medok, but she favoured the path of independence and something about Hesdar's relationship with Bars made her feel uneasy.

But now, she back-tracked mentally. No matter how strongly she had felt about Bars' influence on Hesdar, she had to own that the present state of affairs was far worse. Hesdar thought and reasoned clearly and fairly, for sure, but now Hesdar was being fed one-sided information that could only lead her to one conclusion: That the Elders must be stopped at all costs.

Bars would not have let this happen. What did Yorgish mean, "find Medok?" Did he mean Floom? It seemed unlikely that the Elder would have referred to a female non-Minister simply by her surname. Did Yorgish believe Bars to be alive? And surely he was not simply at his retreat, Norvesh-side? Surely they would have searched there for him already?

If Bars were alive and well, this would call into question a lot of the recent events at the Congregation, for good or ill. Was his disappearance engineered to bring about a shift in power? And if so, by whom? Was Bars part of a conspiracy, or a pawn in someone else's war game?

As the scenery flashed by, so did the thoughts. She did not have time to reach a conclusion, before they arrived at the Lovel residence.

Rez shook her head as she approached the main entrance. It had been a grander home at one time. There was evidence that there had been at least three more rooms attached to the property in years past.

Those resources had been allocated away from the Lovels and Rez knew only too well that the reason for this reallocation had been Graye's gambling addiction.

Still, Madam Lovel had made good use of the space and her spare time. Everywhere about the building Resar saw freshly planted flowers and shrubs, in addition to some well-established plants. A lot of thought had gone into the planning and arranging of the garden and from the amount of work demonstrated here, Rez could tell that Graye loved her garden.

She wound the door rattle. There was no response in the house. Rez walked round the building, looking in. There was no sign of life.

Graye was known for her reclusive ways. Since her recent decline, she avoided public places and travelled little. Graye reputedly was extremely hospitable to guests—perhaps her way of atoning for wrongs—but she did not actively seek out company away from home. It was unusual to find the home abandoned during the day.

Rez made enquiries of the neighbours, but these were inconclusive. Few people were in and those that were had not seen much of Graye that day. One lady believed that Graye had left the house early that morning, with a young friend, but where they had gone she could not say.

She returned to the waiting vehicle and instructed the driver to take her to Plykar's department at the Seat.

Plyk's reaction did nothing to lessen Resar's growing alarm. When Rez explained that she had been unable to locate his wife, he stumbled and fell into a chair, wide eyed, ashen and fearful. Rez suggested that perhaps Graye may have gone to visit somewhere with the young friend?

"No, that can't be so. Even if Graye went out whilst I was working, she would always send a message to me telling me of her movements. She feels more secure if I know where she is going." He put one hand to his forehead and started massaging it vigorously. "She would only go out without telling me, if she didn't want me to know where she was bound." He looked at Rez sharply and demanded, "Where is she?"

"I honestly do not know. Yorgish considered it important that I speak to her."

Plyk stiffened at the Elder's name. "Please do not say she has been conspiring with him; please do not say that."

Rez thought quickly. "She has not, as far as I know. Why otherwise might Yorgish wish to speak with her?"

In a hollow voice, Plykar said, "Because she has been Hearing again. She was clean. She had a message for the Elders and they were very excited by it. Maybe they wished to ask her more questions? To see if she had heard anything else?"

Something triggered in the back of Rez's mind. *In times of peace as in times of trouble, listen to the Hearer.* It was something she had read during her spiritual studies as a young woman. Just a phrase that had stuck in her mind: you should never neglect your spiritual duties. Never be complacent.

This was certainly a time of trouble for Yorgish. He would want to speak to a Hearer. *What of the young friend who was with Graye?* Rez wondered. She asked Plyk if he knew anything about this person.

He shrugged. She was young, very pretty but a bit childish. She had some history with gambling and Graye was trying to help her.

An awful thought struck him, just as it struck Rez. His face turned greyer yet; hers became more determined.

"This is all part of the same conspiracy," she said aloud.

"But where is my wife?" Plykar asked again.

"We cannot know the answer to that now. Master Lovel, listen to me. The work that you are engaged upon—do you believe in it? Do you not see where it is leading?" Rez asked him urgently, on a mission.

"Is it wrong to find useful employment for the Ethereans?" Plyk asked, almost as a child would ask her mother if it were wrong to try and consume all the sand in her play pit. Rez looked at him steadily, not answering. Plykar sighed. "Will you find Graye? If you will promise me that, I will do what I can here."

Rez set her face. "I am not in a position to promise anything Plykar. I am about to embark on a course in direct opposition to the decisions and decrees of the High Congregation. I cannot now guarantee to fulfil any promise that I give; I may not be in a position to do so. But I will try."

Plykar reached out to hold Rez's elbow. "Then so will I," he said.

During the previous three journeys it had not once occurred to Resar to ask herself whether or not she trusted her Etherean chauffeur. But now, as she prepared to journey to Norvesh, to find Bars Medok—if that were possible—she found herself questioning the wisdom of letting any individual know her whereabouts. Of course she could not hope to evade any Ethereans who may now be looking for her, but she could at least make some wise choices before she set off on this journey.

She concocted a convincing story about business that called her to another of Deb's cities. The chauffeur showed no sign of interest, one way or the other, but took her there without question. She then dismissed him. From that point, Rez picked up another transport, to another station and in this manner she arrived at Norvesh after several changes. With each leg of the journey she felt that she became more anonymous.

Finally, she took a short-distance transport to the mountain where she knew she would find the Medok holiday retreat. It was late afternoon and the occupants of that home were enjoying the last of the sun, sat between the front of the home and a stream running down the mountain. Of the five people there assembled, she recognised three:

Floom Medok, the Elder Garmon Weir and in full health and evidently high spirits, none other than Bars Medok.

The party greeted her with surprise, but that surprise was shortly to turn into shock.

"Hesdar jointly preparing a statement indicting the lead Elder? I cannot believe that," Bars said. Jonathan was trying hard to follow the conversation. Resar looked at Jon and then back at Bars, questioningly. "Anything you have to say to me, you may say in the presence of my son." Rez's eyes widened.

Rez's flow cut short, Bars Medok saw fit to fill the space with an explanation of how he and his family came to be at their retreat home with one of the Elders and a high-ranking member of the Guard. Rez could not take in the description of the Belee'an dungeon or the horrors that Bars and his son Chankwar had faced there. Of the possibilities she had been considering, Bars as co-conspirator seemed ever less likely. No matter what her feelings may have been towards Bars, she had always trusted him. His story did fit with her preconceived ideas of his nature.

The mood of the party took a serious turn with Rez's arrival. Ulsa, who had been distant, now took an active interest in the conversation.

Rez continued with her story, "I do not know if this is related, but I must tell you since it appears to be significant. In the brief time that I had with Yorgish he told me that I should seek out Graye Lovel."

"The Hearer?" Ulsa asked, diplomatically making no reference to her well known disgrace.

"The same," interjected Garmon. "It would be the instinctive reaction of any Elder in a time of crisis to make enquiries of a Hearer. Even though regrettably, we have previously neglected this action." He turned to Rez. "But you have not been able to find her, have you?"

Resar frowned slightly wondering how Garmon might have guessed this, but she knew that he had insight far beyond most, where Yershowsh was concerned. "I attended her home, but she was not there. Her husband did not know where she was, but told me of a guest who had lately stayed with them. This guest was a gambler and Graye was trying to help her.

"Graye would usually tell her husband if she were to leave the house, but on this occasion she did not. I can only surmise that she and the guest have sought out a gambling den and are wallowing there together."

"If Graye has returned to her addiction, she will be of no assistance to the Elders," Bars observed. "Are there any other Hearers with whom we may consult?"

"Only Mekly Sur could answer that," Garmon said. "Traditionally Hearers have confined themselves to matters touching their immediate locale. Since the Elders are based nominally at the Seat, protocol would require that we consult with Madam Lovel, the only Hearer in our area. We have no direct contacts with Hearers from other vicinities. But Mek would know where to find them."

"But unfortunately Elder Sur is cited as a co-accused. You all are, Elder Weir. The only reason that you are not also under arrest is that no one knows that you are here. We would not be permitted to consult with your administrator." Rez was feeling stressed and out of control. It was not a feeling with which she was accustomed and she was not enjoying it.

"Then we must proceed as best we can without the benefit of a Hearing," Bars said, instinctively reaching for the reins. Leadership was his natural state.

"But Bars, something concerns me yet about Madam Lovel's absence," Rez said, her hand raised. She did not continue. Her words tailed off as she concentrated as if on a puzzle.

Floom, who had been silent thus far now spoke, "I am sorry to interrupt, but do you think that Graye also may have been abducted? The timing seems so convenient."

Bars looked at his wife intently. She looked away, embarrassed.

She did not consider herself to be any match for the minds of politicians and Elders. He started nodding slowly. Still looking at his wife, he spoke to Rez, "Rez, you were most recently at the capital. You have more current insight into the undercurrents there." Turning now to look at Rez, he asked, "Please tell me that my wife is not as brilliant as I believe her to be."

Rez frowned and then caught Bars' meaning. "I am afraid to say Minister that I believe she is. That explanation would be compelling."

"I agree." Bars concurred, affectionately rubbing his wife's knee. "Elder Weir?"

But Garmon was barely with them. He was looking up to the mountain and his lips were moving, although no sound could be heard. Bars was about to say his name, but Garmon held up his hand to stop him.

Alternately looking at one another, at Garmon and at the mountain, the party sat in silence for some time, whilst Garmon continued in his abstracted meditation. Jon was watching Garmon in particular fascination and was in turn watched by Ulsa, with as much interest.

At length, Garmon's lips stopped moving and he turned to face Jon, with sad eyes. "There is a significance to this that I do not wish to overlook." Without explaining he then turned to the rest of the group. "Graye has indeed been abducted by the forces of Belee'al, I am convinced of it. I believe that she is still alive, but in peril. Similarly every member of the Guard's Eldership is in peril. If we are to be Enveloped, we may also be destroyed. There are others capable of leadership who share the Elders' ideals, but at this time, I feel sure that the High Congregation would take over the task of appointing fresh Elders, bringing an inappropriate political agenda to bear. I fear the worst for the Etherean Guard. It stands in a position of incredible power upon Deb. Without the appropriate checks, without the safeguard of a scrupulous leadership, I cannot begin to imagine what damage may be done to our cause."

"Then we must..." Jon began. All eyes turned to him and he felt suddenly very self-conscious. He stopped speaking and started stammering. "I mean... don't you think... we should..." His cheeks started to glow. Who was he to make suggestions to this illustrious body of men and women. He was a complete outsider, here as on earth.

Rez was about to speak, to solicit Bars' view of the action that they should take when Bars stopped her. "Minister Playne, I have recently discovered that my son Chankwar is a Guardian." He let the words sink in.

"A Guardian? A Guardian of the Insensate?" Rez spoke the phrase with awe. She had learnt the history of the Guardians and felt the same wonder that every scholar feels upon hearing of their exploits through the ages. No one could predict when a Guardian would appear, but it always augured good and bad news. One could be sure that when a Guardian was discovered amongst the Ethereans, the planet would shortly face a period of crisis. And that Guardian would rise to fight against the crisis.

Rez had never taken kindly to the designation, 'Insensate'. In modern times, the expression was avoided. Non-Ethereans did not need to be reminded that they lacked the extra senses of the Ethereans. Even amongst themselves, Ethereans chose not to use the word to describe their non-Etherean brethren. But in this one expression, 'The Guardian of the Insensate,' the word endured. And this could be forgiven and understood, since the Guardians were truly outstanding amongst humans.

Rez fell silent and Bars indicated that Jon should continue speaking. Feeling no more confident, Jon complied. As he spoke, he found that Deban words became unlocked from his subconscious. He spoke with a clarity and ultimately an authority that he had never before experienced.

"Garmon speaks of Graye's significance. I believe that your enemy—our enemy sees some of this significance. We may be led by that. We know that the Belee'ans do not always immediately dispose of their enemies, even when it is in their power to do so," Bars nodded, "and there is hope that Graye is still alive. We must find her." Jon arose as if compelled to bring more force to bear on his words.

"The first place that we will look is that foul dungeon where I have been. They will expect a rescue attempt—indeed this may be their sole reason for capturing the Hearer. Nevertheless, we will attempt this. Ulsa and I together can do far more damage to the Belee'ans than they imagine." Ulsa blushed imperceptibly and sat slightly more upright in her seat.

"Once we have released Madam Lovel, we may then find the will of Yershowsh," Jonathan was surprised to hear himself say these words, but they seemed to flow naturally under the circumstances, "and for our next steps, we may be guided by that."

Having made this speech, Jon sat down sheepishly. Garmon turned away and smiled and then setting his face straight again, he asked Ulsa, "What is your opinion of the readiness of your pupil?"

This was not a question that Ulsa seemed ready to answer. She looked in every possible direction except at Jonathan or Garmon. Her dusky skin reddened and she filled the space with 'ums' and 'ahs'. Noting her discomfort, Floom, motherly instincts activated, arose and walked over to Ulsa. She took one of Ulsa's hands and looked down at the bracarpium master lovingly as if she were her own daughter. Ulsa stopped searching for words and looked up at Floom. No words passed between them. Ulsa blushed even more fiercely, but then this subsided and she composed herself and spoke to the party, still holding Floom's hand.

"As most of you know, I am the three times and current bracarpium champion of Deb. Before this moon sequence I truly believed myself to be the most able warrior on the planet, excepting only the Elders. There is much security in that." She sighed and looked at Jon, her cheeks reddening again.

"After only three days of training, Jonathan Chankwar threatens to surpass me. Every time I increase the pace, he is but two steps behind. Every trick I employ, he learns with ease. *Even during battle* he yet improves. His capacity for Ether combat is, in my opinion unparalleled amongst Ethereans. We have not yet studied spreading, but if he masters that with the ease with which he mastered threading, he will quickly become all but godlike in his skill within the Ether." Jon was looking at Ulsa in amazement and she returned his gaze, shyly.

Garmon chuckled. "And if any further confirmation were required that Chankwar is the Guardian..." He did not complete his sentence, but his old eyes were twinkling.

An immensely proud look in his eyes, Bars clapped his hands together and said with finality, "Then let us make our plans and may Yershowsh be with us!"

22

Though trembling, Graye had remained calm even whilst she was bound and gagged and forced to sit upon the crut—which was uncomfortable. Her peaceful composure appeared to suit the disposition of her jailer Jerud, who watched her from one side of the room, swords lowered. Bravish Ha'ware had left the two women alone, after whispering some instructions to Jerud. Although Graye had feared that those instructions concerned the manner of her torture, Jerud had made no move in her direction and Graye was beginning to think that she was for the time being merely a prisoner—not also a plaything.

She felt inclined to attempt to strike up a conversation with Jerud and would already have attempted this had it not been for the rag in her mouth. She could see that Jerud was looking at her often with an expression of intense fascination. Whilst Graye could not understand the reason for that, she was sure that she could exploit this, were she able to talk. Graye underestimated perhaps the extent of Jerud's devotion to Belee'al.

At length, Jerud seemed to relax a little. Other than shifting uncomfortably on the studded crut, Graye had made no attempt to struggle or free herself. Jerud caught Graye's eye and nodded her head upwards, to indicate that she required Graye's attention. "Would you prefer to stand? Or lean against a wall perhaps?" she said.

Graye nodded, apprehensively. Jerud walked towards her and Graye felt her entire body stiffen, involuntarily. Jerud moved to the rear of the crut, to release the bindings, but before she did this, she leant forward and spoke quietly into Graye's ear. "It would be greatly to my preference if you behaved. Make any attempt to resist me or flee and I will be obliged to relieve you of three of your fingers. Do you understand and agree?"

Graye took a sobbing breath and nodded, vigorously. "Thank you," Jerud said. Graye felt the bindings being cut. Then Jerud walked back to where she had been standing before, facing Graye. "You may stand, or sit, in that corner." Jerud pointed with her sword to the furthest corner of the room. Slowly Graye arose and walked to the corner as instructed. She lowered herself to the ground and rested there, her head on her knees, feeling marginally less nervous. This seemed to Graye an ideal opportunity to meditate.

And so it was that when Klushere materialised within the room, Graye was looking at the floor and did not at first note his appearance. Her head jerked up when she heard the sound of her son's voice saying, "Mother, I wish you would not persist in defying Belee'al." As those words and the awful fact of Klushere's presence in these circumstances sunk in, Graye began to cry.

Klushere looked sharply at Jerud. "Is she hurt?" he snapped.

"No my Lord," Jerud replied, with lowered eyes.

"Good. Come mother. We are hopeful that this unpleasantness will be over soon." Graye felt herself lifted up, one arm held by Klushere and the other held by Jerud. And then quite suddenly the whole world vanished.

It was an alarming sensation. Or lack of sensation. Her mind still functioned, but there was a total absence of sensory data for it to process. A thousand different emotions filled her mind at once, but without the associated production of hormones creating also a physical reaction within her body, she felt strangely detached from the feelings of loneliness, emptiness, hate, pity, doubt, despair, grief, anxiety and terror that she now experienced. She was herself and yet not herself.

She could not see—but it was not as if her eyes were closed. It was as if suddenly she lacked the apparatus to see or even to process visual information. Images filled her mind, but they were random and unconnected with anything that she might ordinarily see.

Similarly smell, taste, touch and hearing all eluded her. She was a non-person and yet she was still aware of her own existence. Might this be what it was to be blind, deaf and mute? She tried to produce a sound, but she had no means to do this. So this must be why the Ethereans many, many centuries ago began to refer to non-Ethereans as 'the Insensate'. For here, in the Ether, where she presumed she must be, she was just that. Completely without senses.

What was that she was feeling? It was panic. It flitted through her mind like a frolian redwing insect, hovering around her id and then flapping away erratically. Would she ever be a person again? She did not know. She had no way of telling. She hoped that this experience would be short lived, but with a loss of sensation came a loss of awareness of time. There was no time, no universe, no physical world. She was simply a mind. A spiritual entity, alone in her non-world.

Could she reach out and touch other beings, she wondered? Were there any other beings? Had there ever been any other existence than this? And on her mind sped, unfettered by the chains of physical constraints.

In reality she spent very little time in the Ether. Before long, she regained her senses, but like a drunk man suddenly sobered, she could not take in her surroundings. In this mentally weakened state she meekly allowed herself to be guided through tunnels and passageways and down a circular staircase. She was then manacled and chained, in the dingiest of rooms, with only a dimly flickering candle for company.

As the door to the dungeon closed behind her son and his companion, she reached out with her spirit to Yershowsh. *Is this all part of Your plan?* she asked.

This is not my *plan, daughter. My plan is yet to be revealed. But I am with you. When you are released, you will be sought out for a Hearing. Tell them that the ghost is to stand before the Congregation.*

With a profound sense of bafflement, but nevertheless reassured, Graye waited.

It was not often that Klushere had sufficient courage to argue with Al'aran Kytone. Circumstances had to be particularly strained for him even to consider it. Any other mortal who dared to argue with the Grand Preceptor would be beaten senseless in a trice. But Klushere was privileged and this privilege meant that on occasion, Al'aran would tolerate an argument from his foremost disciple, the leader and Preceptor of the Central Elect.

"Why must we keep her here? Of what benefit is it? This will surely be the last place that my enemy would search—and why would he be searching for her?" Klushere was careful not to invade Al'aran's personal space. He gesticulated and danced on the edge of it. "This was not Belee'al's command."

Al'aran pounded his stick on the floor. "Be still! I judge this to be correct. Dare you question my authority?"

"So Belee'al did not give this order? I will not be responsible for his wrath when it burns against you, Preceptor." Klushere's face was contorted, an outward sign of his inner turmoil.

Pointing his stick towards the stairway to the dungeon, Al'aran said in a menacing voice, "I believe that I will kill her now!" But he made no move towards the dungeon.

Nevertheless Klushere became enraged by this. "No! I will not allow it! She can be contained and she is no threat to our cause."

"Your attachment to this blasphemer will destroy our cause with no assistance being required from her." Al'aran pulled back his staff as if to strike his disciple. But rather than inflicting a blow, he instead chose to inflict his pungent breath on Klushere, approaching him closely and blasting his words up at the other man.

"Attachment is not forbidden by the precepts, so long as it does not rule. I am the master of my emotions and I will not have you or anyone else question my commitment." Klushere reached his hand up to touch the hilt of his sword. "If you wish to add action to your insult, you will find me ready."

Al'aran laughed at this and lowered his staff. In a surprisingly placatory tone he soothed his disciple, "Contain your anger. You will have need of it yet. Are the Chosen ready?"

Seething, Klushere managed to respond, "Yes."

"Many years have I instructed you. On any serious matter have you ever known me to be mistaken?"

After a pause, Klushere conceded, "I have not."

"Our enemy bayle Prout is resourceful. He has already sent word to the boy. The boy is young, inexperienced and in his foolishness he will come to rescue your mother." With a conspiratorial look he added, "bayle Prout believes that she is essential to their cause. The young one will be caught up in their plans for rescue and will accompany them on their mission. Their forces are weakened; they will require all of their allies to assist. You know I am right."

"This plan of yours. I do not like it." Klushere stamped to the stairs, to look in on his mother.

Al'aran smiled to himself. In the tongue of Belee'al, he said quietly, "Do not let his single track mind interfere with his duty, my Ultimate Preceptor."

In the corridors and chambers of the underground network, the Chosen waited. There had never been a better opportunity to meet

Ethereans on the Chosen's own territory. Here, where the skills of their enemies would be hampered by the pervasive shroud of Enveloping, they would at last have the upper hand. No matter how many or how few attempted to rescue the Lovel woman, the Chosen would be ready and the Chosen would be victorious.

Bewildered and alarmed at the prospect that faced him, Jonathan barely noticed that all of the party had drifted into the house. All except Garmon. Garmon remained, patiently watching Jon, waiting for an opportunity to speak. It had been agreed that he would spend some time passing on final instruction to Jonathan, before they executed their plan.

The sun's last rays had not long disappeared over the horizon and two of the planet's moons were visible at opposite ends of the sky. Jonathan looked at first one and then the other and then spoke. "We only have one moon on earth." He gazed across the brook. "There are so many things here that are different, Garmon. How can I hope to be of assistance? How can I make the slightest difference in the outcome of the conflict now facing your planet?"

Garmon picked up his chair and brought it close to Jonathan, facing him, but to one side. He reached out and touched Jon's chair, drawing both of them and both chairs into the Ether. "Tell me Chankwar. Does not your life come into focus now? Do not many mysteries now have an explanation?"

Jon listened for a moment to the strange sounds about him and looked at Garmon's Ether presence, noting the characteristic corona, which if they moved, would fade into a footprint. "Yes, I have found more explanations than I ever could have expected to encounter in one lifetime, I confess. But with those explanations have come yet more questions."

"No man knows all the answers, Chankwar. It is not given to us to be all-knowing. Too much knowledge can be a dangerous thing."

Garmon chuckled.

"Yes and too little can be dangerous also." Jon sniffed. "That is an expression on my planet."

"But Yershowsh reveals His mysteries at His own pace. No more than you can handle. And no less than you need." Garmon gestured around him. "All this is opened up to you now, for a purpose. You are a Guardian and that should give you a profound sense of destiny."

"Should it?" Jonathan asked. "I do not even know what that means. What is a Guardian and what marks me out as one?" He laughed and said, "And how can I pass on this responsibility?"

Garmon leaned forward and looked into Jon's eyes. "The Guardian is ordained by Yershowsh to save the people from themselves. A Guardian is given great power and great responsibility. That is not something that can be passed on. And no man can aspire to be a Guardian." A meaningful smile passed over Garmon's lips.

"Why is that?" Jon asked.

"Because the very thing that makes you well qualified for the task is the fact that you do not desire it. You do not desire the responsibility and more importantly you do not thirst for the power." Garmon adjusted his sash, unconsciously referring to his own position of power. "If a Guardian were to turn against Yershowsh, that would be a grave matter indeed."

"But I don't even know Yershowsh!" Jonathan cried in despair.

Garmon merely smiled at this. He paused for a moment and then continued, "Chankwar, remember to listen to His voice. And before you embark on this task, please *force* yourself to believe that you are almost unbeatable. No Etherean can challenge you and hope to be victorious."

"What do you mean? Ulsa beat me consistently." Jon frowned.

"You have progressed so much. Believe me, if it were a matter of great import, you would now have no difficulty in overcoming the brack master." Garmon's eyes twinkled and he looked away.

"Is that why Ulsa feels so embarrassed in my presence?" Jon asked.

Not turning to look at his pupil, Garmon answered in a faraway voice, "For the last three years, Ulsa has been competing in the bracarpium championships. For as long as she has been a competitor, she has also been a winner. No one has ever defeated her." Garmon paused, wondering whether it would be in Jon's interests to reveal at this point the remainder of the reason for Ulsa's behaviour. Could any man, even a Guardian, allow the news to leave him unaffected?

Jon spared him the decision, nodding with understanding. "And Ulsa is single and perhaps no man has yet been her equal—in her eyes."

"I would counsel you not to let that knowledge interfere with your duty," Garmon said sternly.

"There is no danger of that," Jonathan said sadly. "I am far from being ready to contemplate enjoying the company of another woman."

Neither man spoke for a while. Jon allowed Garmon's words to pass through his mind, taking in the significance of every last syllable. Before this week, he would not have believed any of it. But events had combined to give him a belief in himself that he had not previously known. It was not arrogance, or self-obsession; he had become self-aware and he knew that what Garmon said was true. As to Ulsa, well he had enjoyed her company, no matter what he said. But he was not about to begin a relationship, so soon after the loss of his wife.

"It *is* flattering though," he said to Garmon. Both men smiled.

23

The plan was insane and Bars told Jonathan exactly what he thought of it. "You cannot hope to succeed if only two of you try to take on superior numbers. I will lose my son again and I am not prepared to allow that to happen!" He pounded the table, where the six were breaking their fast and then stood, looking down at Jon, allowing a small amount of paternal anger to burn against him.

Jonathan was unperturbed. "Remember that we cannot be sure which of the Ethereans are for us and which have been compromised. Minister Playne said that Yorgish thought the Guard had been infiltrated. We do not have the time to weed out our enemies in search of true allies. We must act quickly; therefore we must take the few allies we can be sure of. I do not mean to fight all of the Belee'ans simultaneously, nor attempt to conquer by dint of superior numbers."

A strange shift in the balance of power within the house had taken place overnight. Much as Bars hated to admit it, protective as he felt towards his son, Jon was very much taking control of the situation. And this was not an area in which his considerable political skills could assist.

Jon continued, outlining the reasoning behind his chosen strategy. "Garmon cannot be involved in the fighting. We have to assume that the remaining Elders have been Enveloped; we cannot risk that happening also to him. Our only option is for Ulsa and I to approach the dungeons alone, praying that stealth will give us the upper hand."

Floom did not trust herself to speak. It sounded to her that the plan relied very much on hope and very little on sense.

Garmon broke from his accustomed morning reverie to interject, "Yershowsh is in this plan." Before anyone could argue or question him further, he quietly left the table and walked away, fading as he went. He wished to prepare himself for the part that he had to play in Jon's plan.

Jon was not a master strategist. His plan was simple and straightforward. He and Ulsa would rescue Graye Lovel, whilst Garmon attempted covertly to identify the locations of the incarcerated Elders. He and Jon would then rendezvous; they would ask Graye to Hear and they would act on Yershowsh's direction.

After breakfast, Floom was very loving towards Jonathan whilst Bars was tensely formal. They were reluctant indeed to release him to this suicidal course of action. But release him they did.

Garmon took Rez to the Norvesh station, so that she could obtain transport back to Rebke. She would return to the Seat, her "business" concluded. Garmon then set off on his mission. Jonathan and Ulsa made for the temple of Belee'al, barely a word passing between them. Before they commenced their journey, Jonathan simply said this: "You have been an excellent teacher. I owe much to you. It will be an honour to enter battle with you." Ulsa had not responded to this, except by way of a slight nod.

There being nothing further to discuss and no reason to delay, they threaded their way to the temple. In a short space of time, they arrived at the clearing, where Jon had first emerged when he escaped days ago.

"How are we to obtain ingress?" Ulsa asked. They had not

discussed this obvious part of the plan.

"The same way I left. Through the ground. We will head straight to the dungeon. I have no doubt that is where Graye is being held." Jon pointed directly downwards.

"But you said that it was Enveloped?"

"I believe I can break that."

"Impossible," Ulsa remarked, shaking her head.

"And yet I escaped," Jon replied simply. Then, taking her hand to draw her through the barriers of Enveloping, he entered the Ether and began his descent.

Jon tried to remember the direction he had taken on his way out of the dungeons, but this was an impossible task. When he had left, all he had to think about was moving upwards towards the surface. It had not been necessary to chose a precise direction. Now on the reverse journey, it was unsurprising that he failed to retrace his steps precisely.

And so, rather than arriving at the intersection of corridors, he and Ulsa overshot and emerged, tumbling out of the Ether by force of intense Enveloping, directly into Al'aran's personal chamber. Jonathan and Ulsa looked about themselves, disorientated. Equally disorientated were the other occupants of the room. Somehow the watchful Chosen had been completely bypassed and now standing before Klushere, Jerud, Al'aran and the treacherous, once more favoured Delturn, were two enemies of Belee'al.

For a moment, no one moved. And then with a shriek, Kytone charged.

When contrasted with his rapid learning and movements in the Ether, Jon felt sluggish out of the Ether. Released from the burden of transporting Ulsa however, Jon found that he was able to lift the shroud of Enveloping round his person, just sufficiently to compensate for his sluggishness. Of those in the room, Jon alone was untrained in non-Ether combat. But also of those in the room, Jon alone was able to break the spell of Enveloping. But for this fact, he would surely have been vanquished easily.

Ulsa was something else. Jon could not help admire her, even in the intensity of the battle. When Al'aran charged, Ulsa was far from being caught unawares. In a flash her brack was activated and in her hands in pole form. Though Al'aran moved his staff with blinding inhuman speed, Ulsa parried his strikes with ease.

It did not take long for the other Belee'ans to enter the fray. Delturn noticeably hung back, but Jerud and Klushere came to the aid of Al'aran quickly.

Uttering a brief prayer to a god he did not know, Jonathan added his brack to the mêlée. As soon as he made his intention to fight known, Klushere and Jerud peeled away from Delturn and Al'aran to concentrate on Jonathan. Before Jon had time to think he had four blades to content with—the two of Klushere's twin-bladed sword and Jerud's dual rapiers. Becoming only partly intangible and remaining visible, Jon was able to move at sufficient speed to be able to parry the attacks. But it was all he could do to defend himself—attack was impossible.

Ulsa fared rather better than Jonathan. Notwithstanding his sprightliness, Al'aran was an old, decrepit man and Ulsa was a fraction of his age and in the peak of her physical abilities. On the whole of the planet no Deban was her equal in combat with a brack.

Delturn was of little assistance to Al'aran in close combat. He was quickly overcome and knocked to the ground senseless. The final sickening blow that marked his exit from this mortal stage came not from Ulsa's brack, however. Al'aran decided that he would experience less interference in his fight, if Delturn were not flailing his sword wildly. In a moment when Ulsa was concentrating more on Delturn than on Al'aran, Al'aran struck Delturn on the back of the head, fatally splitting his skull. Delturn crumpled in a heap, despised and rejected at the last by both sides.

The brack champion could not help smiling grimly. Strategically she appreciated the reason for Al'aran to turn on his own. Delturn was seriously cramping his style. With the younger man no longer hampering him at his right, Al'aran moved up a gear, moving his staff in ever increasing sweeps, until at last, he connected with Ulsa's flesh.

It would not have been hard enough to cause any pain, had it not been for the fact that at the last instant, with a flick of his wrist, the end of the staff slid away, revealing a razor sharp cutting edge. Ulsa felt the wound and chided herself for being complacent about her opponent's weapon. But it was not a deep gash and it did not affect her momentum in the slightest.

In the meantime Jon was struggling. Klushere and Jerud had succeeded in pushing him back against a wall. Jon was unable to snatch enough Ether to launch himself through them and had to content himself with continuing to parry their increasingly ferocious joint assault.

Jonathan feared that he would shortly be bettered, but a gasp from Al'aran gave him hope. Ulsa had connected with Al'aran's chest and he had for a moment toppled backwards. Ulsa was quick to pursue, but a signal from Klushere caused Jerud to leave his side and come to the aid of the Grand Preceptor. In alarm, Jon wished to run to the side of Ulsa to protect her, but Klushere would not allow it. Klushere had no use of the Ether, but clearly he was an expert swordsman. His tempo increased in the absence of Jerud and Jon found that he was struggling just as hard to keep the blades away. He was panting with the exertion and sweat was pouring down his brow, stinging at his eyes.

The battle continued, neither side gaining much ground for a while, but then the Belee'ans found a chink in the Ethereans' armour. In a double-act that must previously have been rehearsed, Al'aran made a low attack at Ulsa, whilst Jerud attacked high. Ulsa parried both attacks, but whilst her brack was extended in this position, Jerud spun round and reverse kicked her in the side, knocking her flying. She dropped her brack and weaponless with two Belee'ans approaching, Ulsa saw no possible way out.

As if on cue, Klushere backed away from Jon, whilst Jerud shouted, "We have her! Drop your weapon or she dies here and now." To add force to her words, Jerud leapt to Ulsa's side and held one of her rapiers to Ulsa's throat.

Jon froze. Klushere lowered his sword and smiled at Jon. "Tell me this, Sewer-discharge: Are you prepared to die that your friend might live?"

A hundred images rushed into Jon's mind of former encounters with Klushere—the attack on his wife, the escape from the dungeon, the arrival of Martin—if only he were here now! And then his mind settled on his wife's rings. Jon felt the anger rise.

Not lowering his brack, Jon asked quietly, "Why did you take my wife's rings?" He was seething at this relentless psychotic man.

Klushere was taken by surprise at the question. He seemed puzzled for a moment and then laughed, as if remembering a hilarious joke. He reached into an inner pocket with his left hand and then withdrew it. He opened his hand to show to Jonathan Isobel's wedding and engagement rings. "You mean these trinkets?" he asked, mocking Jonathan.

He sneered at Jonathan and Jon felt his entire body fill with hate and loathing. *Peace*, a now familiar voice said in Jon's head. Jon tried valiantly to calm himself.

Klushere continued taunting Jon. "That woman—your whore was she? She *really* did not want me to take these. She revealed to me their significance early on. Like a fool, she kept toying with them. Are they a memento of your union?" Jon said nothing and tried not to boil inwardly. Klushere took that as an affirmative sign. "I thought as much," he sneered. "Well it is of no consequence. She has no further need of them."

His anger now contained, Jon experienced a new sensation. Something was building up inside him like pressure in a combustion chamber. The feeling increased, growing stronger the more Klushere leered and jeered, until Jon felt that he could contain it no longer.

And then, at the point when he felt that his innards would explode, a marvellous thing happened. Jon was looking beyond Klushere, at the triumphant Al'aran and Jerud and at the mixture of defiant pride with a trace of fear on the face of Ulsa. Astoundingly, whilst he watched, he saw his own hands shoot forwards like pistons towards Al'aran and Jerud, each hand holding a half-section of his brack. Klushere was looking at Jon in amazement and disbelief, but he had no opportunity to act for in a split second, the brack sections connected with the heads of Al'aran and Jerud, driving onwards through their brains, killing them instantly. Klushere dropped the rings in alarm.

In a mixture of awe and shock, Jon's watched as his hands retracted towards his body and he became whole again. He flexed his arms and then looked at the stunned Klushere and said slowly and precisely, "Now, tell me this: Why do you wish to kill me?"

Klushere screamed and hurled his sword at Jonathan. Jon was delayed deflecting the weapon and Klushere ran out of the room into the corridors beyond and was gone. Whilst he was looking after Klushere, Ulsa emitted a single sob and then started to laugh. In her laugh was a mixture of euphoria, tears, delight and wonder. "You learnt to spread—you learnt to spread without even being trained!" she cried.

"Ulsa!" Jon said to her sternly. She paused for a moment, gasping for breath. "We must barricade this door." Together they worked at speed to ensure that no Belee'an could now, or ever, return to this room by means of the door.

That job done, Jon scooped up the beloved rings, kissed them, pocketed them and said, "Now we must free Madam Lovel." He took the key for the chains from the same hook they had been hanging on when he was yet a captive. He stepped over the inert body of Jerud and walked to the trapdoor. As he lifted it, he felt a shudder of unpleasant remembrance. The peaceful voice came again, *All of your experiences led you to this. Do not be fearful.*

Jon felt calmed and strengthened emotionally by these few words. He could almost see events clicking into place for him within a plan and a purpose. He lifted the trapdoor and gesturing for Ulsa to wait, walked down the spiral staircase to the waiting prisoner.

In the gloom he could make out the form of a woman, huddled into a corner. Her body language suggested that she was wary. It was no wonder. She would have heard the sounds of a pitched battle above her.

Jon called out to reassure her as he approached, saying, "Do not be afraid; your captors have been defeated."

A quavering voice called out, "Who are you?"

Jon did not think he could easily explain that. "We're here to rescue you," he said.

Graye responded with a sob. "My son—is he alive?"

"Your son?" Jon asked, crouching down at her feet to remove the manacles about her ankles.

Graye looked down at Jon as he looked up at her and then screamed. It was an incredible noise, just short in magnitude of the sound of a supersonic jet engine at close proximity. Jon winced, but continued unlocking the chains. He well knew the effect being in the dungeon could have.

As soon as Graye had a free hand, she tightly grasped hold of Jonathan's arm and began weeping noisily. She was also trying to say something but the more hysterically she cried the less coherent she became. When her second arm was released she entwined that around Jon's neck and buried her face in his shoulder, still crying loudly.

Feeling as though he were separated from his body, looking upon this from afar, he watched himself half-carry the lady back up the spiral staircase to where Ulsa was waiting. She was looking warily at the entrance to the room. From the other side of the door, there was a sound of loud pounding. But the barricade was holding.

"Are you sure you can break through the Enveloping again?" she asked, with a grim expression. She had retrieved her brack and was holding it ready for action. She frowned as she became aware of how much Graye was sobbing.

With a confidence he did not feel, Jon replied, "Certainly. We will combine our efforts." Ulsa looked at him uncertainly, not knowing how she could assist. "Trust me," Jon cooed. "Brace yourself Madam Lovel—we are about to escape through the Ether." Graye gulped in mid sob. She had been through this before.

Ulsa held Jon's free hand and made what to her seemed a futile effort to enter the Ether. But it appeared to work. In an instant, they were travelling together through the ground. Once above the surface, they released hands and both threaded towards their agreed rendezvous in order to avoid leaving Ether footprints, Jon carrying the Hearer with him. The rendezvous point was an underground room at the Seat. Garmon had provided directions to the rarely used room, judging that this was perhaps the least likely place that anyone would look for him. It also was conveniently close to the rooms of judgment and punishment where the Etherean Elders would most likely be tried. Garmon hoped that the trial had not already taken place. Events had been moving on at an alarming pace since he left for the Medok holiday residence. In any case, from the little he had been able to discover, the Elders were being held at the Seat.

When Jon, Ulsa and Graye arrived, they found Garmon in meditation, instilled in the Ether. When they materialised, Graye continued to hold on tightly to Jon. Jon was beginning to feel distinctly uncomfortable with this treatment, but it became worse when Graye stopped crying and instead began kissing him on his cheek.

Jonathan looked at Ulsa with an expression of bafflement, only to note that she was staring angrily at Graye. Feeling helpless again, he next looked to Garmon for assistance. Garmon opened his eyes, materialised and walked over to Jon. He gently prised Graye away from the Guardian, allowing Jon to sit down unencumbered for a minute.

His suspicions now confirmed by Graye's behaviour, he rendered the explanation that Jon could not possibly have anticipated. Holding Jon's gaze, he gestured to Graye's tear streaked face. Jon saw Graye's face properly for the first time and goggled in wonder, feeling as though he were looking in a mirror as Garmon said, "Behold your birth mother."

24

There was no time for explanations. Much as Jon wished to investigate this new revelation, it would have to wait. They needed to execute the next stage of their plan. Garmon spoke to Graye in soothing tones, explaining the predicament of the Elders, much to Graye's consternation. They needed her to Hear from Yershowsh, since they had no idea how they should next proceed. There were no precedents for action in a case such as this.

These words deflected Graye from her hysteria. Avoiding looking at Jon for the moment, she replied to Garmon's request. "Whilst I was in chains, Yershowsh spoke to me. He told me that He would be with me. And then He told me that when I was released I would be sought out for a Hearing immediately. The message I was to give was, 'Let the ghost stand before the High Congregation.'" She looked at Garmon apologetically. She had never understood why Yershowsh chose at times to speak in riddles. She hoped that the meaning to the riddle would be clear to her rescuers.

Jon wondered whether this were yet another Deban puzzle that he could not hope to solve. He looked to Garmon, praying that the answer would be clear to the contemplative Elder, but on Garmon's face he saw even more puzzlement than he himself experienced. Ulsa was not even attempting to consider the problem, thinking herself to be out of her depth in such matters.

"Could it be that someone else might know the meaning of this?" Jon asked Garmon and Graye, hopefully.

Graye responded with a firm, "No." Then she added, "The message was for those who first sought a Hearing. One of you," she gestured at all three, "must have the answer."

In modest embarrassment Ulsa stuttered, "Do not include me. I will be of no assistance. I do not believe in ghosts!" Then she quietly gasped and raised her hand to her mouth. Graye, Garmon and Jonathan looked at her questioningly.

After a pause, Ulsa said, "This must surely be a coincidence, but I said the same thing upon seeing Bars Medok: that it was like seeing a ghost, but that I do not believe in ghosts."

"That would make sense," Jon murmured, unconsciously switching to English. No one noticed, since they were all lost in their own thoughts.

At length Garmon raised his voice in agreement. "I believe Madam Grabe is correct. I have no other answer. My own wisdom, for what it is worth, says that we should not introduce Bars Medok into the High Congregation at this time." He laughed. "But I am old enough now to know that my wisdom is less reliable than Yershowsh's." Addressing Jonathan, he continued, "You are least likely to be recognised or apprehended by the Etherean Guard. Do you believe that you can bring Bars Medok here?"

An indescribable excitement began to build within Jon. He felt at that moment he could single-handedly transport the Medoks, building and all and deposit them in the courtyard within the Seat, no matter what resistance he might face. The feeling of freedom—and yes, also power—was almost intoxicating. "Yes," he replied, smiling at Garmon, including Graye and Ulsa in that smile. And then in a flash, he disappeared.

Clearly the Medoks did not require much persuasion or explanation, because after a short space of time, Jonathan reappeared, with an adoptive parent on either arm. Jonathan longed to discuss with Garmon and the Medoks the question of his true heritage, but more pressing was the need for Bars to show himself to the High Congregation, in accordance with the command of Yershowsh.

It was one of the few times of day when the majority of the Congregation could be found in one place: one of the regular debating sessions. Garmon saw no advantage in entering the principal debating chamber quietly or cautiously, so the entire group, three Ethereans, three non-Ethereans, materialised simultaneously before the thrones of the Chair and the Director.

Several things happened at once.

Firstly, the majority of the minsters began talking at the same time, with great animation. Expressions ranged from confusion, to hate, to joy, to outrage, but one feeling was held in common: intense surprise.

Secondly, Ti'par ru Masal turned white and made no attempt whatsoever to bring order to the Congregation.

Thirdly, Hesdar called for Guards to arrest Garmon. Her order could not be heard above the hubbub, but nevertheless some Guards and some of the non-Etherean security corps came forward to take Elder Weir into custody.

Fourthly, upon seeing this, Ulsa and Jonathan drew their bracarpiums ready to protect the Elder.

Rightly sensing that chaos would ensue if this situation remained unchecked, Bars Medok did for him what was natural and instinctive and ascended the platform, standing before Hesdar, Ti'par and their retinue. He stretched out his hands, to indicate that the Congregation should come to order.

Such was the respect that most felt for Bars, silence fell upon the chamber and Guards and security held their places. Raising his sonorous, authoritative voice, Bars addressed the assembly.

"Esteemed ministers, ladies and gentlemen, honoured Elders," Bars began in the customary greeting, "it is a privilege once more to stand before you. May Yershowsh guide my mouth and your thoughts."

Ti'par made an effort to stand and looked as though he were about to attempt to physically restrain Bars, but Hesdar held his arm and told him to be still. Bars continued, unperturbed. This was his arena.

"I cannot tell you how it gladdens my heart to be able once more to address you. And yet at the same time, the present circumstances cause me great distress." He gestured to the right of the platform, where Yorgish, Ruith, Gylan, Jish and Mekly were being held, surrounded by ten visible Etherean Guards and twenty invisible Guards. "Clearly, much has happened in my absence." He said this with disapproval. A few ministers slapped the desks before them with their issue portfolios, to indicate agreement.

"Before I turn my attention to those matters though, I would be grateful if my esteemed friends would indulge for a moment a proud father's whim." More murmurings. Most of the Congregation well knew that there was no child in the Medok household.

Bars stepped down from the platform towards Jonathan. Hundreds of eyes followed him, spellbound. He took Jonathan's hand and then drew his suddenly bashful son and his even more embarrassed wife onto the platform alongside him.

One arm around Jon's shoulders and one hand holding onto Floom, Bars continued, "Twenty-five years ago, my wife and I were asked to take into our care a newborn baby. The circumstances surrounding that need not concern us," he glanced at Graye, who returned his gaze steadily, with a hint of gratitude, "suffice it to say that we took the child and raised him as our own.

"Five years after that, the Cull began. No one here was unaffected by that. Like everyone, Floom and I were deeply concerned for the safety of our son, whom we named Chankwar. The more so because of the peculiar nature of our charge. We consulted with the Elders and asked if they may be able to assist in the protection of our son." Bars looked towards Yorgish, whose right hand was firmly entwined in his beard. He was nodding, appreciatively.

"I make no apology for the fact that I thought our son merited special protection. His heritage was unusual and his prospects were considerable. We believed it to be in the best interests of the citizens of Deb that he be protected. I now know this to be true." At this, several minsters and members of the public became outraged and might have leapt up to attack Bars, had he not continued in a placatory tone.

"The horrors of the Cull were many. Floom and I shared those horrors, since shortly after our meetings with the Elders, Chankwar disappeared without trace." Bars allowed a deep sadness to colour the tone of his voice. "The following years were dark beyond description for the people of Deb. Even now, we have not fully recovered.

"I know that the Elders did all they could to bring the murderers to justice. I know that many years were spent in what transpired to be a fruitless search. The person or persons who had murdered thousands of innocent children of the age of five, were never brought to justice."

A moment of understanding came to Jonathan. He interrupted his father and whispered in his ear, "I know who that villain was. I shall bring him to justice." Before Bars could utter a word of protest, Jonathan was gone. Garmon looked at Bars in concern. Struggling for a moment to collect his thoughts, Bars drew a worried Floom closer to him. He then continued to speak.

Of course as Bars had recounted this horrendous segment of Deban history, Jonathan had clearly seen how it all related to him. He could imagine himself, for reasons he had yet to discover, being adopted by this amazing couple, in absolute secrecy. He could see a man, a figure of consummate evil, searching for the missing child five years later. Not finding him, that man began systematically to destroy all children of the same approximate age. It reminded Jon of stories he had heard before. In this story, Jon was the child who escaped death at the hands of the evil one.

There could be absolutely no doubt in Jon's mind, who that evil one was. Klushere had made it abundantly clear that he would prize the death of Jon more highly than anything. Klushere was responsible for the deaths of countless thousands of innocent children. *And so*, Jon concluded with determination and a righteous anger, *Klushere must die.*

It occurred to Jon briefly to attempt to take Klushere, to bring him before the Congregation to answer the charges. But he saw the futility of that. In this matter he could trust no one but himself. He did not know where he would find Klushere, but he believed in his ever expanding Etherean abilities and he would now employ all of them to one purpose. To find and destroy Klushere.

Jonathan sped to the upper edge of the atmosphere on the Norvesh side of the planet and concentrated. His Ether senses were becoming increasingly attuned. This had happened gradually since the day Klushere took Isobel from him. As he watched and looked with all his senses, he felt myriad pulsations of Ether surges as his brothers and sisters moved about in the Ether. He looked down and saw the trails leading in all directions.

He felt sure that Klushere was afraid of him. He had fled from Jonathan, leaving behind his sword, having seen that Jon had become so much more powerful. It was unexpected. Klushere would regroup as far from Jon as he could, finding evil allies and they would then try and take Jonathan together. Jon would pre-empt them.

He started threading now, slowly over the surface of the planet, noting where Ethereans were grouped together. There were no barriers. He could detect them all, whether they were in the Ether or not, above the ground or below it, in a building or in the open air.

And then Jon came upon a remote forest, away from civilisation. There were Ethereans there. It had to be them.

"For twenty years, Floom and I have thought our son to be dead. For twenty years I have fought for justice. I was proud when the people elected me to be a minister. I was proud when you elected me as Director. I was not proud for myself. I was proud for my son, Chankwar." Bars' eyes became watery. Round the room, some ministers were moved enough to cough, covering over their own emotion.

"Of late I have felt increasing struggles. There will always be opposing views wherever politicians are gathered. But some views started to come to my attention that were diametrically opposed to my notions of justice and equality." He raised his voice. "I feel bound by my duty to the people of Deb to stand against this. It seems however that there are those who wish to win their arguments by use of force rather than honest debate. I was taken captive, removed from your illustrious company and subjected to appalling treatment."

Some of the ministers now looking at Medok started to draw the conclusion that Bars was fantasising. He showed no outward signs of ill treatment and he had not been away long enough to heal completely, if he had been physically abused. Bars was already aware of where his colleagues minds would tend.

"The fact that I come before you whole, is a testimony in itself to the wondrous miracle that Yershowsh has performed." He gave his wife another reassuring squeeze. "Whilst I was in bondage, there was brought into my cell a man who was evidently an enemy of my captors. They tortured and humiliated him, but his spirit would not break. To this day I do not know what they wanted with him.

"We were comrades; brothers in adverse times, in a place where no Etherean could venture, since my dungeon was covered by a strong blanket of Enveloping." Bars noticed that the Elders and their visible jailers were paying close attention to him now.

"This man Heard Yershowsh and exercising a power I could only dream of, worked his way free of the chains that bound him. He released me and when I stood before him, any doubt that may have existed in my mind now fled. There before me, a beaten, bloodied man, but unmistakeable nevertheless, was my lost son.

"Together we left that cell. He carried me into the Ether and there caused me to heal. That should not be possible for a non-Etherean, except in one case." Seeking out a friendly face amongst the ministers and finding Resar Playne's, he addressed her. "Minister Playne, for the benefit of our friends who may have forgotten their childhood studies, would you kindly explain how a non-Etherean might find healing in the Ether?"

Rez was a perceptive woman. She could detect the tide turning in favour of Bars. She dared to respond in a controversial manner to the man whom she believed should be returned to his position of authority. "*Director* Medok," she started, ignoring the few frowns and muttered objections, noting instead the indications of agreement from the majority, "as I recall, a non-Etherean may be healed within the Ether if taken there by a Guardian."

Everyone in the Congregation knew what this meant. Bars picked up the thread, laughing with glee. "Yes it would appear that my son was hidden in a safe place by the Elders, away from the Cull, unaware of his abilities and his role in life. The role given to him by Yershowsh. When he took me into the Ether and I became whole, it was then that I realised that Yershowsh sees far into the future and protects His plans. No man may thwart Him.

"For the Guardian of the Insensate has returned." Bars then turned and plucking the issue portfolio from the now almost witless Masal added, gesturing at the incarcerated Elders, "And as usual, it would appear to be not a moment too soon."

—»»»»—

Jonathan closed in on the shadowy figures. They were hunched in a makeshift hut, nestling amongst some trees, far off any beaten track in this forest. *Another grand residence for Belee'al*, Jon thought, not really knowing who or what Belee'al might be.

As soon as he unthreaded himself into the vicinity, he sensed the reaction of the people in the hut. They emerged, warily, a variety of weapons drawn. Amongst them was Klushere.

Raising his voice as loud as he could manage Jon cried with emotion, "I have no argument with any besides Klushere. You cannot protect him from me. If you leave now, I will not follow you. If you remain, I cannot vouch for your safety." He brought his wrists together, activating his brack. As soon as it was in his hands in pole form, he reshaped it with a blade at both ends. One end or the other would part Klushere's head from his body, Jon was determined.

Without hesitation, every member of the Belee'an party entered the Ether, surrounding Klushere. Jon nodded briefly, saying quietly, "As you wish." And then he propelled himself towards them.

Now that he was able to do battle against Ethereans without any effects of Enveloping constraining him, Jon saw that Garmon's words were correct. *No Etherean can challenge you and hope to be victorious*, he had said. To Jon's eyes, the movements of his enemies were slow and predictable. They came at him with spears, swords and clubs. But not a single blow, not a single thrust or slash could penetrate his defences. One, two or three at a time, he battled them, brushing them aside as he fought to come between them and the master they protected.

He saw Ethereans tumbling about him, each one scrambling to regain his or her position, trying to recover from the blows they were receiving from Jon, in and out of the Ether. They could neither elude him nor better him. He hounded them so quickly that they had no time to recover. When they came to the point of fearing for their lives, they were obliged to retreat to allow the Ether to heal them.

Jonathan did not care that they healed. He cared that they retreated from his goal. He could smell Klushere and could feel his mounting fear. But not for a moment did Jonathan feel a trace of mercy towards this mass-murderer.

At length he stood before Klushere. He had disciples to either side and behind Jon, all doing their best to protect their Preceptor. But their best was inadequate. In a move that Jon had planned from the start and had kept until the last, once more relying on surprise to be his ally when so outnumbered, he used the technique called spreading. Waiting for the precise moment when Klushere ducked out of the Ether to avoid Jon's brack, he extended his arms so that his hands flew through the Ether, attached to him by spiritual tendrils, round to the back of Klushere. There they took with them Jon's brack. And there, they materialised and severed the head of the vile man.

His mission accomplished, Jon threaded away from the scene, not caring what might be the reaction of the disciples.

Taking the issue portfolio with him, Bars Medok walked off the platform towards the Elders. The Guards did not challenge him. Indeed, most of them were looking distinctly uncomfortable. Looking down at the portfolio, Bars announced, "The Elders are on trial, it would appear!"

Unable to contain himself any longer, Ti'par shouted, "By their own admission they have conspired to commit acts of Grand Anarchy and must be punished accordingly."

Bars again studied the portfolio. Lifting his head, he commented quietly, "Yes, that is what it says here, is it not?" Addressing the Congregation, he said passionately, "From whence does the authority of the High Congregation originate? Does it come from the will of the people? Or rather, does it issue from the will of Yershowsh, who rules over all?

"We believe that the Congregation has the right to rule over men, but who has the right to rule over the Congregation? Is the highest authority in this land a collection of fallible men? Is that what we believe?

"Since we were babes, we have been taught that the will of Yershowsh is pure. We must choose for ourselves whether or not we follow that will, but I for one am satisfied that He is right and He is just. And therefore, if we arrive at a crisis where one group, that claims to carry the authority and rule of Yershowsh, challenges another group that makes the same claims, to whom do we turn for guidance?

"By virtue of the events here, it would appear that the stronger group must rule the weaker group. Is this the monarchic democracy we have fought so hard for? Or is it tyranny? Where there are opposing views, there is balance. Where there is balance, there is Yershowsh.

"My esteemed friends, the crime of the Elders is that they foresaw grave jeopardy to the justice and law of Deb. The Elders are of the view that they are commissioned by Yershowsh to protect His people. They have striven to do everything in their power to continue with that commission.

"Ladies and gentlemen, in what respect is that 'Grand Anarchy?' Do you really believe that you should take from your protectors their ability to protect you? Please Yershowsh may it not be so."

Breathing heavily, Bars placed his hands on the shoulders of Yorgish and Ruith and faced the High Congregation. One by one, they rose from their seats and began to clap. Sivian unobtrusively left the Elders he was guarding and exited the Seat. There was nothing further he could do here. He would now attempt to locate his leader. For Sivian, it was not a happy day. For Bars and the Elders, a moment's insanity was now being banished from the High Congregation.

25

Jonathan was spending time at the home of Plykar and Graye Lovel. Although he had felt all but invincible three days earlier, he had come to realise that the recent weeks had taken a heavy toll, physically, mentally, spiritually, but most of all, emotionally. He was bewildered as may be expected, by the array of parents with whom he was now acquainted. The only person left to complete the picture was his natural father. Plykar had quickly made it clear that he was not Jon's father. But the Lovels had decided that it would not be to Jon's advantage to know his real father. They made their views clear to Jon and he did not press the issue.

It is not always the case that estranged children connect with their birth parents, but Jon felt an incredible bond with his mother. Perhaps this was because of the traumatic times they had both experienced of late. Perhaps it was because they were both unusually gifted in their different ways.

Graye admitted to Jon that she did not dare to be proud of him. She had done nothing to deserve to be the mother of a Guardian. She had no hand in raising Jon; circumstances had required her to give Jon away soon after he was born. With a deep sense of shame, Graye told him that for her marriage to survive, it had to be so. She had friends in the High Congregation who had ensured that Jon was placed with a loving family.

If he had been able to take it in, Jon would have reeled with shock from the revelation that Klushere was his older brother. It seemed to him however, to be an abstract fact that had no connection with his life or reality. He never had a sibling.

This evening, Graye picked up her narrative as she attempted to explain to Jonathan some of the ways of the Ethereans and in particular the reason why Klushere was so hell-bent on destroying his brother.

"History shows and we have no reason to question it, that to every mother may be born one and only one Etherean. There is no pattern that we have been able to detect—no reason of heritage. Ethereans do not 'run in the family.'" Jon was sipping rynyn, blowing out the steam quietly and enjoying his mother's tales. Plykar sat quietly in one corner of the room, allowing his wife to enjoy intimacy with her son. His eye had a misty look. His wife had gained a son she thought lost. But Plykar had simply lost a son.

"Yershowsh blesses where he see fit," Graye mused. "This much we can observe: if a second child is born before the first child reaches the age of onset, the first child's chance of becoming an Etherean is substantially decreased. The same is true for all subsequent children."

"Onset?" Jon asked.

"This is the time when a child starts to show signs of being an Etherean, usually in the twelfth or thirteenth year. Your brother," Graye gulped back a sob and her eyes became watery, "was devoted to the idea of becoming an Etherean. He wanted nothing more in life. When his thirteenth birthday came and went and then his fourteenth and his fifteenth, Klushere became obsessed with the notion that I must have another child, hidden somewhere. He felt that he had been passed over." Graye sighed. "How could I tell him that he was right? For all we knew none of my children would become Ethereans. There would have been no advantage in Klushere knowing that he had an illegitimate brother. His family was disgraced enough already."

Graye looked at her beloved husband and her eyes were apologetic. He shook his head a little and forced a smile for the woman he loved. He had long since forgiven her for this, but occasionally she needed reminding of that fact.

"And so Klushere became attached to some wicked people. He sought out other means of obtaining Etherean-like powers. I believe that it is possible, although I know not how. I imagine that arcane practices are entailed." A sob that she could not repress rose. "He must have become as evil as he was powerful," she managed to say through her tears.

What a tragic story, Jonathan thought to himself repeatedly. He wished that he could have prevented all this heartache. Perhaps if he had not been born... But then he remembered all the things that he had to be grateful for. He had no less than five parents who all seemed to care for him deeply. He had experienced in his life a love that was, to his mind, beyond compare. His wife had been devoted, but more than that, she had been a true inspiration to Jon to become a better person. He knew that she would be pleased if she could see him now. He wished that he could tell her all that had happened. Sometimes at night, he did exactly that, although he did not believe she could hear him.

The next morning Graye seemed very distracted. She had been an excellent host anticipating every need of Jonathan's before he had chance to speak it. But today she was far away and thoughtful and somewhat neglectful.

After Plykar left for work, Jon amused himself by looking at some of the books the Lovels had in their library. Although some of the language had come back to him and he had learnt more in a short space of time, this was only in the realm of speech. Deban books were a jumbled mass of meaningless characters and symbols. Perhaps he would learn to read this one day.

Graye came upon Jon engrossed in a book. She noted with a secret but kind smile that he was holding upside down one of her rehabilitation textbooks—one that she had edited. Jon was sat on a bench; Graye quietly sat next to him.

Jon spoke first. "I stupidly thought that I might at least recognise a letter—but it seems I must have forgotten everything I learnt. I cannot remember much from my first five years." Jon reached out for his mother's hand. She took his hand and studied it closely. It was hard for her to believe that this full grown man was the fruit of her womb.

"Jon," she said, timidly. Graye preferred to use the name with which Jonathan felt most comfortable. "I am sorry I have been distracted this morning."

Jon smiled. "It is no problem Graye." He had to call her by her name. It was far too confusing to call her, 'mother'—now that he had three of them. "These have been crazy days."

Graye shook her head and then brushed back her long grey hair. "It is not that. Yershowsh has spoken to me this morning. His words trouble me. But they are for you. I wish..." she tailed off. Her emotions were rising and her eyes reddened. "I wish," she continued, "that I did not have to relay this message. But my reasons are selfish." She hung her head. Jon listened intently.

Graye collected herself and spoke. "You are a Guardian, Jon and you must go where Yershowsh sends you if you are to be fulfilled and if the world is to benefit from your calling. But I do not think that you are *Deb's* Guardian." She let these words sink in.

"Deb has been a training ground—you will have other training grounds. And I believe that they will all lead you back to the homeland that you love." Graye sighed. "For selfish reasons I gave you away and for selfish reasons I now want to keep you here. But I will not be selfish with your life twice."

Jon was puzzled. "Is this what Yershowsh has told you? That I am to return to my planet and be a Guardian there? How can I do that without other Ethereans to guide me?"

Graye arose from the bench, came round in front of Jonathan and then knelt down at his feet, looking into his eyes. Jon could palpably feel her love for him and the tearing within her heart as she continued to speak to him earnestly. "No, Yershowsh has not said this—it is my own conclusion. What he has said I feel afraid to tell you."

She reached out for his hands and holding them both tightly said, "I have two pieces of news that will bring you joy and sadness. You are not permitted to act on the first. On the second, you must act immediately." Jon braced himself.

"The first thing Yershowsh would have me tell you is that the man you sought to kill by means of your own will and your own judgment, lives. He deceived you and was not defeated as you had thought." Jon shuddered. He had been content with the thought of Klushere being dead and no longer able to haunt him. And he was not permitted to act on this? This seemed to him supremely unjust, but he did not have time to dwell on it. Graye continued.

"The second thing I must tell you is a bittersweet message, for me. The message will bring you joy even whilst its implications mar my own happiness. You still have a life on your own planet and this will carry you away from Deb. For Yershowsh says that the person you most loved, whom you thought lost forever, is merely sleeping, awaiting your return."

Every hair on Jon's body stood on end. His eyes filled up with tears, whilst his heart leapt with a combination of joy and alarm. Adrenaline coursed through his body. Graye was saying that Isobel was alive!

How could this be? But then Jon thought about all the things he had learnt since he left earth. He was a Guardian and he had the power to enable non-Ethereans to access the healing properties of the Ether. When he had picked up the inert body of his wife, she must have been barely alive, but nevertheless alive. And somehow, she had been healing even as he carried her to her temporary grave.

"My wife is alive?" Jon asked, not daring to believe it. He searched his mother's face for a sign that she was lying. He found no such sign. Graye nodded.

Looking into his mother's eyes one last time, Jon kissed her on the cheek and then said, "Please say goodbye for me. I will return when I can. But I must go. I have a promise to fulfil."

He hugged his mother and then was gone.

Epilogue

Over the weeks since Isobel's disappearance, her parents Gordon and Faith had become distant with each other. They both felt it. They both felt helpless about it. They found that their love for each other was stifled and they now only felt empty and bitter. If only things could return to normal. But that would never happen.

Tonight as on other occasions, they allowed the television to anaesthetise their emotions whilst they ate their dinner together, silently. They didn't speak because there was nothing left to say.

It was easy to see how they had come to this point. The circumstances did not create any definite moment for their grief to begin. All they had were assumptions and implication. The police had not found their beloved daughter's body, but the search had been scaled down. Appeals had been made, but there were simply no leads. No one involved had even been able to hypothesize a convincing motive.

Gordon has refused to believe that their darling Isobel could be dead. Faith had accepted this belief too readily for Gordon's liking. They sunk into a vague gloomy animosity towards each other. For now, they remained together, but this was purely out of habit.

And yet this couple were strong; they had many wonderful shared experiences and a good friendship. Their friends individually tried to encourage them to seek counselling or other assistance, but somehow they both lacked the motivation. A desire for help is the first step towards help. The desire was not there.

They interacted with one another simply because it was part of their routine. Plates were gathered, dishes washed, choice of viewing discussed. All very civilised and polite. But real feeling was missing. Isobel had been an irrepressible whirlwind of emotions at times. With her gone, Gordon and Faith felt that their own emotions had also died.

Faith arose first to retire to bed. They no longer went to their bedroom simultaneously. The idea of getting undressed together was distasteful. So they would not normally be found in the hall together at this time of night. It was merely a coincidence that when the doorbell rang and Gordon arose to answer it, Faith was just starting to climb the stairs. She looked round with interest as her husband opened the door, wondering who might wish to intrude upon their lives at this late hour.

Faith watched as Gordon undid the latch, pulled the door towards him and then froze. He had not opened it far enough for Faith to be able to see who the visitor was. Gordon turned and looked up at Faith and his face was contorted. His mouth was opening, but only gurgling sounds were coming out.

Intrigued and alarmed, Faith moved down the stairs and stopped at the bottom. She saw who the visitor was and she had to reach out for the banisters to support her. She tried to scream, but like Gordon, her vocal cords were not responding correctly.

And then the moment broke and Gordon and Faith rushed forward simultaneously to hug and kiss their beautiful, healthy and very much alive only daughter. Unseen and unheard, from within the Ether Jon said, "See you later." He flitted away, with many errands on his mind.

He had much to do and many responsibilities to attend to. For he was back on earth and he was the Guardian of the Insensate.

Glossary

Bracarpium	Created from Ebullene, combined with miniaturised power sources and magnets. The weapon of the Ethereans, worn as twin bracelets.
The Central Elect	The foremost disciples of Belee'al
The Chosen	Highly secretive followers of Belee'al who engage in violent and illegal activities in his name.
Crut	A low-standing, high-backed stool, popular in some parts of Deb.
Deb	The planet of the Ethereans.
Door-rattle	A device found on Deban front doors, which is intended when wound to attract the attention of the residents within.
Ebullene	A naturally occurring liquid element found on Deb. When alloyed with a certain base metal, its molecules can be reformed by electrical and magnetic means. When solidified, it is super-hard.
Envelope	A spiritual technique, covering an area or person, which makes the use of Etherean powers impossible.
Etherean	In every family one child has the opportunity to receive the "power seed" and become an Etherean; a resident of Deb with extraordinary abilities.
Flektor	A creature found on the Norvesh side of Deb, renowned for its twice yearly, headlong, full speed migratory habit.

redwing	A small winged insect of rapid, erratic flight, found in abundance in certain quarters of Deb.
The Etherean Guard	A military body composed entirely of Ethereans.
Hearer	One who hears directly from Yershowsh.
The High Congregation	The planet-wide governing body on Deb.
Rey	A bicycle-like transportation device used on Deb.
Rynyn	An energy-giving Deban drink.
Serj	A Deban stimulant narcotic.
Ti'alor	A multi-player game of skill and chance, popular within Deb's gambling community.